Hell's *Chimney*

Derek Smith

Earlham Books

Published 2010 by Earlham Books

Book design & cover art by Lia at Free Your Words
(*www.freeyourwords.com*)

ISBN: 978-0-9536283-7-7

Contents

Part One

The Hunted Prince

Chapter 1

The darkness was total. Not a chink of light, no indication of walls or ceiling. No window. Straw was under his puffed up hands, tied too tightly behind his back. He could feel the blueness, the pins and needles in the fingers as he tried to move them in the damp straw. His ankles too were bound. Was he in a barn? The urine from a horse, or was it his own? He groaned and rolled in a sea of pain: bloated hands, ankles, his right eye throbbed, flashing deep redness. The side of his face ached. Patches of his body cried out their bruising.

He remembered the kicking. They grabbed him, he had struggled – and they came in punching with fists and boots. He'd tried to protect his head with his hands but they'd ripped his arms away. They trod on his fingers and they went for his helplessness. He'd screamed and yelled for his mother, of all people. Dead three years. Mother – to come and stop them, to rip them away. To save him, to make it stop.

The thought brought tears. Perhaps for his mother, but mainly for his sorry self, trussed like a chicken, kicked into unconsciousness. He tugged at his wrist bonds. There was no give. The circulation must be almost cut off; he could lose his hands. He tried wriggling the fingers and groaned as if they were still kicking him.

Toby was on his side, his ear and cheek in the pungent straw. How long before they came? They must come soon. Was this simply a lesson? He had stormed out of his father's presence declaring he could never respect that woman. That woman, who had bewitched his father and now insisted on replacing his mother. 'Call me Mother,' she had declared. And he yelled, 'I'll call you bitch.'

Fool. There are things which must not be said. It was the drink. And the sight of Zeke, her crow ugly son, loving it as his own father dressed him down. And she, sweet loveliness herself. The bitch. She had his father on a string. She pulled and Father yelled and screamed and ranted at him. It was like a pummelling with hot coals, with the lady nodding, smiling reassurance while Father harangued.

Until he broke.

He had thrown his plate at her. The chicken flopped into her lap. Onion and gravy besmirched her face and her yellow dress. She was not smiling then. Her lips pressed thin, her eyes blazing at him. Oh no, she was not smiling then.

He must apologise. Eat crow, lick boots. How it had all burst out of him! Wine words, wine insults – and on top of it – throwing the plate. This was the result. Beaten up, tied up in this stink hole. He groaned and rolled, wanting to rub his jaw, scratch his ribs. He yanked himself to sitting position but it was no better. The ache and pain moved round him as he moved. From jaw to belly, to ribs, to hands.

He wanted his mother. She would have interceded, taken his part. She would cool down his father's temper. She would.

But she wouldn't. Never could. Wouldn't. Dead is dead.

In fury, he had ridden away into the forest. Rode the horse too fast until he had to stop and walk the animal. By the stream, as the horse drank and its flanks steamed, he knew he was trapped, at least for the next few years. He must do her bidding, keep out of his stepbrother's way. Be dutiful, be respectful. Honour his father the King and accept his Queen and her son.

Damn them both.

Pity took him over. He rolled and wallowed. He yelled out, 'Help me! Help me!' He was beaten. He would give in. The point was made. He would respect her. The bitch. She would be his new mother. The crow's vomit. He would love her. The pig's dung.

He had ridden back, determined to make amends. Over the drawbridge, into the courtyard. And instantly they had set upon him. Dragged him from the horse. Kicked him, smashed him. Such brutality, like a man set on by robbers. Though he noted there had been no swords or knives. So surely the purpose was to punish him? Humiliate him.

It had worked.

He rolled over and crushed his hand, and cried out in pain. Surely, they would drop off. The fingers were losing feeling. They must be going black. Let them come soon. He would agree to anything. Please, Father – whatever you say. I am your obedient son.

Chapter 2

He heard the sounds, metal grating metal. Someone had at last come. He sat up, wincing at the pain in his wrists. He couldn't see his body but he could map it out in aches. As the metal continued grating, he hoped this would be the end of it. A key in a lock, he guessed, someone having trouble with it.

The door slowly opened. A wedge of light thickened from a strip, and fanned out until it took him in. Framed within the doorway was a stubby man in a tunic, carrying a lantern. He lifted the lantern high and peered into the cell. For that was clearly what it was. There was a small window high up in the far wall, but showing no light as it must be night outside, a cloudy dark night. The walls were black with some scrapings here and there. And on the earthy floor a puddle of scattered straw.

The man came in and stood over Toby. He was bare-armed with thick fat fingers, the finger nails black with dirt.

'You alright, lad?' he said, revealing a few rotten teeth. His face was pitted, and the nose squashed as if it had been hit with something heavy.

'I'm not alright,' said Toby shaking himself.

The man smiled, showing his gaps and a thick wet tongue. 'You're alive. That counts as alright down here.'

Toby shuffled in the straw, trying to show his bound hands. 'Can you undo these ropes? They're killing me.'

The man pursed his lips, then shook his head. 'Can't, sonny. It's not down to me.'

'Do you know who I am?'

The man grinned again, like a schoolboy pleased at knowing the answer. 'You're that prince. What's his face.' He flicked a grubby finger and the lantern shook, rocking the light. 'Prince Toby – that's you.' He peered closely at the young man, sucking his lower lip under a couple of blackened teeth. 'Don't often get a prince.' He broke into a cackle, his body shaking in his enjoyment. 'In fact, never had a prince. Had a Chancellor once.' He shook his head and sucked through his teeth. 'Nasty man, but dead scared. Afraid of torture. Didn't stay long.' He winked a bloodshot eye and wiped down his nose with a grubby index finger. 'They say money changed hands. A house even. I don't know about that. I just hear bits and pieces down here. They come, most stay. Everyone goes in the end, of course.'

'Please untie these bonds.'

The man shook his head as if he cared. 'Can't. Orders.' His tongue lolled thoughtfully in his cheek. 'Though, don't see a lot of use for 'em. But it ain't down to me.'

'Will you loosen them?' Toby's eyes pleaded.

The man walked round him sniffing. 'You do go on.' He wiped his nose with the back of his hand. 'You got some good gear there. Dirtying up a bit. But be worth something.' He rubbed Toby's sleeve between a couple of fingers. 'Prince's gear. Someone'll want that, be sure of it.'

The candle flickered in the lantern, shaking the light and shadows. The man peered in at the candle, and flicked some wax off the edge with a finger.

Toby said, 'I'm a prince.' He paused then said with deliberation, 'I'm going to be freed soon.'

The man considered this then shook his head. 'Doubt that.'

'You don't know it.'

He smiled toothily. 'What do I know, down here? They might free you. Might. Most likely not.'

'When they free me,' said Toby firmly, 'I shall have you whipped.'

The man stood back startled. 'What have I done?'

Toby looked hard into his eyes. 'Untie my bonds.'

The man trembled, the light shaking on the walls and floor. 'Can't, sir. Can't do it. If they found you all undone they'd have me. Can't do it, sir.'

Toby watched his twitching face, and the shudder going through the man's body. The man was afraid of what Toby might do – but more afraid of what others certainly would.

'Loosen the bonds then,' said Toby quietly.

The man looked about him as if someone might come through the walls. 'I'll do it a bit. Just a bit so it don't show.' He crouched to do it then stopped. 'Only promise – you won't tell.'

'On my honour,' said Toby. 'You'll be rewarded.'

'We'll see about that,' mumbled the man and set about the bonds around Toby's wrists.

He put the lantern on the straw which brought the light down with it. As he tugged at the ropes with his fingers, Toby winced.

'Go easy.'

'Bugger me,' cursed the gaoler. 'They done these tight.' He was on his knees now, behind Toby's back. 'I shall have to get me teeth into 'em.'

Toby could smell his oniony breath. The man spat into the straw then pulled Toby's arms up. Tony groaned. His wrist hurt awfully but he could barely feel his hands at all. All at once he felt some give – and he was yelling in pain.

The man drew a grubby hand over Toby's mouth and hissed, 'Keep it down, master. Keep it down.'

'Pins and needles,' moaned Toby. 'Ooh – they're killing me.'

The man began rubbing Toby's fingers. At some other time he might have objected to the filthy hands but now he was only grateful.

'That's as much as I can do, master.' The gaoler had stopped and was getting to his feet.

'Thank you,' said Toby still breathing heavily but the pain was easing. 'Do the ankles.'

The man hesitated, licked his lips and then bent to them. They weren't quite as tight and in a combination of fingers and teeth, he was able to loosen them.

'That'll have to do,' he said standing up.

'Thank you,' said Toby, wriggling to make the most of the looser bonds.

'You won't say nothing?'

'Nothing,' said Toby.

The man relaxed. 'Now what I really come for. Your breakfast tomorrow.'

It was Toby's turn to smile. 'Do I get a choice?'

The man nodded. 'You can have what you want.'

Toby looked hard into the man's eyes. He didn't seem to be joking. 'Why?' he said.

The man shrugged. 'Cus they said.'

'Who?'

'Fruff. The Head Gaoler,' he said.

'Who said it to him?'

The man shrugged. 'Someone. Some messenger was talking to him. Dunno who. All I know is you get what you want for breakfast.'

Toby tried once more. 'Do you know why?'

The man smiled. 'Seems a bit of a waste to me. If you're going to get your head chopped off...'

Toby wasn't sure he had heard correctly. 'Who is going to get his head chopped off?'

'You.'

'Me?' A shudder gripped his body. He felt prickly round the neck. 'I am going to be executed tomorrow? Me?'

The man nodded. 'At noon. The executioner is here already. I seen him sharpening his axe in the blacksmith's shop. Won't hurt. He's good. They cover your eyes if you want. Then one smack and it's off. He's good. Used to be a woodcutter. Says it's no different from chopping a log – except for all the blood spurting. So what about bacon?'

'At noon,' mumbled Toby, very aware of his neck, the bones and the veins within, the bridge between head and body.

'I'll put you down for bacon then. Ham? Best ham? Anything in the kitchen you can have. Eggs? Goose eggs even. A jug of beer? I would. Not too much. Don't want to be peeing while you're waiting.'

Toby's teeth were chattering. He could barely think, hardly make words. 'Are you sure of this?' he managed to say.

'Yeh,' said the man. 'Anything you like. Chicken. Bread just out the oven soaked in butter.' The man slobbered. 'Almost worth losing your head for. Go on, feed up. Anything you don't have – I'll finish.'

Toby lowered his head. His knees had a life of their own, the blood was pumping in his ears. It couldn't be true. How did this man know?

'Why?' he whispered, and then to prevent more additions to the menu, added, 'why am I going to be executed?'

The man lifted the lantern and chewed a fingernail thoughtfully. 'Well, if you kill a king – what do you expect?'

Toby stared at him. 'Kill a king?'

The man sucked in a breath and licked round his teeth. 'Did you think you'd just injured him? No such luck, mate. You done a real good job. He's dead and proper is the King. And you're going to join him tomorrow. Did you say you wanted the ham? I'll put you down for four eggs, and the blood sausage...'

'Put me down for...' said Toby, stopping as the tears welled in his eyes. Suddenly he was sobbing, his body shuddering. His father was dead. Could that really be true? Then why else had he been kicked and bound like a felon? Because, it could only be, there was no other possibility – because he was to die too. On the executioner's block.

He wept for his father. He wept for his neck. The gaoler made further suggestions: porridge, pork scratchings and apples. And as the young man didn't reject them, he added them, wondering aloud how big a breakfast he would be permitted. But then a prince was a prince. There was royal blood in that neck.

At last he left, locking the door. Leaving Toby in his own darkness.

Chapter 3

It was impossible to sleep tied up. And even if he wasn't, too much had happened. He ached all over, his head buzzed like a hive. His weeping was over. And he began to think.

Why did he believe the gaoler? Because he told him. But why believe him? Because in his miserable state, he would believe anything. Tied up, abandoned in the dark on stinking straw – any explanation would have worked. So perhaps the man was lying. He certainly was about breakfast. Toby could not believe he would get a magnificent feast an hour before they cut his head off. For what reason? It was a gaoler's joke. The man would have a good laugh when he brought in the stale bread and water. So, if he was lying about breakfast, then it could be he was lying about his father being dead. And if he wasn't dead Toby couldn't be accused of the murder.

Except.

Was he really in the dungeon because he had thrown a plate of food at his stepmother? And tied up? And beaten up like a common criminal? It was not impossible. His father had a temper and maybe wanted to teach him a lesson. But his father also believed in family honour – would he so publicly humiliate his son, a prince of the realm? Never. If he was going to lock him up, he'd lock him up in his chamber. He could take away his horses. There were ways to punish princes who were badly behaved. And there were ways to punish murderers.

Which was most likely?

All he had was the word of one man. One filthy, nail biting, onion smelling, toothless gaoler. A man who had tortured, bullied and starved hundreds of prisoners. The word of the lowest of the low. He could be told anything by such vermin – and how would he ever know what was true?

He convinced himself his father was alive. Then convinced himself his father was dead. He convinced himself he didn't know anything about anything – that he had been too proud, too sulky, too rude to his stepmother and her son. He would go on his knees before her. He would beg her forgiveness. He would tell his father he had changed.

That is – if his father was still alive. And if his head stayed on his neck at one minute past noon.

How could they think he had killed his father? He went on that tack. Supposing the awful story was true, that his father had been murdered. It had to have been at the time while he was off riding in the forest. He'd have to have come back to do it. The guards at the drawbridge would have seen him if he had. The stable boys... You can't sneak into a castle with a horse. Could you sneak in without one? Suppose he had been planning to kill his father? Then riding off to the forest might have been a good idea – his alibi. And then somehow get back in without being seen. And then back out again – so he could return from his ride pretending to know nothing.

It could be done. By bribing a guard or two.

Did they really think he had done that? Planned all that. And what about the guards? Could he have risked leaving them alive? It was all so much nonsense.

He must steel himself. Let time pass. This would all come right.

Toby was in this frame when his visitors arrived.

The door creaked wide and the gaoler stood between the jambs holding a lantern. Just behind him were two guards, both with an upright spear in one hand and a lantern in the other. Behind them were others he couldn't make out, one of them also holding a light.

The gaoler stepped into the cell, followed by the guards. They peeled away like curtains, to allow those behind to come between. One was Councillor Higgs in his ermine robe and the soft black hat that had always reminded Toby of a sleeping cat. Around his neck was his ornate chain of office, indicating his importance. He was the King's first Councillor. Beside him were the Queen and her son, Prince Zeke.

For an instant, he thought: now it will come right. But she was in black, her long robe almost scraped the ground, and covered her shoulders. The sleeves were half-length and puffed at the end. The dress had a velvety sheen in the lamplight. There was a thick black band around her forehead and brown hair, and her long pigtails draping over her shoulders were tied in black ribbon.

He groaned inwardly. The dress of a widow.

Her son too was in black: cloak, leggings and shirt. A sword showed under the cloak as if he needed it, even with a tied prisoner and armed guards. He was taller than his mother, thin and lanky. His hair was blonde and straight, his face white, with pink showing through. His lips thin and pale, and down the left cheek a long scar from below his eye to the corner of his mouth. It gave him a fighting look, added to by his central missing tooth. But neither were won in battle, Toby knew, but from a childhood accident when he fell from a rope swing.

The Queen stood over Toby with Councillor Higgs and the lantern. The later solemn, his droopy chops attempting to roll off his face. Toby expected no sympathy there, he had never liked him. He caught the Queen's eye – what mood was she in? She was changeable. It was possible, he thought. Besides, no matter what, she must know it wasn't him.

'The guard has confessed,' she said.

This threw Toby, his tongue and lips struggled to respond.

'Your confederate,' she went on. 'Under torture he told us everything.' She shook her head and smiled sadly. 'He told us how you came back secretly, how he distracted the other guard...'

'He's lying,' Toby at last said.

'I'll cut his throat, Mother,' exclaimed Zeke, rushing forward, hand on his sword.

She held her son's arm. 'No need, dearest.' She turned back to the Toby. 'The truth is in the boot and the thumb screw,' she said. She looked to the Councillor. 'The man is dead – is he not?'

'He is, Your Majesty. He died on the rack.'

'One less to draw and quarter.'

Toby's neck ached from looking up at her. Her sternness, her solidity, her black – and Higgs who wouldn't know a jest if it hit him on the nose... This was all true! His father was dead. Murdered.

'I didn't do it, Your Majesty,' he said just audibly.

She widened her eyes. 'And the guard lied?'

'Yes, Your Majesty.'

'And the dagger we found under the cushion in your room?' shouted Zeke into his face, the spit causing Toby to shut his eyes.

He could hardly breath. The more they said the worse it was... He began to shake, trembling from head to foot. Bound, he could not stop himself.

Zeke grasped him tightly by the nose.

'Tell us about the bloody footprint in the hallway outside your father's chamber from your shoe?' he yelled as he twisted Toby's nose.

'I was out riding,' screamed Toby.

Zeke cracked him round the face with a gloved hand. And as his head swung, Zeke hit him on the other side. His eyes filled with tears, his cheeks stung. While he was still rocking, Zeke grabbed him by the hair and yanked his head back.

'It is only because my mother is soft you will not be tortured,' he hissed, inches from his face.

'I am innocent!' he screamed in red pain.

With a push, the Prince released him.

'See?' said the Queen to her Councillor, 'How he will deny to the grave.'

'I would never have believed this,' said Higgs shaking his grey locks. 'You shame us, boy.' He waved a teacherly finger. 'You shame our very country.'

Toby's head was lowered like a penitent. What could he say to them that wouldn't get him kicked?

'I tried to be your mother,' said the Queen wearily. 'My son tried to be your brother. But your rudeness, your hostility, your hatred were boundless. I tried again and again. I loved your father. I wanted to love his son...' she stopped in a sob. 'And now I am a widow.'

She dabbed her eyes.

'Let me kill the rat,' exclaimed Zeke, striding around kicking straw. 'Let me stick him. Let me smash his brains against the wall.'

'I am innocent,' said Toby feebly, drool dribbling down his chin.

'I have lost my dear husband,' sighed the Queen as if she had not heard. She wiped away the tear rolling down her cheek. She straightened, sniffed, her weeping over, and held a hand on Toby's head like a high priestess about to bless him. 'These are crimes so hateful, that I can only pity you.' She flicked at one of the guards. 'Untie him.'

'Mother! No!' exclaimed Zeke.

The guard looked in bewilderment, not knowing whom to obey.

'Do as I say,' insisted the Queen.

Toby watched. He wanted to wipe his chin. He'd seen these mother-son battles many times. She would win.

'But, Mother, please...' Zeke cajoled. 'He needs to suffer.'

The Queen shook her head. 'Don't argue with me, dearest. I know what's best.'

Zeke stamped his foot and bit his lower lip. Then turned away.

The guard had laid down his spear and crossed to the prone youth. He took his knife from his belt.

'Your last hours,' she intoned to Toby, 'should be spent in prayer. Beg forgiveness for your patricide. Be on your knees to God.'

The guard cut the wrist bonds. Toby wriggled his hands, twisted his wrists as the guard worked on the ankle ropes. He wiped his chin on his sleeve. He sucked his swollen fingers, he licked his red wrists.

A cry of agony escaped from the Queen.

'Turn back the sun!' she wailed. She covered her face in her hands. 'Take us back 24 hours when I woke with your father...'

Zeke ran in and kicked Toby in the chest even as the ankle rope was falling away. He fell back on the straw, winded.

'I'd like to torture you myself,' snarled Zeke, one foot on Toby's chest like a victorious wrestler. 'Hour on hour until you begged for death. And then we would really begin.'

'Believe me,' gasped Toby, 'on my honour, Your Majesty...'

Councillor Higgs stepped forward. 'Patricide forfeits all claim to honour.'

The Queen nodded.

'Poor child, poor child,' she murmured. 'Leave him, dearest.'

Zeke dug deep with his heel, then stepped away reluctantly. 'Mother, let me smack the lies out of him... Please.'

She shook her head. 'It is not seemly.'

Zeke threw his arm up in rage. 'Why did I bother to come – if you are going to mollycoddle him!'

With an anguished sigh, he strode out of the cell.

The Queen called after him, 'Dearest...' She stopped and shook her head with a long sigh. Then flicked at the guards and indicated the door. The gaoler and the guards quickly marched out, taking most of the light with them. Higgs looked to the Queen for direction. Her attention was on the prince in the straw, rubbing his chest between massaging his ankles and wrists.

'I will not speak with you again,' she said.

Toby tugged at her robe like an infant. 'I am innocent. I swear it.'

'Enough, I think,' said Higgs to the Queen.

She nodded at the old man. 'I had to see him.'

'I understand.'

'I could not believe. Barely a man...'

'I understand completely, Your Majesty.'

'I still do not believe...'

They were walking to the door, leaving Toby in shadow.

'Evil is beyond belief, Your Majesty.'

Higgs stepped out first and waited in the corridor. Zeke had already gone, his stride ringing on distant flagstones. The Queen lingered in the doorway, the light behind her. She was complete blackness, a spectre in a long robe.

'I shall see you for the last time at noon,' she said. 'Make the most of your final hours.'

She turned and walked out of his sight.

The door slammed shut.

Chapter 4

Earl Gomm shuffled down the wide stairway, shivering.

'I'm coming, I'm coming.'

He carried a candle. With his other hand he held his dressing gown to him, beneath it could be seen the hem of his night-shirt and below that his bare legs. He wore a night-cap with a tassel and bed-socks.

In the wide hallway were two men. One was in night attire with a lantern. Plainly his sleep had been disturbed too. The other wore outdoor dress, a hat in one hand at his side, a coat to the knees and riding boots.

Earl Gomm joined them. He put his candle on a sideboard and clutched at his upper arms.

'It's icy,' he exclaimed.

'There's a thick frost, my lord,' said the man in outdoor gear.

Frost patterns covered the windows of the hallway. The wood surrounds were dark stained, two portraits of over-dressed men were cast in shadow.

'Winter's early,' shivered Earl Gomm. He shook himself, sleep still heavy in his eyes.

'I am sorry to disturb your sleep, sir.' The man stamped his cold feet.

'Not as sorry as I am to be disturbed. Your hammering would have woken the devil.'

'I could get no response, sir.' He was rubbing his red hands.

'Well, you have woken the house. What's your news?'
Before the man could respond, he turned to the other man.
'Benjamin – let's have a fire in the sitting room. And hot
water and lemon for myself and this man.'

Benjamin nodded and shuffled off.

'We'll soon have you warm,' said Earl Gomm rubbing his
palms. 'What's your news? And I withdraw the hot drink if
it's not important.'

The man chewed his lower lip for a second or two,
thinking how to phrase the difficult words he had to convey.
This was his third visit that night and there'd been shocks
enough at each household. But there were no easy words.

'The King is dead, sir.'

Earl Gomm staggered against the sideboard, almost
knocking the candle over.

'How, who, when...?' he burbled. 'This cannot be true.'

'In the afternoon, sir,' went on the messenger. 'Murdered.
Stabbed in the back by his son.'

Earl Gomm's hands had gone to his head, he twisted
around in his incoherence. 'I cannot believe this. The King.
Murdered. By his son.' He stopped his dance. 'Which son?
Prince Toby?'

The man nodded. 'Yes sir.'

'This is madness. I always liked the boy.' He rocked
against a wall, which barely supported him. 'The King dead.
Murdered.' His hands again clutched his head. 'What is
going to happen to us all?'

'The Queen now rules,' said the messenger.

'God bless her,' said Earl Gomm. Breathing heavily, he
was lifting himself against the wall. 'Thirty years of peace
we've had. Now what?'

'The Prince is to be beheaded tomorrow...' The man
halted and corrected himself, 'Today, at noon. The Queen
requests your attendance.'

'I shall be there.' His heart was beating rapidly, his hands
supporting him against the wall. He was seeing the battle-
field where he'd been wounded as a young man in the War

of Succession. Where he nearly died. Friends and relatives had not been so fortunate, including his own father. Thirty years ago.

'How do they know it was the Prince?' he said weakly.

'He'd had an argument with his father and the Prince left in a temper...' the messenger hesitated. 'I don't know the details sir, but a guard, a confederate of his, confessed under torture. A bloodstained dagger was found under a pillow in his room...' He paused for an instant. 'I can tell you no more.'

Earl Gomm held up his hands. 'That's enough. Too much. Far too much.' He steadied himself and stood unsupported. 'Thank you. I am sure it distresses you giving such terrible news.'

The man nodded.

'Stay for some breakfast,' went on Earl Gomm.

'It must be speedy,' said the man. 'I have four more visits yet.'

Earl Gomm clapped his hands. 'Benjamin! Benjamin!' he yelled. 'Here at once.'

The old manservant came running from a side room.

'Wake the servants. Everyone. Wake the family. The night is over.'

Thirty minutes later, the family were seated round the large table in the dining room. A fire was blazing in the hearth though the room was still chilly. A candelabra was in the middle of the polished oak table and other candles had been placed round the room. The long drapes had been drawn but it was still dark outside. A thick frost blocked the window, like the jewelled web of a giant spider.

The family were dressed but half asleep. They were clutching mugs of warm milk. Earl Gomm had already told them the news. He was in the black robes of mourning; the rest of the family had simply picked up the clothes by their beds.

'The carriage is being made ready,' he said. 'I must leave in thirty minutes.'

'Have you spoken to the servants?' asked Countess Gomm.

He shook his head. 'Barely. I've had the odd word with Benjamin. And I dare say he has given them some garbled version. I'll leave that to you, my dear.'

She nodded.

Martin, his son, said, 'I'd like to come with you to the execution, Father.'

Earl Gomm shook his head. 'Important as it is, I want you here. You must wake the priest. Everyone on the estate. There must be a service for the King. Everyone must attend.' He turned to his wife. 'You must make sure all the household goes, everyone – every kitchen boy and girl, every stable hand. All suitably attired. Any black they have, worn. You must make up ribbon for armbands.'

His wife nodded. She was already calculating. Thinking about clothing for everyone and the ribbon.

'What shall I do, Father?' said Orly, his daughter.

'You, my dear, will help Martin inform the estate. We are all in mourning. Have the flags at half mast. Take off these clothes and find your blacks. We are loyal subjects.' He waved a severe finger. 'Never let it be said otherwise.'

'What's the Queen like?' said Orly.

'When I have spoken to her – she has been charming. But I have only known her as the King's consort.'

'Is she as beautiful as they say?' asked Orly.

Earl Gomm nodded. 'She is. I have never seen a more beautiful woman...' He stopped for an instant, a thin smile escaped. 'With the exception of your mother...'

Countess Gomm shook her head rapidly. 'You've picked a strange time for your flattery.'

The smile had gone from Earl Gomm. Smothered as inappropriate. 'I don't know what she'll be like as head of state.' He gazed round at them all. His wife, his son, his daughter – only the toddler was not here. How vulnerable they were. His wife knew. She had grown up in the war – but his children knew only peace. Heaven help them.

Quietly, he said, 'We are loyal subjects of the Queen. She is our monarch. Express no disloyalty. Express no doubts. I did not say those words earlier. She is the best of Queens. God save Her.'

'God save Her,' they repeated after him.

Orly caught Martin's eye. She had heard the fear in her father's voice and was not used to it. He was the protector. He was the Lord of the estate and the family. Nothing could go wrong with him in place. He was her safety, the foundation of her life.

But a murder in a high place had cracked those foundations.

Chapter 5

Toby was in the straw, lying sideways, his knees clutched to his chest, shivering. There wasn't enough straw to get completely under it, and by trying to pull it over, he would draw it off somewhere else. He had given up trying. His teeth chattered, his body shook. He wanted the night to end, he wanted it to go on forever. He was enveloped in misery.

But the cold could not be ignored. It had sunk through to his bones. He rose stiffly and began thrashing his arms, lifting his knees and twisting about. In the dark he hit a wall, turned rapidly back and did the three and a half paces to the wall opposite. He turned and did it again. He could not see the walls he was meeting; they met his outstretched fingers. Then he circled the cell. A rapid walk in the dark. He was brother to all the others, in all these dungeon cells, walking round and round, seeing nothing, trying to keep warm, filled with hopelessness.

Who had killed his father? The answer took no working out. The instant the question was posed, the response was hurled like a lightning bolt. Her. The Queen had killed him. This was no mystery. Who else could it be? The Queen had planted the dagger under his pillow. She or Zeke; it didn't matter. They were in it together. Easy enough to smear blood on a shoe and put a print outside the King's chamber. And to torture a guard until he screamed out that he was Toby's accomplice. And in case he should change his mind, rack him until he died.

Easy.

To wear widow's weeds. To weep on cue. And to chop her stepson's head off to clear her son's way to the throne.

Easy as cutting bread.

He stopped walking, feeling dizzy, and leaned against a wall. She had the kingdom. She had the succession. Zeke would rule after her. Find him a wife, breed from him – and she would go on forever.

His forehead rested against the damp wall. He wanted to howl. How long was this night? It seemed as if he'd been born in the dark and would never come out of it, like an insect under a stone. He had lost his eyes at birth. There was no light. He continued circling, like the other blind men in their cells, walking time away, a hand scraping the wall to make contact with something solid.

Why had she come to see him? It wasn't necessary with all the trumped-up evidence against him and the guard screaming his name... Why?

To show him she could, perhaps that was it. And her untying him – that was her being merciful. She needed a witness. So she brought Councillor Higgs. He will tell of the visit and Toby's wickedness.

Claiming innocence to the end.

What could be more wicked?

He tottered, almost overcome with dizziness. And in an instant felt very afraid. The darkness was full of demons. He had lost himself in the space. Where was the door? Where was the window? He was filled with panic, his heart beating in his ears. Was there a door? Was there a window at all? Out of the darkness, a red thing with pointed teeth, a barbed tail and a trident was coming for him. He closed his eyes. It was still there. He had left his cell. This was the anteroom of Hell.

He screamed and ran into a wall. He turned and raced and bashed into another. The imp was after him. It would rip his soul from his body. It would prick him like a sausage. Into the wall. And off and back. And into the wall...

But this was no wall. It moved, it creaked. It was true. He was in Hell.

He backed off. Standing still. He counted to twenty. He pressed his nails into his hands. A little calmer, he moved forward and pushed. He had felt it move again.

His fingers were against metal and bolts. It was the door. He shouldered it. It had a looseness. Slackness in the lock perhaps... He worked his fingers to the edge of the door. Pressing them into the groove, he pulled with his fingertips.

The door opened with an agonizing groan.

Just a few inches, but enough for a dull strip of light to enter the cell. He dare not believe it. The door was open. Was this really Hell? Could there be devils out there ready to roast him? Was he already dead?

He battled with the dream world, conjured out of fear and darkness. It was the real door. He could see the outline. He could feel its realness. He listened intently, and could hear nothing outside.

This was still the living world.

But why was the door open? Accident – could it be so? That the gaoler had been so in awe of the Queen that he had forgotten to lock up after him. A man who locked scores of doors daily... It seemed so unlikely. Gaolers do not leave doors open. If it was deliberate – then why? Why would they have left his cell door open?

It hit him. She wanted him to escape. To run for it. And then he could be chased and speared like a rat. She had men out there, waiting for him to come out.

Then let them kill me, he thought. Rather than go mad, chased by devils, rather than be axed at noon. Let them cut me down now.

He opened the door a little more, and slid into the corridor.

Chapter 6

A lantern hung on the wall, just outside his cell. He was a privileged prisoner, a prince. Ordinary prisoners did not have lights outside their cells. Of course he would have liked it within. But not even princes were granted that.

Toby took down the lantern from its hook. And walked slowly into the gloom of the corridor. He kept close to the wall, creeping on the flagstones to silence his footsteps. He had been down in the dungeons once before. Curious as boys were, his father had asked the Captain of the Guard to show him round. He'd loved the torture chamber, and had even put his foot in the boot.

Three corridors, he remembered, came off the end of the stairs. So he must just trace this one to their foot. He could so easily be caught. There was nowhere to go, no way off the corridor. He stopped for an instant; if they were waiting for him – where would they pounce?

He continued walking, and his heart jumped in his chest. He'd heard a grunt. He stopped, listened. It was rhythmic. Someone was snoring somewhere. He crept on, and in a little while came to him in a recess. The gaoler was slumped on a bench, a jug on the floor by a flickering lantern. His mouth was open, the bloated tongue almost out. Each snore lifted his chest and threw back his head. By him, on a large ring, was a set of keys.

There was just two on it. The Captain of the Guard had explained to Toby – all the cells had the same key. And the other was for the door at the top of the stairs that opened out into the courtyard.

Toby inched his way to the sleeping man. He could smash the jug over his head – but perhaps that skull was so thick, it would simply wake him up. The gaoler groaned, waved his arms and fell back into his slump. Toby could smell drink. All the better.

He took the keys, squeezed them in his hand to stop them clinking. He was about to go forward to the stairs when he had a thought. Instead, he turned about, crept back along the corridor to his cell. Which key was it? He tried one. It fitted. He turned it and locked his cell door.

Back he went up the corridor, past the sleeping gaoler. He wondered whether he should blow the man's lantern out. Better not, it would make his own more obvious. He crept on, listening to the darkness, looking deep into the shadow ahead. Expecting every instant to be jumped upon.

At the foot of the stairs two other corridors ran off like mine shafts into blackness. The stairs were well worn. 54 of them or 55 – he had counted them on his visit. On his way up, on his way down – and had been one out. He began his ascent. They curled round like the stairs of a lighthouse. He could only see a little way ahead, to the round of the bend. The stairs were narrow, well worn, barely wide enough for one person. If they came for him now, one from the top, one from the bottom – he could be skewered between them.

Rounding each bend he expected a guard to be standing there, spear at the ready. Perhaps someone was coming up after him. He forced himself to stop. There was no sound. For a few seconds he was frightened to go on. At least in this space he was temporarily safe. He took another step, and another. He counted them upwards. It didn't matter that he hadn't begun from one. He wasn't counting stairs.

It was then he heard a yell and running footsteps below. Another cry, even as he raced up. It was the gaoler after him. Toby took them two at a time. The gaoler had reached the bottom stairs and knew the prince was ahead from the spilling light. There was no point putting it out now.

'Come back 'ere! I'll get you, you dog!'

The screech rang round the walls as Toby raced upwards. If anyone was ahead – he'd race straight into their arms. The gaoler had reached the stairs. Toby could hear his heavy tread behind him.

'I'll strangle you when I catch yer! I'll put your eyes out!'

Toby ran in terror. There were no tiptoes now. Up and round as fast as he could manage. He hoped the man was very drunk. But what had woken him? His own snoring perhaps...

Ahead was the door. Toby put down the lamp. Which key was it? There were only two but they looked so alike. Why hadn't he remembered when he'd locked his cell?

His sweaty fingers fumbled. Which? He put one in the lock. It wouldn't turn. Was it the wrong one or was it just difficult? He tried twisting it again. And once again. And then pulled it out.

The footsteps were clattering up.

'I'll tie you in knots. I'll turn you inside out like a sack!'

The other key was in the lock. He twisted. It worked. The night air hit him as he pulled the door open. Toby took the key out and was out into the courtyard. He turned, he could see the gaoler with just about eight steps to go. Breathless, cursing, his great hands reaching out for him.

'I'll twist your bleedin' head off!'

Toby slammed the door shut. He rammed the key in the lock and turned it. At the same time there was a thump against the door. But he had locked it.

Toby took the key out. He could hear yelling and thumping. The door though was thick. The sound wouldn't carry too far.

This was no time to stick around.

Chapter 7

He edged around the courtyard of the castle, keeping tight to the wall. It was very dark; there were few stars, no moon and a lot of cloud. The wind was icy. There was always a guard in the courtyard, he knew. The guard would patrol the courtyard and then take a break in his cubbyhole. Toby could hear nothing. Perhaps this was his break. Or the wind was keeping him longer.

He must get out of the castle. The obvious way was across the drawbridge. That might be down, sometimes it was at night. They weren't at war and often supplies came late. But there were always two guards at the drawbridge, and others sleeping in the guardhouse. He'd never get out that way.

This, though, was his castle. He had lived here all his life and he knew a way down the castle wall. He and his cousin Kev used to use it to escape from lessons. It was dangerous. And when his father heard about it, he'd had them both thrashed.

He needed to get up to the battlements. There were five ways up, not counting the two at the drawbridge which he ruled out. Too close to the guard and the guardhouse.

Footsteps clinked on the cobblestones. The guard had begun his patrol. Toby couldn't see him and the echo of the sound made it difficult to know where he was. If he'd just left his base, it would be perhaps a minute before he was round here.

A few steps ahead was a way up to the battlement. But he found it barred by a stout wooden door. He pushed at with his shoulder. Locked. Toby groaned. The others would be locked too.

The footsteps were closer.

The keys of course. It was possible one might work. He tried one. It didn't turn and didn't want to come out. No-one oiled these damn things. The guard was whistling and closer still. The key came out. There was not time for the second. He would be caught.

But the guard had stopped. Why? The reason didn't matter, the fact was enough. Toby put the other key in. It wouldn't turn. The guard would be on him. Why had he stopped?

The dungeon of course. The gaoler's thumping.

The key turned stiffly. He pulled the door open, took out the key and stepped into the stairwell. At the other side, he locked the door behind him.

With some relief, he took the stone steps two at a time. There were perhaps twenty which led him up to the battlement. From the top, kneeling down, he looked below into the courtyard. He couldn't make out the guard, but if he was at the dungeon – how long would it take him to get a key and find out what was happening?

Not long. Not long enough.

The battlements were about ten feet wide, with a low wall on the outside with rectangular cutouts for archers to shoot through. There would be two guards up here, he knew; they walked in opposite directions patrolling the wall. Toby could easily be caught by either of them or by both in a scissors.

He listened.

There were footsteps, but only in one direction. Two sets. They were together. Naughty, naughty. Some other time he might report them for that – but now he was grateful they'd got together for a chat.

Toby was ahead of them. He knew where he had to go. And, if he stayed ahead, would be there in perhaps a minute. He stepped along as speedily as silence would allow. He was aware of every sound of the night, the intense cold and the danger he was in. An escaped prisoner could be killed. Rarely were they brought back alive.

Toby had reached the section of the wall where he and his cousin used to climb down to the moat. That was in daylight of course. Well, he couldn't wait. He was over the top and hanging by his fingertips. His feet had to find the ledge. There it was, above a long narrow window. Now he had to lower a foot, low as he could get it, extend the toe, hanging by the very tips of his fingers. Where was it? Got it. Then find a crack for one hand. Feeling along the wall. Got it. Now take the other hand down. This was the awful bit. One foot on the ledge, the other stretched down to the bottom of the window. One set of fingers in the tiniest of grooves, the other searching... His legs began to shake. Not now please. His fingers found a cleft. And he lowered his other leg into the safety of the window.

He could now bring his hands down, one at a time, to the ledge about the window. This bit was easier. Now, he drew his hands into the window, pushing on either sides to keep a grip, and lowered his feet to the next ledge above the middle window. There were three in all, and then a short drop to the outcrop above the moat.

A voice came from courtyard, just heard by Toby hanging from the outside wall.

'Oi! Guard on the rampart!'

A reply came from the top quite close to Toby. 'Yes? What's up?'

'Something's going on in the dungeon. There's thumping on the door.'

'The silly sod has lost his keys again. Drunk I bet.'

'What shall I do?'

'Hang about. We'll come down...'

Toby thought, they must have keys to open the door at the bottom. And those keys would fit the dungeon door. And the gaoler, once free, would tell them soon enough what was going on.

He was down to the mid window. Time was short. The rampart guard must be already in the courtyard. Could he drop into the moat? He'd make a splash but they probably wouldn't hear – and he was quite a way from the draw-bridge guard.

Toby lowered himself into a crouch in the window. Then, with his hands on the ledge, let his feet and body down. His legs were dangling in space. Now was the time to drop, but he was afraid he'd hit the edge of the moat.

He couldn't hang much longer. He let go and pushed off the wall with one foot. It tumbled him half backwards. In a second, he was in the icy water. It closed over his head, and then he hit bottom. He pushed himself up and struck out for the far side, not waiting to hear whether he had been heard or not. Too late for that. Toby was not the best of swimmers – but he was freezing and time was desperately short. He splashed hands and feet until he bumped into the bank.

The sides were muddy. He had to grasp tufts of grass to get any leverage. He slipped back, grabbed ahead and dug his fingers into the mud and pulled himself out.

He stood up and looked back at the castle gasping. He could hear no alarm. Not yet. But it couldn't be long.

He began to run.

Chapter 8

'This key's useless.'

The three guards were at the door down to the dungeon. One of them was trying to turn the key, another holding a lantern over him, the third watching.

'Let me have a go.'

The first shrugged and shifted aside. The second took the key.

'Hell, it's stiff. I keep telling them about these keys. That new blacksmith is a heap of manure. Half the doors won't open.' He tried twisting with both hands. 'Useless.'

'Let me have a go,' said the third.

'It's a waste of time,' said the one at the door.

'Let me have a go then,' insisted the third.

'What d'you think you've got? Magic fingers? Go on then – show us how it's done.'

'What could be going on down there?' said the courtyard guard who was holding the lamp.

'The gaoler's a drunken sot. He's lost his keys before. Why should we help him out?'

'Hopeless flaming key,' said the man at the door. 'You sure this is the right one?'

'Must be. I think,' said his mate.

'That makes me feel confident.' He stopped trying to twist it. 'We've all three tried it. It's a dud. So we'd better get another...'

'We could leave him,' said his mate.

'What, leave him locked in?'

'We're off watch in an hour – ain't we? Let dawn watch handle it.'

'And how d'you know what's going on down there? Could be a riot.'

His mate put a hand on his shoulder. 'The sod's locked in right? So they're all locked in. What's the problem?'

'I know that but...'

'D'you want to wake the Captain of the Guard at this hour?'

'No.'

'I bet you don't. But how else do we get another key?'

'They could hold us responsible. What's going on down there. We could've stopped it... We've gotta get the key. Then they can't blame us.'

'Who's it going to be then?'

'You, mate. This is your pitch. We're battlements.'

'And it's your junk key...'

Before the guard could reply a call came across the courtyard.

'What's going on there?'

They looked over. Three men were coming over, two with lanterns slightly behind the third. As they drew in, they recognised the one in the centre. Prince Zeke. And lowered their heads respectfully as he approached.

'What's going on here?' said Zeke. His sword was drawn.

'We can't open this door, Your Highness,' said a guard. 'And someone's banging...'

'Is that all?' said Zeke.

'Yes, Your Highness.'

'Does it take three of you?'

'We came to help, Your Highness.'

'Go back on patrol, all three of you. Report to the Captain of the Guard when you go off duty.' He swung his sword. 'Now. Off. Go!'

The three left. Two crossed the courtyard to go up to the battlement, the third continued round the courtyard.

Zeke watched them away. Then he thumped on the door. There came an answering thump. Zeke turned to one of his guards. 'Get me a dozen men. Here.'

'Your Highness.' And he rushed off.

Zeke turned to the other. 'Wake the torturer. I want him here at once.'

'Yes, Your Highness.' And he strode off.

They had left their lamps. Zeke fought his shadow on the wall in swordplay. When he had killed it, he thumped again on the door, three times.

Three thumps came back.

The gaoler was sitting on the top step with the jug he'd brought from below. Might as well finish it while the guard sorted themselves out. There was going to be hell to pay. Someone had escaped. He'd thought at first it was the young Prince. He'd only caught a glimpse before the door slammed. But then he'd gone down and checked; the Prince's cell door was locked. Someone else then. He wondered who it might be. He shrugged, took a swig and sniggered: Quickest way out of the dungeon, this.

In five minutes he was asleep.

He woke quickly enough when Prince Zeke burst in with twelve guards and the torturer.

Chapter 9

Toby had reached the forest. Already, there was a streak of reddish light from the east. Hoarfrost hung from the trees and traced the undergrowth. His teeth chattered. How long had he got? They must have opened the dungeon by now. Surely? He could imagine them saddling horses, the dogs straining at their leashes. He must get far away, deep into the forest, to stand any chance.

It was so cold. His clothes were soaking in icy water from his swim in the moat. It was like being rolled naked in snow. Still on the move, he took off his top and undershirt. His chest and arms were wet and the cold stung. He wrung the undershirt. Water gushed from it. He twisted it and twisted it, until the drips stopped. He put it back on. Damp as it was, it felt better. His body would have some chance at drying it now. He wrung his top, working from the sleeve ends, to the middle, down to the bottom, the icy water numbing his fingers. And then again, wringing. At last he put it back on.

Stopping to sit on a log, he took off his shoes. He poured out the water. He took off his leggings, naked to the waist. Ignoring the indignity, he wrung them out, twisted them, swung them at a tree to batter out the moisture and finally put them on again. Shoes on once more, he began to jog.

He knew this part of the forest as he'd ridden out many times. But then he'd taken the broad rides, now he went for the footpaths. There were more of them, less trod, more chance of losing his pursuers. The leaves had gone from the trees, so he could take his direction from the growing light in the east. He must get into the very thick of the forest.

Where were they?

He had been in this forest only a week ago with his father hunting deer. There had been the two of them, with the master of the hunt. And the outriders, the dog men and beaters on foot. Later, servants had come bringing the midday meal on a wagon. A fire had been lit, and while they ate, a minstrel had sung for them. It was one of those cold, sunlit days. He had loved it, alone with his father. That had not been often since he had taken a Queen.

That woman. And her son.

Hate pushed him on. He wanted to stick them like pigs. Roast them screaming, trample them under the horses. And then, as sudden as it had come, hate was gone. Fear ran it off. He was alone. He would never hunt with his father again. He had no horses.

For the first time in ages he felt hungry. Fear had been too strong before and had filled his stomach. Now that fear had gone. He had seen the dogs work too many times. They could tear a man to pieces in seconds. They were kept hungry for it. The brutes dined on fugitives. But he had not eaten since the row with his father, yesterday at noon. Must be over eighteen hours ago. He stopped at a stream to drink, but water wasn't the problem. The winter forest was no place to forage.

He had to keep the vision of the dogs. He wouldn't die of hunger, not for a long time yet – but the dogs at his heels... See them. Baying, fangs dripping in eagerness. Use them. Be very afraid.

Run.

The track was hard underfoot, with frozen ridges, and between them iced-over puddles. Light seeped between the trees. The shadows were longer than a flagpole. A bright orange sun rolled on the horizon. The watch would be changing at the castle, he thought. Soon all would be awake – and all would know their midday entertainment had forsworn them. He must make distance. He groaned with each stride, the smoke of his breath signalling his fear.

What had he become, in less than twenty-four hours? From beloved Prince to the lowest beast. A pauper had more freedom. Could ask at least for alms. He was quarry. The hunted. The pursued to death. All humanity was on his trail.

Was there anywhere to go? Who would give him shelter?

He must not just die.

Father! he called into the winter forest. A lone bird trilled. He willed his heavy legs on. Father! If he could just get away… then… He dared not think of then. There was but now. He was the running, exhausted hare. Where was home?

Chapter 10

Earl Gomm was in the front row, seated with a blanket over his knees. In the cold midday air, he cradled a mug of hot wine. Alongside were others of the nobility. Behind, also seated, but on benches were lesser lights, knights and so forth, and behind them stood the populace.

In front, against the castle wall a low, wooden stage had been set up. Seated on it were the Queen, Prince Zeke, and to one side Councillor Higgs. Between the Queen and the watching crowd was the block. Everyone had heard Prince Toby was not to be its victim. All morning the castle had been a fire of rumour. Guards had been running about, arrests had been made, the torturers were working overtime. Gomm had been told of the Prince's escape immediately on his arrival. Before he could ask much else, he had been ushered in with a number of other lords to an audience with the Queen. Each in turn had sworn allegiance to her.

Now the circus.

Gomm never liked executions. They brought out the worst in everyone. Blood lust devalued human life. He wanted peace, he had tried to live in peace. There were times the King called for men for his army. Gomm had always sent them with reluctance. And was saddened at those who did not return.

There were four to die today. Poor wretches. Three guards and a gaoler. Gomm had heard they played some part in the escape. The informant was vague as to exactly what. Gomm watched as they stumbled out of the dungeon door, bare to the waist, chained hand and foot with guards on either side. Their backs were stripped of flesh from whipping, bubbling blood. They could barely walk. The boot, thought Gomm. He had met the King's head torturer once, Alec. Alec swore he could get a man to betray his mother in ten minutes. Gomm had asked him why, what was the point? He'd got no coherent reply, but realised it was all a game with Alec. He enjoyed the blood and gore, the screams. Breaking men was the point.

These four were broken. Alec had excelled himself. The whipping, the boot, their faces swollen like pigs' bladders. The gaoler had lost three fingers, one of the guards an ear, another had lost half his nose. They had all confessed to helping Prince Toby escape. And for their reward had their tongues cut out.

Gomm shuddered. What sort of truth was this? How could anyone know whether they had helped Toby or not? It was wise though not to say such things. He went to sip his warm wine but its bloody colour nauseated him. He put it down. Gomm knew he must be a loyal subject. This was a gory start to a reign.

It did not augur well.

The prisoners and their guard had halted by the executioner, who wore black leggings, black shoes, black singlet, as if he were in mourning for the lives he would take. His burly arms were bare and held the double-edged axe over his shoulder. His head was completely covered in a black bag down to his shoulders. Holes had been cut at the front for eyes, nostrils and mouth. He waited patiently. Gomm feared he would have no shortage of work.

The herald blew his horn. The Queen rose. All the audience stood and bowed or curtseyed.

'Be seated,' said the Queen.

They sat. The Queen waited until all eyes were upon her. And then a little longer. She wore clothing suitable for a widow: a black, long-sleeved robe from neck to feet. Around her neck was the full royal regalia and within its semi-circle the smaller yellow jewel she always wore. On her head was the crown of state. She was proud, thought Gomm, she was beautiful. She was dangerous.

'My people,' she began. 'The murder of our beloved King has brought me reluctantly to the throne. I will do my duty. There will be a week of mourning throughout the land. My coronation will be in a month. The Lords have sworn an oath of loyalty.' She looked along the front row, catching an eye here and there. 'Heaven help any who betray me.' She turned to the prisoners. 'These traitors helped Prince Toby to escape. He is now a fugitive.' She returned to the crowd and gazed deep into their midst as if she were seeking out their deepest secrets. 'Prince Toby was the murderer of my dear husband, your King. Anyone who assists Toby shall die. Their family will be slaughtered and their houses burnt. These four traitors await their punishment. Their families have been put to the sword. Let that be my warning to all of you.'

Gomm caught her eye and shuddered. How much blood would there be?

The Queen turned to the executioner.

'Behead them.'

The gaoler was brought forward by a guard, a gurgle was coming from his tongueless mouth. A plea for forgiveness, a protest, or simply a groan of pain – who would know? His chains rattled in his trembling. The executioner took his head by the hair and thrust it on the block. The man did not resist. Gomm wondered what had been done to him in a morning that the man went so willingly to death. The executioner stood back. He held the axe in both hands and gently placed the blade on the back of the gaoler's neck. He raised the handle slowly. Gomm closed his eyes. He was much closer than he wanted to be. He heard the swish, then the chop and the gasp of the crowd. He opened his eyes. There, a few paces away was the headless man in the block, the torn hole gushing blood. Almost at Gomm's feet, in reaching distance, was the bloated head.

The executioner picked it up by the hair and raised it high in the air. The crowd roared as the blood dripped down his arm.

Chapter II

The four had been executed. Their heads were on pikes. The crowd were roaring. How much longer could this go on, thought Gomm. He had come, he had seen, he felt sick – and yet he must stay like a schoolboy until he was dismissed.

He vowed to spend as little time as possible at court. Prince Zeke and the Queen were chatting. Or rather her son was shouting in her ear above the racket. He was smiling, plainly enjoying himself and she was grinning more than a widow should. Gomm grimaced. The Prince enjoyed this, the Queen too. How far would they go?

He must look after his family. Take no sides, make no enemies. Guard his tongue at all times. Life would be cheap at court. He hoped on his estate, he could be left out of things. Be allowed to grow his corn, keep his cattle and sheep, look after his people.

Too easy. He had a vision of blood flowing off the hills into the lakes below.

Zeke was still speaking to his mother. She was nodding. Whose death were they plotting? If he could he would walk away now. But he dare not. He was in the Queen's presence. She dictated the coming and going.

The executioner was standing by his block. He was holding the axe downward, the metal head on the ground. The blood, running down his arms, trickled off his fingers and snaked round the axe handle. He was calm and waiting, his black vest blotched with gore. His family at least were safe, thought Gomm. Father was assured of work. These were the good times. Meat would be on the table, grain in the barn.

The herald was blowing his trumpet. All were silenced. They knew the rules. They knew when they could shout and scream. They knew when they must keep their mouths shut.

Prince Zeke rose. He raised his arms for silence. There was no need. Every eye was on him, every jaw clamped shut. Zeke wore close fitting black, the colour of mourning. But he wore too chain mail, black to be sure – but unusual for the death of a monarch. As was the sword he wore at his waist. On his hands were his customary black gloves. Mourning, or otherwise, he wore these.

'God save the Queen!' he shouted.

'God save the Queen!' came the immediate response from every throat.

'These traitors have received their punishment.' He pointed up to the dripping heads on their pikes to the right of him. 'The Queen's justice will be quick. Slow justice is weak. It allows men to conspire, armies to gather...' He raised a hand, and swung a pointed finger round the crowd. 'There are some here who are already conspiring. The King hardly a day dead, and the crows are gathering. I am the instrument of my mother.'

The Queen behind him nodded.

'I will not allow traitors to bring her down. Already followers of Prince Toby gather. Their leader has killed the King – and they conspire in his name to take the country. My mother and I will nip it in the bud. Followers of Prince Toby will die.'

The crowd cheered. Gomm shouted his yea with the others. He could not been seen tight-lipped.

Prince Zeke waited for silence. Both arms were on his hips, legs slightly apart, his lips closed tightly. The Queen behind was nodding, faintly smiling as she adjusted her headscarf.

'There are traitors here,' shouted Zeke. 'Amongst those voices cheering are serpents whose poison must be cut off. We know who you are.'

Prince Zeke scanned the crowd. Gomm could feel the shudder. Who would he pick out?

'Eight of you,' went on Zeke. 'Eight traitors. Eight followers of Prince Toby.' His hand swung round. 'Eight who will die.'

He turned and the Queen handed him a piece of paper.

Zeke turned back to the crowd. 'I have the list of traitors. Let's begin.' He glanced down at the first name and with a wry smile said, 'Earl Gomm.'

Gomm rose, his legs shaking. It wasn't totally unexpected. As Zeke played out his game he had thought, anybody could be chosen. It was a lottery. Yes, it could be him.

The crowd were hurling abuse.

'Your Majesty...' Further words were lost in the uproar.

Two guards had taken an arm each, a third put a bag on Gomm's head. There were muffled cries as he was dragged to the block. He struggled and pulled. The executioner grabbed him by the hair and slammed his head into place. The guards held his arms to the ground, the third had a foot on his back. Still he struggled.

The axe was lifted and came down swiftly. It missed Gomm's neck but cut his backbone and spinal cord. All movement stopped in his limbs. He was alive but paralysed in all but his head. God save my family, he thought. God save my country...

And thought and word and life were hacked off, in a better aimed chop.

His head fell onto the cobbles.

Chapter 12

Frost was forming again on the branches and undergrowth. In the west were red layers of cloud with an underlay of gold. Toby shivered. It had been a little warmer during the day, but now there was a return to the cold of the night. All he'd eaten that day was a parsnip he had pulled out of the frozen ground. He'd barely stopped. His feet were badly blistered, but he limped on. If he'd been going in a straight line, he must be twenty miles from the castle. But he doubted he had. He was a sack of weariness, tramping so slowly it was pointless going on. Except to stand still would be to freeze. He had to find shelter. A night out in the cold would kill him.

He'd seen few people that day, and those he had – kept out of their way. A woodcutter with a wheelbarrow of logs, a shepherd on a wider trail came along with half a dozen sheep, a priest singing hymns – at the first sound, he had hid behind a tree. He'd waited until they were gone before continuing. No one must see him. He was an outcast, found guilty of the worst crime. The time for his execution had come and gone. He could imagine what a crowd had gathered for a royal execution. And how disappointed they would have been when he didn't show.

In a day he'd gone from prince to prisoner to vagabond. He had no money. He never carried money. Princes don't need it. A valet carries the purse. Not that he would have been left with anything in the dungeon. He halted, leaned against a tree and squeezed a painful foot. His teeth chattered. He could not simply walk and walk. He was walked out. He was starving, blistered and bruised. Could he try a cottage? Not in this embroidered jacket. Muddy it might be, but no peasant wore such finery. Throw it away? And then freeze all the quicker.

He took it off and turned it inside out. It looked odd with the hemming and lining – but he put it on that way. It wouldn't save him if anyone chose to look closely but it might pass a glance. He must find a cottage. He would offer to work for food. Ask to sleep in a cowshed. It was a risk – but likely a small cottage would not have heard the news. Especially one out here in the forest. He must try to talk like them. How did they talk? He didn't know. He had never talked to a peasant.

Wearily he hobbled on. The track was icing up, the hard ridges pressing against his blisters. He scrunched his toes and in a little way found a stick. That was easier but it broke after a quarter of a mile. He wished he had a knife. Found another stick which did him for a short distance before that broke too.

Dogs, he thought to himself. The dogs are coming. It had worked in the morning. The images of baying and ripping teeth had pushed him on through the morning. But it didn't work now. Instead, he couldn't help himself, he thought of sausages spitting in the pan, eggs frying with brilliant yellow yolks and bubbling whites, bread toasted with the butter melting into it. He laughed in spite of his misery, reminded of the breakfast the gaoler had promised him. Had there been anything at all? He'd welcome now even a mouldy crust. Had the gaoler had it? A smile escaped from him when he thought of the instant the gaoler had got to the top of the stairs and he'd slammed the door on him.

No doubt he is being punished.

The sun had gone down but it was not yet dark. A single bright star was following the route of the sun.

'O help me, star!' he cried into falling light. 'Help me find shelter.'

He gazed into its brightness as if it were a god that could grant such things. So light, in so much deep blue. Surely it could perform wonders?

It was then he saw the fox. He hadn't noticed it before. His eyes either on the star or his feet. It came right up to him in the nature of a dog. That surprised him. He had only known foxes as timid creatures, running from the hounds. Whenever he'd come across one, when not out on a hunt, they sped off as soon as seen. This one sensed his weakness. The animal sat in the middle of the path, and gazed up at him with its dark eyes as he approached.

Toby stopped. The fox continued to stare, its ears twitching. Then it turned and began walking slowly along the track, its tail raised. When it had gone a little way, its head turned back. Clearly it meant him to follow.

Or that's what Toby guessed. And what did it matter anyway?

He followed.

Chapter 13

He stumbled on in the growing dark. The fox was about ten yards ahead, adjusting its pace to his. When he stopped, it stopped and waited for him to begin again. And his stops were often. There was clearly some purpose in the fox. And he had none himself. At least it kept him moving.

The fox stopped at a side path, waited until he was close enough, turned down it and a little way along halted again. When Toby was safely along the fox continued. He could by now barely see it in the gloom. But that hardly mattered as the fox with its dark-adjusted eyes could see him – and stopped often enough even for poor human sight.

The sky was filling with stars. Almost above him was the saucepan of the Plough, and across from it the W of Cassiopeia: the cold stars of winter nights on either side of the Pole Star. Astronomy was a subject thought suitable for a Prince. A fit of shivering overcame him. He could not stop himself. It juddered through his body, from his chattering teeth, down his shaking arms and knees.

He was so weary, he was so cold, he was so unhappy. Everything had gone. All that awaited was death. Why delay it? He could simply lay down. Give in to it. It would come. It would be a blessing.

What was left for him in life?

His hands were scratched by brambles. He hardly knew, hardly cared. Blood would go its own way. The path was thinning. Easy for a fox to get through but tight for a person. The brambles were like claws clutching at his clothing, a branch streaked his face. He bunched his hands within the ends of his sleeves to push away what he could.

Part of him wanted to just give up. And part to fight to the very end.

And if to fight, to live – then he needed people. And surely he wanted wide paths. Not this snaggled, overgrown thing but a path that people walked down with their animals. If he disappeared into the thick of the forest then he would die in the thick of the forest. It was an icy night, he was sore and exhausted. Hungry and despairing.

Live or die?

He was hardly sure it was a real fox. The tired mind plays tricks. A fox was not a dog. His own mind was trapping him. He turned about. He must find people. He ran a little way. How long did he have? Stumbling back the way he had come, he felt the fox between his legs. He stopped, he could hardly make out its shape. It was rubbing against him like a cat.

He turned once more. He would trust the fox. It had come back for him. It was taking him somewhere. Please, fox, he pleaded... He followed in hope down the dense path. And in a few minutes, scratched and weary, was minded to turn back again. Stopped, considered. What was the point? What was behind? What was in front? He was completely lost in the forest on a freezing night.

He stumbled against an obstruction, tried to get round it but it went along on both sides. Feeling with his fingers; it was woody and woven. A fence. He peered ahead. There was something there. A full black shape. And a faint smell of wood smoke. Could this be a cottage?

His hands feverishly worked their way along the fence. One over the other, tumble fashion, until he came to the gate. The fox was waiting there. It brushed against his leg, then led him in.

The path was short. He was soon at the cottage door. The wood of the walls was rough on his fingers. He might have stood for an age, pondering, daring himself but the fox was scratching at the door.

Inside he could hear shuffling. He wanted to run. He was an outlaw now. But would be a dead one if he continued roaming. And he couldn't anyway. Exhaustion and cold had run him to earth. Toby held himself to the spot. And the door opened.

An old lady stood there with a lamp held high. Grey hair was spilling out of a red spotted headscarf.

'Why have you been so long?' she said.

Chapter 14

She led him into the one-roomed cottage.

'Sit down, young man,' she said, indicating one of a pair of chairs either side of the fire.

He flopped into it and, as the warmth played over him, began to weep. He could not stop himself. He shook with sobs for the misery of the last day and this simple comfort.

'I'll get you some soup,' said the woman.

Her voice bathed him. It didn't order or scorn him. It offered.

'Thank you, thank you, madam,' he managed to mumble through blue lips.

The woman chuckled. 'Don't madam me. I won't know whom you are talking to. I am Maeg.'

'Thank you, Maeg,' he whispered.

The fire was in a stone fireplace, the only stone in the house. A black pot was on raised stones, licked by the flames. The woman ladled the soup from the pot into a wooden bowl, which she passed to Toby.

He clutched the bowl in both hands. His face was wet, though his weeping had ceased. This fire and soup were real. How beautiful was the heat. He felt like a new leaf stretching to the sun. He gazed into the wonder of the flickering flame. Red and yellow joy flowed into his bones.

She gave him a spoon. He sipped the hot soup. A piece of carrot sang to his tongue. He swallowed the melody and came back for more notes. And it sang from his stomach and sent its chorus into his arms and legs, to his fingers and his tingling toes. It was heavenly soup. Thick with a peppery pea flavour – and within it, soft and hot, pieces of onion, carrot, cabbage and parsnip.

It was soon gone.

She refilled the bowl. And this time gave him a plate of bread, thickly buttered.

There were two chairs at the fireplace. She took the other one, stretched out her thick legs, her hands in her aproned lap – and smiled at his joy.

When he had finished, he put the bowl and plate on the floor.

'Thank you, Maeg,' he sighed. 'You will be rewarded.' And then felt foolish, speaking the words of a prince from the mouth of a vagabond.

'Never mind rewards,' she said, sitting up in the chair. Her face was round and red, pimpled here and there. Hairs came from her thick nose. She had perhaps six teeth.

'There's lots to do,' she went on. 'If they catch you here, your life is not worth a stick, Prince Toby.'

He stared at her, startled. 'How do you know?'

'I know things,' she said. 'Take off your clothes.'

Toby was now alarmed. It seemed he was being offered alms but now threatened...

'I have no others...' he began.

'Take them off,' she said. 'They are princely clothes. How far will you get in those? You think by turning a coat inside out I can't tell how well made it is? Your only hope is to disappear into the people. Take them off.'

Toby hesitated. In fear and shame.

'I've had four sons in this little cottage,' she said. 'Don't worry for your modesty.'

He began to undress. First his coat, then his leggings.

'And the underthings,' she said. 'Who wears such finery here?' And when he hesitated further, she added, 'Your life is at stake.'

Toby took them off and stood naked before the fire.

'You poor boy,' said the woman. 'Those bruises. They certainly roughed you up.'

She rose from her chair and went to a shelf. She returned to him with a blanket and a large pair of scissors.

'Wrap yourself in that.'

Toby did so and sat again in the chair. He watched in horror as she threw his vest on the fire.

'We must burn every scrap,' she said. 'You were never here.'

'What shall I wear?' he said, watching her cut his leggings into pieces.

'I have old clothes here from my sons,' she grinned toothily at him. 'Much more suitable.'

Toby hesitated before he spoke again. 'Are you... a witch?'

She shrugged, throwing a piece of legging on to the fire. 'Some call me that. It's not my word. I have some magic. Less than I used to.' She tapped her forehead with a plump finger. 'It's the memory. It goes. There are things I could do...' She sighed heavily, 'but now...' She stopped and put down the material she was cutting. 'Give me your soup bowl.'

Toby handed it to her.

She kneeled on the floor before the fire and circled her large hands round the bowl. The firelight flickered in her eyes. 'I used to be able to do it.' She looked into the bowl. 'It's finding a starting point...' Her hands were round the bowl in her lap, the thumbs and fingertips touching. Her head was immobile, gazing into the bowl as if it were a deep well.

'Ah here it is.' She swung the bowl side to side to catch some light. 'There are grave times ahead. I see fear.' She tipped the bowl. 'Love. Hate.'

Toby didn't respond but felt disappointment. This was fortune-teller's hokum.

'This is more like it,' said the woman eagerly. 'It comes back.' She was silent for a few moments and then intoned:

'You will rescue someone who lies with the dead. You will walk with the dead. You will destroy the secret of life.'

She looked up at him.

'You have been chosen, Toby. And I have but a little part to play.' She put down the bowl. 'Sleep now, because in the morning you must move on.'

Chapter 15

She made him up a bed by the fire. She put a blanket over the mat, with two more on top. He was certainly warm enough and ten times grateful for that. But could not sleep, rolling from bruise to bruise. There seemed nowhere he could lay comfortably. His legs ached with weariness. He was drained, and yet he could not sleep...

And then he could.

And was gone. Too deep to feel pain. Too deep to dream. Like a fire covered in coal dust, his life was there, burning low, too low to hurt. But low enough to heal. The old lady came once or twice to replace the blanket he'd thrown off. But although he rolled and shuffled he did not wake until well into the morning.

It was light when he opened his eyes. The old lady was working at the wooden table in the centre of the room. She had already re-made her narrow bed under the window. On the table was a wooden bucket and the woman was chopping herbs and throwing them in. She had several corked bottles by her and poured a little in from each from time to time.

'Sleep well?' she asked.

Toby smiled drowsily. 'I must have.'

She went to the pot on the fire and ladled porridge into a bowl. She handed it to him with a spoon. Toby took it gratefully and still in his blanket by the fire began to eat.

'I've sorted some clothes out for you,' she said, indicating the heap on the chair. 'Don't put them on yet.'

Toby wasn't thinking of doing so, too busy with his porridge. And when it was finished, he looked to her for more, like a cat that had just licked out its bowl.

'Help yourself,' she said, adding a pinch of powder to her bucket. She had a dog-eared book in her hand and sucked her lips noisily as she read.

Toby kneeled before the fire. As he picked up the ladle the blanket fell off him. He was naked, all his clothes had been burnt last night. With a bowl in one hand and a ladle in the other he couldn't cope and panicked for an instant. But then he didn't care, because she didn't care. And he ladled himself a bowl of porridge, his body red in the firelight. The old lady did take half a glance between her reading and mixing. Half joy she felt in his appetite, and half a pleasurable envy of the smooth body of youth.

His bowl filled to the brim, Toby sat naked by the fire and spooned his porridge. It was creamy with milk but had no sugar, instead a little salt. Two days ago he would have rejected this peasant fare – but his hunger spared him such fussiness. It was wholesome, it was hot and creamy. It was delicious. He could have eaten the pot.

When he had finished the third bowl, she brought the bucket to him.

'You must wash yourself all over with this. It will ease your bruises. And take away your smell.'

Toby blushed. Did he smell so bad?

'Every smell I mean,' she said putting the bucket down. 'There's magic here. For a full day after you wash yourself with this, you will have no smell. The dogs will lose your trail.' She took the bowl from him. 'Forget food if you can. You are a fugitive. They are out to kill you. You must be away very soon.'

'I have nowhere to go.'

She shook her head. 'Go you must, Toby. Now wash.' She handled him a flannel and tentatively he dipped it in the frothing liquid in the bucket. 'Be vigorous,' she said. 'Wipe it over every inch of your body, from your scalp to the soles of your feet. No smell must escape you.' She went back to her table and picked up a second bucket from the floor. 'I'm going up the path where you came from, to lose your smell near the cottage. Now get on with it yourself. Hurry up. There's men with swords looking for you. There's a reward on your head.'

Toby jumped up. Of course there would be. He soaked the flannel in the bucket and wiped it round his face.

'Don't miss anything,' exclaimed the old woman. She was at the door with the bucket. 'Make haste,' she said as she left, closing the door behind her.

Her preparation smelt of pine needles, of leaf mould, and there was something vinegary in it too. Immediately it touched his skin it dried, leaving the skin feeling hot and stretched as if it were sunburned. Whether it was taking away his own smell he could not tell, but it was certainly taking away his pain. His bruising washed away as the liquid passed over it. As if leached out like mud in fabric. His body was coming back to him. He worked his way from top to bottom, glowing with renewal. No longer creaky-boned with bruised flesh, he felt he could run up a mountain. When he had done the soles of his feet, he started again from the top. His life depended on it.

When he was completely washed, there was no need to dry himself. The liquid had dried over him like a varnish. He stretched and filled his lungs. He would go far today.

Toby sorted through the clothes on the chair. And began with the vest. It was rougher than he was used to and itched his chest. But he knew the old lady was right. He'd done with silk and velvet. He put on the leggings and the brown coarse tunic. She'd left him a cloth belt which he tied round the waist. For shoes, he had clogs. He'd prefer something lighter but he must wear what everyone wore.

He was barely finished when the old lady returned, her bucket empty.

'I've been up the path about a mile or so. Where it meets with the main path. The dogs will lose it there.' She looked at him approvingly. 'Almost the peasant. Better rub some mud in those hands on your way. That hair is a bit fussy. Sit down. Let me cut it on the rough.'

He sat in the chair and she hacked off curls. More than he would have liked.

'You won't be a pretty prince any more,' she said.

She swept up the hair and burnt it in the fire.

'Time to go.'

'Where am I to go?'

She shook her head. 'I cannot tell you. You will go where you go. And if you don't know you can't betray anyone. But I promise it will be safe. Now...' She lifted a finger severely. 'Who are you?'

He began, 'I am...' then stopped. Who was he?

'I am a knight with a sword at your throat,' said the old woman. 'If you don't know who you are, then I will cut your head off.'

'Who am I?' said Toby.

'You are my grandson, Ned,' she said. 'I am Maeg the healer. My son and his wife died of the plague.'

'Could you not heal them?'

'Not when they were across the sea.' She handed him a paper. 'Read this, learn this. It is the names of your brothers and uncles – and what I know of them. Eat it when you know it.'

'Won't it put you at risk?'

'Perhaps. Besides, I am old enough. You can say I am dead if you wish. That's why you are on the road. Your old granny died.'

She went to the table and took up a flour sack. 'Here's bread and cheese, water and a knife for your journey.' She picked up a blanket from the floor. 'And here's a poor man's cloak.'

'Why are you doing all this for me?'

She put a hand on his shoulder and looked into his eyes. 'I knew your mother. I was her wet-nurse. And was with her until she married.' She turned away and wiped an eye. 'You remind me of her. But please, ask me no more. You must be off. There is a hue and cry already, and you have a long way to go.'

The old woman led him out of the cottage, along the small path to the gate. The blanket was rolled on his shoulders, the flour sack of food slung down his back. The fox was waiting, its bushy tail raised.

'Sly will take you,' she said. 'Follow her. You have much to do.'

Chapter 16

As he strode, his breath fumed in front of him. He was still in forest, mostly winter-bare with a few leaves still clinging. The day was bright in a clear sky, the frost melting on the grass and branches. Toby felt strong. He'd eaten, he'd slept, his bruising was gone. No longer in the sorry state he was last night. Then he had been at the end of his tether.

He didn't know where he was going. Getting away was his main motive. Creating space between himself and the castle. As the waves washed out from there, they would become smaller, weaker. And he would be harder to find. He must make distance. The old woman had said he had things to do – but he didn't see how he could do anything. Anything other than stay alive. And distance would keep him alive.

He followed Sly, pleased to have her company. She didn't always take the paths, but sometimes cut across country, into the thickets. These slowed Toby, but he found his way through and caught up.

At one point he was aware of himself whistling. Sly stopped, turned and stared at him, her ears twitching.

'Sorry, Sly.'

Did she nod? Anyway, she turned and continued.

He felt happy. Walking so easily, free of bruises, and the morning so fine and clear. Alone in the forest, he was free.

But a little later he was overcome by misery. How dare he feel happy! His father had been murdered. He had lost everything. His reputation was in tatters. How could anyone but a fool feel happiness after all that?

They must be coming for him. Over that hill, behind that copse, he could walk into a camp of riders and dogs. How long would his new identity last then? Happiness was madness. His life hung by a thread, and if he forgot for an instant – then the next might be his last.

But in spite of himself, every so often, he forgot to be miserable. And had to pinch himself. Had to see the riders and the dogs behind every tree waiting for him.

Happiness was for fools.

But sometimes he was a fool.

After a couple of hours walking, he rested on a log to eat. The old woman had given him half a loaf, which he broke with his hands, saving some till later. He cut a lump off the cheese with the knife. He offered some to Sly but she scorned it.

'I hope you know where we are going,' he said.

While eating, he read the paper the old woman had given him. He repeated the names on it. And when they began walking once more, he continued repeating them. Telling himself who he was. Ned, the grandson of Maeg the Healer.

Would anyone believe him?

They had been on their way for about half an hour since the break, when a scream startled him. It was followed by another of such piercing intensity that it curdled his blood. Happiness flashed off. His instinct was to run like a rabbit. He was trembling and had to steady himself against a tree. Sly stopped, her ears pricked up, sniffing.

He heard the whinny of a horse.

Sly ran off, away from the sound. Toby stayed, trying to quell his terror. Another scream. He could run, should run – but someone was being hurt. He already knew he was a fool and might yet be a dead one – but he couldn't simply leave.

Another scream. Laughter and the bark of a dog.

He crept from tree to tree towards the sound. Sly had stopped, some way off. He beckoned to her. He could see she didn't want to come, but he continued and then slowly, cautiously Sly came. He waited behind a broad oak and she caught him up.

'Good girl,' he whispered.

Toby squeezed his hands tightly to stop them trembling. It didn't work. He took his knife out of his sack and put it in his belt. Much good would it do him.

Another scream. More laughter.

Down on all fours, he inched his way up a bank. He knew the source was close by. Sly wouldn't come, and stayed at the foot of the bank. At the top, he saw ahead of him a clearing. And in it, the cause of the screaming: a youth tied to an overhanging branch of a tree by his hands, dangling there, a few feet off the ground. Under him were two soldiers in what Toby must now call the Queen's uniform. Their horses were a little way off, tied up. Closer in were two dogs chewing at bones.

The soldiers had swords in their belts and wore helmets and chain mail. They were piling sticks under the young man, and every so often one of them would hit him with a stick on his bare legs.

Toby was as close as he dared be.

It was plain they were going to make a fire under the youth. He was about Toby's own age and his build. A peasant, thought Toby, from his tunic. Were they going to kill him? Or was it torture? And then would they kill him?

Why?

One of the soldiers was kneeling by the pile of sticks under the youth. Toby could hear the striking of flint.

'Do you like crackling?' the soldier called to his mate.

'With apple sauce.'

The two of them laughed. The young man was whimpering. Smoke began to come off the heap under him. It curled about, catching the wind. The soldier roughly pulled off the young man's shoes and threw them behind him.

'Don't want you getting cold feet,' called out the soldier.

The fire was catching quickly. The wood was cracking, and flames were coming through the smoke. The heap was piled high and ended just a few inches below the prisoner's bare feet.

What could Toby do but watch?

'Please, please...' the youth was begging.

'You gonna admit it?' said the soldier at the fire.

'Anything! Anything!'

The other soldier struck him on the back with a thick twig, making him swing slightly. The young man screamed. Already he must be feeling hot as he was trying to pull his feet out of the darting flame.

One of the dogs began to bark. Then the other. And they began to run. Past the soldiers and the man hanging from the tree. They were coming for Toby; they must be. More wolf than dog, fierce grey hunters, snarling for meat. Toby lay flat, he drew out his knife. Could he take blood before they did?

Up the bank they came. But to one side; they were not going for him. He lay still, holding his breath. Over they charged, growling. They were after the fox. Sly had raced off, and they were after her, into the thick of the forest.

One of the soldiers was running up the bank yelling.

'Dragon! Hunter! Back here!'

He ran up the bank. Toby pressed himself flat. The soldier was over and after the dogs, which were out of sight, barking off into the thick of trees.

The other soldier was laughing to himself as he fed the fire under the hanging youth.

'Let's have a real blaze while Jack's away.'

The captive was pulling his feet away ineffectually. Whimpering, pleading as the soldier selected pieces for the fire.

Toby wondered, could he stab the man? If he failed – he'd either be dead or cooked.

Quietly, he circled round. He was aiming for the tree where the horses were tied. Using them as cover, he could perhaps come in...

And then what?

Kill him? A soldier? What chance had he? He'd never killed a man. A deer with bow and arrow, from a distance. But a man, in touching distance? His heart beat faster as he circled round. Shrub to shrub, tree to tree. The fire was smoking more heavily, the soldier had crouched down below it. The youth was choking. Toby could hardly see him in the smoke.

In the distance he could hear barking and an occasional shout. He was at the tree where the two horses were tied. One of them was shaking its head and wrinkling its nostrils at the smoke. It then occurred to him that he had no need to kill anyone. Quickly he untied the reins. Then backed off behind the tree. But the freed horses just stood there. He wanted them to run off, for the soldier to chase – but these docile nags just waited for their masters.

He couldn't shout, he didn't want to slap them. Instead he pricked one in the rump with his knife. It drew blood and the horse whinnied and reared. Then came to ground, and, seeing Toby by the tree with the knife – ran off. The other horse watched it go for a few seconds then followed.

The soldier heard and saw the animals galloping off. And was then running too.

'Oi, you two! Peace! Fearful! Back here!'

The horses were off up the path, each pushing the other. The soldier pursued, waving his arms yelling. Toby watched from behind the tree, easing round as the soldier came past. In the distance, he heard a bark. He hoped Sly had outrun the dogs. The horses had rounded a bend and were out of sight. The soldier was still yelling but Toby could hardly hear him. The man stopped to walk, put his hands on his hips, and broke into a run again. And was gone round the bend.

Toby came out of the tree, into the smoke. His eyes streamed and he had to cover them. He ran from memory to the trunk of the young prisoner's tree. Close in, he was able to see again, his fingers rapidly found holds on the trunk. Maybe he couldn't kill a man – but he could climb.

All those years scaling the walls of the castle. Something he could do. He pulled himself into the crutch of the tree and wriggled along the branch. He had to close his eyes again as he was almost above the fire. The heat dried his face.

He felt the ropes, and with his knife cut at them, glad the old woman kept her knives sharp. First one hand, then the other. The youth fell with a scream. He'd fallen on to the fire.

Toby swung under the branch and dropped to the ground. The young man was lying there, howling. Toby pulled him to his feet.

'Come on, run – they'll be back soon!'

And when he wouldn't or couldn't, Toby put his shoulder under the youth's arm and half lifted him away. The young man whimpered, managing to limp a little. And the two staggered into the forest.

Chapter 17

The icy water gurgled swiftly over the stones. Toby watched the youth as he washed a foot in the water, then the other. Toby had wanted to go further but the injured youth couldn't. And Toby was unable to carry him far as he had no shoes and the soles of his feet were badly blistered.

'We can't stay here long,' said Toby.

The young man nodded. 'Thanks for what you did. I'm Far. My family...' He stopped and shook his head. Then covered his face with his hands. A little later he raised a hand. 'Sorry, it's just...' He stopped again. Words hurt as much as his feet.

'I'm Ned,' said Toby. He'd almost said Toby, in spite of practise. Ned Ned Ned, he said in his head.

'I can't walk at all,' said Far uncovering his tear stained face. He turned up a foot to show Toby. It was a total patch of large blisters, the skin bubbled up white and red.

Toby leaned forward and touched one of the blisters. Far squealed and pulled his foot away.

'Sorry,' said Toby. 'Why were they doing that? The soldiers.'

Far chewed his lower lip. He wiped his eyes with the back of his wrist. 'They thought I was him. They burnt down our house. They killed everyone. Mother, Father, my brother and sister...'

'Why?'

'Because they thought I was him,' he said bitterly.

'Who?'

Far spat. 'That pig faced traitor. Prince Toby. Don't you know? I thought everyone knew. He killed the King. They thought I was him.'

Toby was silent, boiling inside but unable to speak. What could he say? Far's family had been slaughtered because they thought he was Toby. How do you answer that? They were the same height and build – true enough. Hair colour was similar, a curly brown. Far's eyebrows were thicker, his nose thinner... But Far wasn't him, it didn't make sense.

'Why?' Toby said at last. 'Why you?'

'The dogs lost the trail,' said Far, flapping a hand. 'I don't know why. Our cottage was nearby... They said I must be him.' He spat again. 'Me! A prince! Can you believe that? Look at these ploughboy hands.' He held them up. 'Has a prince got hands like this?'

'No,' said Toby, sitting on his own.

'They said I had to say I was the Prince. And when I didn't they kicked me and beat me. So I said I was the Prince. I thought they'd stop. But that wasn't enough – they'd already killed my family for hiding the Prince. They tied me to the tree like you found me. I had to talk like the Prince they said.' Far shook his head in puzzlement. 'How do I know what a prince sounds like?'

Toby didn't reply. But it was too late. He'd already said too much.

'How come you speak so grand?' said Far, his eyes screwed up, staring intently at Toby.

Toby shrugged, thinking quickly. Why did Ned speak so grand? He hadn't even thought about it. He knew who was who in Ned's family but hadn't thought about how he spoke. Grand.

'I was brought up by my grandmother, Maeg the Healer,' he said, giving himself time to think.

'I've heard of her,' said Far. 'She doesn't live far from us.'

'When I was little she worked for a lord. She was his healer... Lord Palgrave.' Palgrave would do, though heaven knows where he lived. He went on, 'And she looked after his children. And I played with them and learnt to talk like they did.'

'Grand,' said Far.

Toby forced a grin.

'But how come you still speak it?'

Toby shrugged. 'I expect it's because we lived on our own. No one else about. I never played with other kids after we left Lord Palgrave's.'

The boy bit his nail thoughtfully. It seemed to satisfy him.

'You ever seen the Prince?' said the boy.

'No,' said Toby.

He put a foot in the water. 'Lucky for you, they didn't catch you. That grand voice.'

Toby didn't reply. That had already occurred to him. If they'd have caught him, they might have let Far go. And if they'd caught him earlier enough, Far's family would be still alive.

'All the more reason to get away,' said Toby. 'Those soldiers might have caught their dogs and horses by now.' He hesitated, then said, 'Tell you what though. Just in case they come. The soldiers. You could teach me to speak like you do.'

Instantly he said it, he regretted it.

Far was staring hard at him. 'You are him.'

Toby shook his head. 'Don't be stupid.'

'You're him.'

'Course I'm not. I'm no prince. Look at me.'

'Show us your hands.'

Toby had no choice. Damned if he did, damned if he didn't.

He showed them. If only he hadn't washed them a few minutes ago. Covered in mud, he might have got away with it. But clean and pink...

Far turned them over and looked at the soft palms.

'You're him,' he said triumphant.

Toby didn't know what to say. High class voice, soft hands. He couldn't convince the young man. He should just run off. Leave Far to look after himself...

'If it weren't for you,' said Far bitterly, 'my Mum and Dad'd be alive. My baby sister and my big brother Tom...' Far had his back to him. He was throwing twigs into the stream.

'I didn't kill them,' said Toby quietly.

'You might as well have done. You killed the King.'

'Who says so?'

'Everyone.'

'Then piss on everyone!' Toby kicked the tree they were under. 'I didn't kill anyone. Why do you think I saved your life?'

Far was silent.

'I don't believe you'll save mine,' said Toby. 'In fact you'd sell me out to the first soldier we meet.'

Toby was standing over Far who still had his back to him, his feet over the stream. He was in a fury.

'I'm off then,' he said.

Far turned. And looked up at him. 'What d'you mean? You can't leave me.'

Toby laughed. 'Can't I? If you can't walk, you can crawl.'

'The soldiers,' said Far, 'the dogs...'

'I don't trust you,' said Toby.

Far held up an open hand. 'I promise you.'

'What's your promise worth to me?'

Both were silent. Neither trusting nor trusted. Toby saw Far crawling along the forest paths. Easy meat for baying hounds...

He said, 'If I'd killed the King, the best thing I could do now is cut your throat.'

Far's hand went to his neck. 'You wouldn't do that.'

'Why wouldn't I?'

Far shrugged. Plainly confused.

'You saved my life,' he said.

Chapter 18

The day was warmer, a little windy. The sky had clouded over. The path he was on had come out of the forest into fields. Across them at some distance, there was a big house. The fields must belong to it. The sheep. He'd passed a hut at the edge of the forest. That too. Someone important must own it all. Maybe owned the forest too.

He and Far had finished off the bread and cheese. They hadn't spoken much. Neither was sure of the other. He wanted to be rid of Far. But felt responsible for him. His dead parents, his burnt feet. All somehow his fault. Common sense said – let Far look after himself. Guilt said – Far was his charge. He hadn't yet decided. He had left him hidden under a thick holly in the forest. Far couldn't be seen but dogs might smell him out. Toby had given him his blanket. After leaving Far, Toby had chipped a tree here and there with his knife as he went along, as markers. If he was going to go back for him... But why not simply abandon him? Far would realise soon enough that he'd been deserted. And Toby had his own life to save.

If he could get a wheelbarrow then he could move Far. If he could get a pair of shoes then maybe Far could walk a little... Or he could just tell someone on the estate about an injured man in the forest and leave it to them. And be done with him. It depended whom he met. What they were like. It was risky but he felt better on an estate like this. In the forest he was at the mercy of whoever came. This, though, was someone's home. He was used to such places, visited them often. Often without warning. A Prince could just turn up and be sure of a welcome, especially if with his father. But now he wasn't who he'd been. And needed to get used to it. He was Ned, a young peasant. And peasants could not just go where they wanted. And must not speak grand. Dare not. That could be his undoing. He'd muddied his hands, bit the nails crooked. But the way he spoke... That could get him hanged, sure as cheese was cheese. While walking he'd tried to speak like Far. But it was hard. He practised on 'Yes, sir,' 'No, sir,' and a few other subservient phrases. Peasants got in trouble for speaking too much. So if he acted a bit stupid...

Maybe.

No one seemed to be around. He was coming in towards the back of the house. Those buildings would be the stables. There might be someone there. If he could borrow a wheelbarrow, then he could bring Far in... Let them take him on.

Be free of him.

He came into the yard. There was no one about. A wagon was by the stable buildings, needing a horse. Across the yard, parallel to the stables, was the house. It was long with two floors. Small windows were on this side. They would be the servants' rooms and kitchens. The family rooms would be at the front. He'd been to many houses like this.

He went to the stable and called out.

'Hello!' He poked his head in the door. 'Anyone here?'

A few horses were tethered in their stalls. There was a wheelbarrow full of straw. He thought of just tipping it out and taking the barrow. No – he didn't want to be caught stealing. Better to ask. Except there was no one about to ask. He came back out into the yard.

Where was everyone?

A back door was open in the house. He went across and knocked on the door.

'Hello, masters.' His best Far accent.

When no one answered he peered in. It was a kitchen. In the centre was a large wooden table with food on – bread, cheese, pickle, some plates and knives. Part eaten as if they

had all been called away. A fire was burning in the large fireplace.

He stepped inside and made sure no one was about. This
was a big kitchen, plenty of shelves with pots and pans
hanging. Whoever owned this house would know his father.
Might know Toby himself. Would he recognise him? Surely
not like this. Dirty, in peasant clothes. Who looked at peasants anyway? Toby picked a piece of cheese off the table and
gulped it. Then a bit of bread, it was fresh, still warm – all
the time, watching the far door, to see if anyone came in
from the hallway. He stopped his eating. Too risky to get
caught at it.

He went to the kitchen door and peered out into the hall.
'Hello, masters. Anyone there?'

No reply. He cautiously came out into the wide hall. A
broad staircase came down from the upper floor. There
were side rooms, the doors closed. He was afraid to go in
those. He knew he shouldn't be here. Peasants and servants
stayed at the back unless they had work to do. He could get
in trouble here.

The front door was open. Best go out, as if he'd never
been in.

He strode down the hallway, and the instant he was
through the front door, he was faced by hell.

There were bodies everywhere. And should he doubt
they were all dead, there was an arm, a head, a leg, a hand
lying carelessly about. The lawn was patched with blood,
churned with bootmarks and horses' hooves. This had been
a massacre. There were children here, servants, lying stiff
and bent. All dead. That woman in long gown and headscarf
with blood pouring from her neck and chest could be the
lady of the house. A toddler by her had its head chopped off.
Some lay on top of each other, some separate, sprawled out.
Toby was paralysed with fear. All these people had been put
to the sword. The servants called out from their meal, the
family from the dining hall, the peasants from the fields, the
stable boys... All taken to the front of the house. Surrounded

by horsemen and armed men and attacked. He could smell the terror; it soaked into the ground like the blood.

He turned into the hallway, collapsed onto his hands and vomited.

He must get away from here.

Toby got to his knees, drool hanging from his chin. And thought shoes. There were plenty out there. He rose and ran quickly out amidst the bodies, trying not to see. He wanted a pair for Far. There was a young man without a head, his legs bent as if trying to get up, shoes about the right size. But he was wearing house-shoes with buckles. There – a boy with an apron covered in blood, his shoebacks downtrodden. Useless.

There was a pair. The limbs stuck out from a pile of bodies. The shoes looked good, perhaps too small. He'd take them anyway. One shoe came off easily, the other leg was stuck under an old woman who'd had an arm hacked off. He pulled the leg out – and it kicked.

Definitely kicked.

And a groan.

It was alive. Toby rolled the old woman off the leg, pulled away a stable boy in leather apron and there was a girl. Breathing. He had taken one of her shoes off – but she was alive. How alive, he could not tell. Alive enough to kick, breathe and groan. He had to get away from here, had to get her away.

He raced into the house, through the kitchen and out into the yard. From there across to the stable, where he turned the wheelbarrow out. And back he went pushing the barrow, across the yard, through the kitchen, into the hallway and out into the tip of bodies. He navigated round, in out, past legs, arms, splayed out forms. He skidded in the blood, and slowed, steadier. None of these could touch him. Though looking at a severed head, its bloody eyes staring – he wasn't so sure. That lone hand could scramble crabwise with its pair and grasp him round his ankles, and hold him here forever, while other hands pulled out his teeth, his ears, his tongue...

He whimpered like a kicked dog. Blood was pumping in his ears, and breathing like a broken bellows, he lifted the girl. She was blood-sodden. But bodies had been lying on top of her – so whose blood it was he couldn't say. He laid her in the wheelbarrow as best he could. Her head rested against the back near the handles, her legs like two bent horns over the front. Blood dripped down her white stockings like red ribbon tied round her calves. Her black long dress, mourning clothes reminding Toby of the Queen's visit, were soaked in blood, already drying in. She wore just one shoe.

Toby looked around for the other, but couldn't see it amidst the bodies. She would have to do without. And so would Far. He couldn't stay any longer. He felt weak, sick, terrified. He was stained like a butcher fresh from slaughter. Where were the killers? Who were they? They could come back anytime, swords slashing for any they had missed. Eager to gather their spoil. Toby wheeled his load through the remains. He bumped over things he didn't care to look at. At the door, he had trouble getting up the step and had to back over it, gazing out at the slaughtered. Might there not be another one or two, part alive, amongst those cut up bodies? There might. Why should he find the only one, without even looking?

'I can't do anything,' he mumbled to himself, and perhaps to those who might still possess some life. Fear of charging horses and bloody swords forced him away. He pressed on down the hallway, into the kitchen. There he stopped. A little sense remained in him. He gathered up a flour sack and filled it with whatever lay on the table. And he was off.

Terror-driven.

Chapter 19

The track as far as the forest had been flattened by lots of usage and peasant labour. Toby ran along it with the wheel-barrow which was well greased and balanced. He had never used one before but quickly got the knack of it. The girl had been heavy at first, but he had turned her sideways and she was a lighter load. Where he had to slow down to catch his breath, he didn't stop altogether but walked as fast as he could manage, aware that horsemen with blades stalked the land, and bloody corpses could be in the act of rising up and following him.

The sun was low, trapped in a furnace of red and gold cloud. In half an hour it would set. Then he'd never find Far. And he was desperately in need of him. Someone alive. Trust didn't matter anymore. But a living, talking person to persuade him that corpses don't walk. Or at least to be afraid with.

In the forest, it was still light enough, and he'd cut enough markers to keep to the way. But it kept coming to him: that dreadful sight! The slaughter at the front of the house. He shivered, his teeth chattered. So much death in so few days. His father, those poor people, very nearly his own and Far's. Would there be anyone left alive by morning?

He had not had time to mourn his father. Too frightened for his own life. Though earlier that day, a lifetime ago it seemed, when off with Sly, striding through the forest, he'd felt happy. And now felt amazed that happiness could exist at all in this world. Or had ever existed.

If so, it had since been chopped to bits.

He stopped to examine the girl. It would be pointless carrying a corpse. She was breathing, though unconscious. He wondered who she was. Her hair was dark brown, her face very white, her nose thin, her lips bloodless. She was bleeding at the shoulder and at the calf. Somehow she'd kept all her limbs. Toby could do nothing to help her and so pushed on.

In a little while he came to the holly tree. The evergreen leaves came low to the ground, making a sort of cave inside, where Far sat on the blanket, a scattering of food around him.

'You're back,' said Far, plainly relieved.

'And I've got company.'

Far had crawled half out. He saw the wheelbarrow and its unconscious passenger.

'Who's she?'

'I don't know,' said Toby. And he told him what had happened.

Far was silent while he spoke, biting a fingernail, his eyes cast down. He shook his head silently as Toby told of the massacre at the front of the house, thinking, Toby thought, of his own dead family, their slaughter. Were the two soldiers part of the same band of killers?

It seemed likely.

Toby finished. Neither spoke for a while. Frost was forming on leaves and twigs. Their breath was steamy. The sun had gone down but it was not yet dark.

'How many dead were there?' said Far at last.

Toby held his open hands out. 'I don't know. Fifty maybe. Could be a hundred. Didn't count.'

Far nodded.

'Best bring her in, and the barrow.'

He lifted the branches as high as he could and Toby wheeled her in to their leafy cavern. Inside it was much gloomier. Soon it would be pitch dark. Far was looking at the girl in the wheelbarrow. He examined the material of her dress, turned over her hands.

'One of your lot,' he said. 'Bet she speaks as lordy as you.'

Toby grinned slightly. 'I think she's the daughter of the house.'

'Most likely. Servants don't wear dresses like that,' said Far. 'And her hands are like yours. She doesn't wash her own clothes.'

'Do you blame her for that?' said Toby angrily.

Far didn't reply.

'I can't help it,' Toby went on, 'if I was born a prince and you a peasant. Those decisions were made by God.'

'Would you have brought her if she was a servant?'

Toby hesitated. It was quite possible he wouldn't. But he wasn't going to admit that.

'I saved you,' he said.

'You did,' said Far. 'And I'm grateful.'

'She may have been born a lady,' said Toby, 'but her family are just as dead as yours.'

Far nodded.

Neither spoke for a minute or so. Both thinking on death.

'I've got nowhere to go,' said Far shaking his head.

'Neither have I,' said Toby. He looked at the girl in the wheelbarrow, head resting on the side, legs sticking over the edge. 'And I don't suppose she wants to go home.'

'She can't be very comfortable.'

'No.'

Toby lifted her and laid her on the ground. Far folded a flour sack and put it under her head.

'She can have the blanket,' he said.

'Put it under her,' said Toby. He lifted her and Far did so. Toby put her down and folded her in the blanket.

He could barely see her face. Just an outline in the dark. Was this all in vain? Would she still be alive in the morning? Feeling chilly, he cupped his hands and blew into them.

'We're going to freeze,' said Far.

'I'll bring some leaves in and some bracken before it's totally dark,' said Toby. 'If we squish up, we might get through the night.'

Chapter 20

It was as black as his cell. And as cold. The bracken and leaves were little help, and made a racket as they rolled and twisted in their discomfort. Neither of them could sleep. They cursed and moaned. From time to time they talked, then relapsed into private miseries. It couldn't be half as bad for Far, thought Toby resentfully. It must often be cold in a peasant's hut, while he had never been cold in his life. Not for long anyway. There was always a servant to get another blanket, light a fire, draw the curtains. But here, he was stripped of rank. And of fire and of blankets.

He tried to distract himself. To think of his father. Knew he should weep for him. But he was too cold. It had soaked through to his very heart. He grasped his knees to his chest, stuck his hands up his sleeves to his elbows – but the cold attacked, like biting insects that would never be full.

He couldn't see the girl or hear her. She was to one side of him, Far the other. If she were dead, then he could have the blanket. It was his anyway – and why wrap a corpse? He put his hand over her mouth, to check whether she was breathing. She was, lightly, and he resented it. So cold, so cold.

'I can hear horses,' whispered Far.

Both listened. There was a distant galloping, the odd whinny. Was it approaching? Difficult to tell where they were. Some on that side, some on the other. How many? Who were they? Toby bit his lip and thought of the slashing horsemen at the estate. Who were they going to slaughter tonight?

'They're coming for us?' winced Far.

Toby punched him. 'Shut up!' he hissed.

Closer came the sound of hooves, hard on the frosty ground. The fugitives dare not speak. It was like drumming, building up from that first barely heard beat to a furious dance. Now almost outside. Toby pressed his nails into his palms.

Ride past! Ride past!

Are they out for me, he thought? Come to finish the execution. Far was breathing rapidly, his teeth chattering. Men on horses had killed his family and then hung him from a tree. Thinking he was Toby. But here was Toby, as helpless as a babe.

Fear galloped though their hearts.

Past came the riders. And a shadowy light swept through their cavern. They must be carrying flaming torches. What houses had they set alight? How many had they put to the sword?

They heard the cries of the riders, the snort of the horses. The rattle of stirrups and swords. Toby held his breath. He closed his eyes to block out the flashing light, he pressed his ears to block out the thundering hooves...

And then they were dying away. Past. On to a more distant mission.

'What are we going to do?' whispered Far.

'I don't know.'

'We'll be murdered here. Hacked to bits like my mum and dad.'

Toby moaned. 'What can we do? Three of us and three shoes between us. Two can't walk and one wheelbarrow.'

He was thinking, I should save myself. I can't do anything for these two. I'm the only decent pair of legs. What good would it do if the three of us died? How stupid to be killed because I want company!

He thought of his father. How he needed his help! How he would never help him again.

I must save myself, he thought. Without delay.

Far yelled. 'There's a dog! There's a dog in here.'

Toby could hear it walking in the leaves. Smell its furry musk. A rough tongue was licking his hand. He felt along its fur with the other hand. The tail gave it away. The long, bushy brush.

'It's a fox,' he said, stroking the animal. 'It's Sly. She's come for us.'

Chapter 21

She had come to complete the journey. Perhaps she'd heard his thoughts. Perhaps she'd made his thoughts. For whatever reason she was here. And he knew he could trust her completely.

Toby rose, stamped his feet and swung his arms to and fro. The leaves rustled under foot, his hand hit a bough.

'You're not going to leave me?' said Far.

Easily done. Harden his heart and go. How much help could he give? How much help did a peasant deserve?

'Are you taking me?' said Far.

Toby stood tall, grasping a branch above him. 'If I take you,' he said deliberately, 'I want respect. None of this talking back and questioning me.'

'Yes,' said Far. 'I promise.'

'You promise what?' hissed Toby.

Far was gripping his ankles. 'I promise, sir. I promise, master...' He stopped, tried again. 'I promise, your highness.'

'Sir will do,' said Toby.

'Thank you, sir.'

'Get in the wheelbarrow.'

Far stood up and Toby helped him in. Moved him a little, hunted for the sack of food. He found it and gave it to Far.

'What about her?' said Far, adding quickly, 'Sir.'

Toby shook his head. 'I can't take two.'

He gripped the barrow handles and wheeled the barrow through the leafy curtain, scraping his brow on the prickles.

'She'll be dead by morning, sir.'

Outside, there was a little light in the air. Toby wiped his brow with the back of his hand, he could feel blood. He could just make it out on his arms. He felt his tunic, it was stiff – it must be covered in blood from his contact with the girl. She couldn't last much longer. Ahead was the outline of the fox, her tail raised.

Toby looked back into the depths. He hesitated.

'Someone'll help her, sir,' insisted Far.

Toby bit his lip. She was a girl. Not quite of his class, but well-born. He still had his honour. His father said, be princely.

His father was dead.

'I've done all I can for her,' he said grimly.

And he began pushing the wheelbarrow.

Chapter 22

Over the next hour the forest revealed itself. The trees and undergrowth returned, coated in a patina of frost. Toby soon warmed up pushing the wheelbarrow, while Far shivered. Toby realised the beast of burden sometimes had the best of it.

They stopped by a stream to eat and drink. Toby washed his arms in the icy water. He splashed some on his tunic, enlarging the bloody stains.

'I'm going to freeze to death,' said Far.

Toby was about to remind him to say 'sir' – but Far was such a sorry sight, lack of sleep heavy in his eyes, his teeth chattering, that he couldn't find it in him. Besides, he felt less of a 'sir' now. Less in need to be lifted. The walking had done it, the warming up, the exercise and food in his belly. He wiped his face in the cold water, washing away the remnants of the sleepless night. He felt quite human. And a little chilly himself after all that splashing.

They set off once more. The sky was bright blue, the low sun seeping into the woods, the frost dripping off the trees. Sly was taking them by the smaller paths, as if knowing that horses couldn't go that way. In places it was hardly wide enough for a wheelbarrow and the passenger added to his woes by being scratched by brambles. There was little Toby could do, the barrow had to go first and deal with whatever came.

The path they were on met a wide ride, pitted by horses' hooves. Sly peered both ways and scampered across. Toby looked one way, no one in sight. Then the other.

A body lay out on the ride, just a few yards along.

Toby left the wheelbarrow and ran to it. The corpse was of a middle-aged man, well dressed and presumably well-born. A puddle of thickening blood was on his chest. His head was back, his mouth wide open, full of blood. There was no sign of life.

Toby was about to leave him when Far called out, 'Get me his coat, sir.'

'It's all bloody.'

'I don't care. I'm freezing, sir. Please.'

'Alright,' said Toby.

And began pulling the man's coat away. First one arm, then the other. He had to turn him to pull the coat away, and from the pool of blood underneath it was obvious the man had been pierced right through.

'And his boots, sir. Please.'

Toby took off the boots. They were soft leather, well made.

'And the hat, sir. If you please.'

The hat was lying a little way off. Toby picked it up and ran back to the wheelbarrow. He threw the articles to Far.

'Let's get away from here,' he said, taking up the handles, and pushing across the ride into the side path where Sly awaited.

Far put on the boots. They were a little big but certainly warmer than no boots. The hat was soft with a floppy pointed end. Far was able to pull it down over his ears. The coat was ample, the man had been quite stout. It fitted Far almost like a blanket, and had strings at the front to close it. It was handsome with embroidery, spoiled by the large bloodstain that covered a good portion of the front. Far though was pleased with his new wardrobe, his hands tucked deep into the sleeves. And he cheered up considerably.

'You look like a master butcher,' said Toby. 'And I must be your apprentice,' he added, looking down at his own blood stained garb.

'It's so good to feel my hands again,' sighed Far.

He had dropped the 'sir' and Toby neglected to chastise him. The corpse had reminded him of his true rank: renegade of the realm. On the run. Where was the fox taking them? Would it be safe?

Far was weeping. It had come out of nowhere. A minute before he had been so happy with his warm clothes. His head was bowed and sobs broke from his chest.

'What is it, Far?'

Far gazed up at him, tears streaming down his cheeks. 'My family, sir. My father, my mother, my big brother, my little sister...'

'I am so sorry, Far.'

He stopped pushing the barrow and put his hand on Far's shoulder, feeling quite useless.

'I was looking at those sheep,' said Far, indicating a few, very woolly sheep in a field. 'And I remembered my little sister chasing them...' He heaved with a sob. 'Mostly they would run from her, but if they wouldn't then she would push them from behind or pull their ears... How she would laugh.'

'I grieve with you.'

Far wiped his eyes with his sleeve.

'You're no better off, sir.'

Toby bowed his head, a nail hammered by despair. In an instant he had lost all strength.

'I wish I were dead,' he said.

And he sank to the ground. His head pressed to his knees and he howled. For himself, for his father, for all he had lost. For the vagabond pushing a wheelbarrow in fear of his life. His chest heaved and the tears flowed. He was nobody in the world. How could he go on?

The darkness in him swirled, the unhappiness heaved. It filled him from head to foot. There was nowhere to go. He might as well die here as anywhere else.

He felt a hand on his shoulder. He looked up and there was Far standing over him. He had limped on his heels from the wheelbarrow a few yards away.

'Please don't stay out here, sir. Someone might come.'

'Does it matter?'

Far nodded. 'It matters to me, sir. Not just because I need you to push the wheelbarrow...' He hesitated, then went on, 'I've got no one but you now.'

Toby lifted his head. And looked hard at Far, caught his eye. The old distrust wasn't there. In his quivering face there was need, respect perhaps. There was someone like himself.

Toby nodded.

'I shall have to think of you, Far. My duty to you.'

'You have no duty to me, sir.'

Toby gripped him by the wrist. 'I saved your life. I am not now going to give it away.' He rose and wiped his eyes with his fingers. 'If I can't live for me then I shall live for others.' He was silent a while, the despair ebbing away like rain drying off hot earth. 'You must save me, Far.'

'I can hardly save myself, sir.'

'Then we'll save each other. Don't call me sir anymore. You're my brother now.'

Far grinned sheepishly. And Toby grinned back at him.

'Now we must put something right.' Toby pointed across the field. 'You see that haystack?' Far nodded. 'I am going to take you there. You can rest up and sleep.'

'What will you do?'

'I shall go back for the girl.'

Chapter 23

In no time he was soaked. And still it rained. He was cold and sodden, walking in water, squelching in his shoes. His hair was a sponge that he shook from time to time to throw off rain. Toby looked up at the sky, squeezing his eyes to keep out the darts of water. The heavy, dark cloud gave no hint of better weather. He slipped on, the wheelbarrow skidding in the mud.

His one consolation was that he was less likely to meet others. Who would be out by choice? He shivered, he was icy cold, walking as fast as he could. Ahead of him was Sly, her head turned back towards him, ears alert, dark eyes watching, red and black fur glistening in the rain. She had immediately known where he was going. At first he was fearful she might be leading him somewhere else. Anywhere. But then he recognised a pond, a church in the distance, a gate. She was taking him back.

His food was soggy in the flour sack. He had split it with Far, leaving him also the bottle of water. Toby could manage from streams, though in this weather all he needed to do was turn his head up and open his mouth. He might die of a hundred other things, but not of thirst.

He decided to eat the food. The bread was mush in his mouth, the cheese at least held together. He thought of whom it was intended for and shuddered. The pile of corpses. Every single one of them slaughtered: servants, stable boys, farmhands, cooks, the family, their children –

slashed to pieces. Heads, hands, feet lying on the lawn, blood everywhere.

Why?

While engulfed by the horror, eating, head held down from the rain, he bashed into him. He had crossed a main path, deviated slightly to avoid a rut with his wheelbarrow. And his head collided with the bare feet of a hanging man. And set him swinging from the bough he was suspended from. Toby took a startled step back. He couldn't make out the man's face as his head was slung back by the noose. He wore a long, rough tunic, his shoes had slipped off and were on the ground beneath him. Rain dripped off him in rivu-lets, down his pendulous hands, and hung in drips from his blue bare toes. Across his chest was a piece of rough linen, tucked in at his neck almost like a bib. On it was written a word in blood: Tobard.

He heard the horses too late. Caught up in the hanging corpse, their approach lost in the rain, he didn't see them until they had clear sight of him. He left the barrow and raced into the woods. He could have got away from the horses easily enough. But not the dog. He could hear it barking and slathering behind him, closing in. It floored him at the foot of a wide oak tree. A large black and brown dog with sharp, drooling teeth that may well have ripped him apart, had not one of the soldiers rapidly arrived on foot.

Toby was pulled roughly to his feet and ordered to march ahead of the soldier. If Toby slowed, a knife dug in his ribs and he was slapped about the head. He cursed his stupidity for hanging about on the main path. He should have been across it and into the forest, instead of staring at a hanged man, too dead to be helped. The dog growled at his heels, nuzzling the back of his legs.

He was in big trouble. And might not get out of it alive. He had seen too much death the last few days to believe these men had any feelings of mercy. They chopped heads off, they hanged and sometimes they tortured beforehand.

'What we got here then?'

He was back on the main path, close by the hanged man. Two horses stood at the edge of the ride, with a second soldier. Both wore tunics and mail; the one with the horses was bearded, while his companion who had caught Toby in the woods was grizzled with a couple of days' growth. The dog snarled around, frustrated at not being allowed to get at Toby.

The bearded soldier grabbed Toby by the hair and held a knife close to his throat.

'You a Tobard, boy?'

Toby instantly said No. He didn't know what a Tobard was, but if there was one hanging a few feet away – then it couldn't be right to say Yes. Don't speak too much, he told himself, try to sound like Far. Not lordly. Though whether it would make any difference...

'Have you seen him?' said the soldier, the knife blade under Toby's nose.

'Seen who?' he couldn't help but say.

The second soldier kicked him in the back. 'The Prince, you dozy pig!'

Toby was lying in the mud, the dog snarling above him, the two soldiers on either side, both with knives pointed at him.

'I haven't seen him,' said Toby, turning over to face them. 'I'm just a poor peasant. Getting turnips.'

The grizzled soldier glanced at the wheelbarrow. The bearded one kicked him in the stomach.

'Stealing food more like!'

Toby winced and clasped his stomach, just as he received a boot to the ribs. Toby rolled about, mud splashing over him, fearing the next blow, hands covering his face.

'What do we do with him?' said the bearded one.

'Cut his head off.'

Toby looked between his hands. One of the soldiers was crossing to his horse. There, he drew a sword out of the scabbard. Any minute, there'd be another headless corpse.

But what could he do unarmed, faced by two soldiers and a dog? If he tried to talk them out of it – he'd give himself away as the prince. If he didn't they'd chop his head off.

'Let's hang him,' said the bearded one, looking up at the one they'd hanged earlier.

'Waste of rope,' said his mate coming back with the sword, his preference clear.

'Plenty there.' The soldier pointed out the hanging man with his knife.

The grizzled soldier grinned. 'Use the same noose.'

'I like a hanging,' said his mate. 'Seeing the legs kicking and the way the hands throw out. The last jerk of life. It always fascinates me.'

'You're quite a scholar of such things,' said the grizzled soldier as he led his horse under the hanged man. He climbed on the animal's back. 'Hold the body,' he said. He could have been a butcher arranging a carcass.

His mate came under and held the dead man by his legs. While both were busy, Toby thought of escape but the dog was watching him. He wouldn't get a yard.

The untying was completed and the corpse fell into the soldier's hands. He let it fall to the ground where the body splattered in the mud, ending up face up, the mouth wide open. Then matters proceeded quickly. Toby was forced to his feet at knifepoint. The noose was put round his neck.

'Got one of those Tobard sheets?' said the soldier holding him.

The other was sitting in the branch of the tree, ready to tie the rope. 'He's not worth one. Bloody rain.' He wiped the water off his forehead with his sleeve. 'Let's get a move on. I'm starving.'

'Get on the horse, boy,' ordered the bearded soldier.

'Please,' appealed Toby, barely able to get out the words. 'I'm just a nobody...'

The knife pressed tight against his windpipe.

'On that horse, nobody.'

Toby gripped the saddle, and tried to lift himself but fell back, lacking the strength in his trembling arms. The soldier cursed and pulled the knife across the back of his neck. He felt the sear and the drip of blood. The soldier pushed him against the saddle. I must extend my life, thought Toby. Delay extinction. Death by knife or by rope. Rope would give him seconds longer. He gripped the saddle and this time pulled himself on, knowing a failure would result in a cut throat.

The soldier on the grounds had the reins and directed the horse under his mate seated astride the branch. The dog suddenly snarled, and all three looked to him. He was eating one of the bare feet of the corpse.

'Oi! Leave off!' yelled the soldier at the reins.

'Let him have it,' said the other. 'It's better meat than we give him.'

'Dog's got to know who's master.'

The man dropped the reins for an instant to lunge at the dog. And Toby kicked hard at the haunches of the horse and pressed with his knees. The horse started forward. Fear gave Toby strength and he kicked again with his heels.

'Go, girl!' he shrieked.

She was away, with Toby head down, digging in, pressing her onwards.

Behind, the soldiers were yelling. The one on the ground ran after, shaking his knife. His mate on the tree dropped down.

'Come back here, Tobard!'

That was not a likelihood. Toby turned briefly. The soldier on foot had just stopped, realising he stood no chance. The dog was eating his meal uninterrupted. And the soldier who had dropped from the branch was climbing on the second horse.

Ride!

Maybe princes can't do much, but they know horses. He'd practically been born riding them. If this horse was half decent... He hoped this was the stronger of the two. He had a start and was lighter than the soldiers. There wouldn't be another chance; he must get away. If he were outrun, he'd be chopped down in the saddle.

Toby dug in his heels and lay forward on the horse's neck. 'Good girl. Run for me. Run hard!'

Chapter 24

The rain flew into his face as he bounced with the rhythm of the horse. This horse was going to run until she dropped. Owned by those soldiers, she was terrorised. She obeyed. She'd run into fire if ordered. That was to his advantage. If he'd have been on an animal that doubted him for even a second, they'd have had him. He gripped tight with his knees and patted her neck.

'Go, girl.'

He suspected he had the better of the two horses. Certainly, he was pulling away. The other was a good hundred yards behind. Now he had choices. He could leave the horse and dive into the forest. That would be the safest thing to do. The dog was busy, and once the soldiers had got their horse back they'd be in no mood for a chase on foot in the forest. He wasn't important to them.

But he wanted to keep the horse. And that was more difficult. A horse might be faster but a horse needed space. She couldn't go down the narrow tracks in the forest, not at any speed. To keep the horse he had to outpace his follower and that had the risk that he might run into someone.

More soldiers.

There seemed plenty out and about, killing almost anyone. Who were the Tobards?

He suddenly realised where he was. This was near the estate, the site of the massacre. He had crossed this path when leaving the estate. The holly tree must be close by.

This must be one of the trails where the riders had gone by in the night.

He rounded a bend. There was another a little way ahead. He halted the horse, jumped off and rapidly pulled her into a gap in the thicket. Then stilled her. He held his breath and waited, hoping he couldn't be seen. If he was, then he'd have to hare off on foot. Easy enough, the soldier would have two horses to handle and so probably wouldn't bother with him. But that wasn't the plan... A few seconds later the soldier came past, kicking his horse in the flanks, bashing her neck with his fist. Too intent on his animal's speed to notice them half hidden in the woodland.

He watched them away and round the bend. And hoped there was another couple of bends beyond so that the soldier would continue to believe he was on Toby's trail. And maybe a crossroad ahead to confuse him further.

Wishing wouldn't help. He took the horse's reins and led her deeper into the forest. In a few minutes he'd picked up the track. There was a branch he'd chipped. And there another. He was very close. Looking back though he could see the tracks of the horse on the muddy track. He led the horse down to a stream where impatiently he had to allow her to drink. He drank himself. The cut at the back of his neck was drying in a string of blood. Quickly he washed it in the cold water, knowing it would bleed more – but he'd learnt out on the hunt with his father that it was less likely to fester. He took the reins. The stream was fast-moving but shallow and he walked along it for a few hundred yards, hoping to sow a little confusion in anyone who might follow, as they'd lose his trail at least for a little way.

He pulled out of the stream.

'Good girl.'

He slapped her flank and she pulled away startled, as if she expected a nastier blow. He halted her, still holding the reins and smoothed her neck, talking gently, knowing it might have little effect. This animal had learnt that human beings were cruel. Their punishment came out of the blue. Reversal would take time. And who knew how much he had?

He was at the holly tree. He tied the animal to a bough a few yards away. And crept under its curtain.

'Hello?'

'Hello,' came the startled reply.

In the cavern of the tree, it was bright enough in daylight to see the pale-faced girl, shivering in the blanket. Her hair was dark and long, unbraided. The blanket was up to her chin. And it was sodden from the rain. She was staring at him as intensely as he was at her.

'Who are you?' she said, barely able to keep her teeth from rattling. Far was right; she did speak lordy.

In a rapid second, Toby had decided.

'I am Ned,' he said. 'From a cottage back yonder.' In his best Far-talk. If he couldn't fool her then he couldn't fool anyone. 'Who are you?'

'I am Lady Orly Gomm,' she said, recollecting her class, and the haughtiness to go with it. 'You may call me Mistress or My Lady.'

Toby hadn't expected this, but if it was the way of things... 'Yes, My Lady.'

She indicated about her, a puzzled tone. 'What am I doing here, boy?'

Toby widened his eyes. 'Boy' now, was it? She couldn't be any older than he was. 'I brought you here,' he said adding as an afterthought, 'My Lady.'

She tried to sit up, then fell back into a fit of coughing. Toby searched about him helplessly. He had no water, he had no cloth. And he didn't know what he was allowed to do. In his role, he was not of her class.

At last she said croakily, 'Why did you bring me, boy?'

'Ned,' he said. And when she didn't respond, he explained helpfully. 'My name is Ned.'

'Aren't you a boy?' she said, her head wearily back on the flour sack.

'Not since I became a man,' he said, 'so please don't use the word.'

'Someone of your station is a boy, no matter what his age. It's not what you like to be called,' she snapped. 'But what you are.' The words exhausted her. She was breathing rapidly. More quietly but with the same haughtiness, she said, 'Who is your master?'

Toby did not know. Maeg hadn't said who was Lord of the Manor where she lived. Probably the same as Far's – but he hadn't said either.

'Lord Jerome,' he said, plucking at a name, the Lord of an estate he had visited.

'I shall talk to him about your manners, boy.'

Toby shook his head and sighed. There was something rather sad and silly about this. He couldn't go on this way.

'My manners may need improving, My Lady,' he said, 'but this isn't the time for me to learn. You are lying under a wet blanket, badly hurt, your family has been slaughtered...'

He was about to explain more when she broke into tears.

'Tell me it's not true,' she begged. 'Tell me, boy.'

Toby was unsure what to say. But he couldn't lie to her. What would be the point pretending her family were still alive? He began slowly. 'Do you live on the estate back there?'

She nodded, not correcting the lack of title.

'I was there yesterday,' he went on cautiously. 'I came for food, to find some work...' the latter not quite true but he didn't want to mention Far. 'And there, at the front of the house...' he stopped. Did she really not remember?

She shook her head, sobbing. 'I thought it was the most terrible dream. When I woke here... I hoped it hadn't happened.' She was a flood of tears, her body shaking.

Toby waited for her to subside, then said quietly, 'You were the only one I found alive.' He didn't add that he hadn't looked very hard. How would that help? And what could he have done besides?

She was bawling now. Toby was fearful of the noise. The soldiers might be about, though he hoped they were far off. Or others, as bad or worse.

But he let her sob, and hoped.

In a while, she quietened and he said, 'Why did they do it?'

She looked at him fiercely, wiping a tear with a knuckle. 'They said we were Tobards.'

That word again. Bad enough to be slaughtered for.

'What is a Tobard?'

She clenched her fist. 'You stupid boy. I pity your master. Don't you know what is happening?'

Plainly he didn't. And not wanting to appear more stupid he kept quiet. She was so annoying. He had come back to help her, and she treated him like he was some despised dog at her feet. Easily done, he thought. He'd done it himself. Yell at a servant. Order a peasant whipped. Not that she could have him whipped, and her yelling was rather subdued – but the loss of respect pierced him.

'Tobards,' she said slowly, to make sure even he understood, 'are the followers of Prince Toby.'

'Oh,' he emitted, feeling somewhat stupid at not working it out, and for not knowing he had followers.

'He killed the King,' she went on, 'and with his followers was ready to take over the land... but the Queen...' She stopped in a fit of coughing that seemed as if it would throw her insides out.

Toby's mind was a whirl. His followers were being slaughtered. But he had no followers. Hadn't thought of it. Hadn't had time. Were there really men and women rising up in his name?

For the first time he felt a little hope.

'My father has always been loyal,' said the girl at the end of a cough. 'How could they believe we were followers of that filthy traitor!'

Toby's hope flickered out.

He said, 'You are not Tobards? Definitely not Tobards?'

'You insolent boy...' she began, but was unable to go on.

'Then why kill you all, every single one of you, My Lady?' He added the title to lessen her distress, as its omission seemed to be as important to her as the death of her family. Killed as Tobards – but they weren't Tobards.

Why?

She didn't answer his question, but she hadn't needed to. Lady Orly's family were slaughtered as Tobards. Far was about to be, and so was he himself. And none of them were. It was clear to Toby what he had known when she'd begun to explain. There were no Tobards. He had done no conspiring. He had no bands of armed men about the countryside. There were no followers rising in his name. But this girl, whose family had been slaughtered for being Tobards, still believed they existed...

It hit him like a clout round the head. He had been allowed to escape the dungeon. The cell door left open, the drunken gaoler, the reduced guard... They were no accidents. With Prince Toby free, the Queen could do exactly what she wanted and blame it on the Tobards.

As for Earl Gomm's estate – well that was simple. Kill them as Tobards. Then blame the killing on the Tobards. And, of course, take the estate.

He almost smiled at the cunning.

Instead he said, 'My Lady, please accept my sorrow at the terrible death of your family. But we must leave here. You are ill and we have no food or water...'

Chapter 25

Toby lifted the canopy of leaves; it had stopped raining, the sky was clearing. Orly wanted to walk the short distance to the horse. She didn't want to be assisted by a 'boy'. Impatiently, Toby let her try. She couldn't even stand unassisted. But when at last she was up, one hand on his shoulder, the other holding a branch overhead, still she wanted to walk herself. And it was only in steps he got to carry her, as she resisted her dependency. The hand on Toby's shoulder became an arm round his shoulder – and, when that was hardly better, his arm round her waist, her full weight against him. Finally the carry. She did not say a word in her humiliation and tried to suppress her groans. Toby knew better than to chide her. Peasants simply do not carry ladies. They would be whipped for it. Lady Orly would only allow her mother or her maid to touch her. She was the mistress here – but she wasn't at all.

He attempted to sit her on the horse, but she fell to the side and he was just able to catch her. Instead, he laid her over the horse's back. She had given up her struggle to be ladylike. This gave him the opportunity to wring out the sodden blanket, more for comfort than for warmth. He twisted it, working from both ends to the middle. Then again until the wringing hurt his hands. He put it back on her, hoping that the warmth of the horse would dry it properly. She was asleep or at least pretending to be.

Toby could sit behind her, but only if they travelled on the broad rides. And those were dangerous, especially with her, as there would be no escape. No outrunning his pursuers on a double-burdened horse.

They must take the paths. And he would have to walk, to assist the horse through.

By the time they set off, she was obviously unconscious, her efforts had utterly exhausted her. She lay over the back of the horse like a large rag doll, her hands hanging limply below her head. Toby walked ahead, the reins of the horse in one hand, looking back constantly to make sure she wasn't slipping off. Water dripped on them from the trees and sprayed from the undergrowth as they pushed through.

He stopped at a stream to water the horse. He drank himself, cupping it in his hands. He couldn't do anything for the girl. He'd only choke her. What was he going to do about food? Merely hungry at present, but a long walk on a cold day would soon empty his stomach. There were three to feed including Far, and not counting the horse who would have to forage for herself.

Toby was about to set off again, when he heard a rustle in a hedge. When he looked, he saw the familiar face of Sly, ears alert, nose twitching – and those dark, mysterious eyes. What power was behind them?

He was immediately grateful for her presence. He had only vaguest notion of the way back to Far – and there was every chance he'd get lost. But here was his guide once more. How did she find him?

The fox went ahead, as ever, waiting to make sure they were following. They walked with caution. Any sound and Toby would stop the horse. Mostly it was nothing: a bird, a deer, but once horsemen, some way off – but close enough to still them for quarter of an hour.

He stopped once more to look at the girl. And at once felt concerned; her face was going blue. Upside down, it must be all the blood going to her head. With difficulty, he sat her on the horse, she kept trying to flop off. He leaned her forward against the neck – and had to hold her there as they continued. It was an arduous way to walk, leaning over, holding her, directing the horse. He wished he had some rope to tie her on.

But given wishes, there were better things than rope.

By the time, they got to Far's field, Toby's back and legs were aching. The girl was breathing weakly and he was starving. Far though was not there. And neither was the haystack.

He took the horse into the field where the haystack had been. And found evidence enough that it had been there. Remnants of hay were scattered around. What had happened was easy to work out. The ground about was churned up by hoofprints. They'd taken the hay for fodder. A band of soldiers he guessed. Had they taken Far too? Or killed him? He couldn't run. Or even walk. Would Toby find his strung up body hanging from a tree?

He almost collapsed with weariness.

The horse was eating hay, the remnants of the haystack. She was a brown, sleek animal and he had grown quite fond of her. On her rump was an army brand. That would get him killed – that is if they needed another reason.

He examined the girl. Fresh blood was trickling down her leg, her face was bluish white. He could not detect any breathing. Had she gone at last? This rude, haughty girl. At last to join her family. He placed his hand over her mouth. She might still be breathing. He wasn't sure. Yes, there was a little life left in her.

What had they done to Far? Caught him asleep, then cut him up for sport? Why was there so much murder and terror in this land? It seemed anyone walking or travelling could be its victim. He had escaped long enough. It was his turn. And would it matter? There had to be an end for him too.

How he needed his father. His strength, his certainty, his temper even. With him gone the world had shattered, smashed like a cup under a blacksmith's hammer. And now the pieces were being smashed too. All to dust. Who would ever know what they once were?

He crouched down on the ground playing with the straw. Tying it in knots, making a weak and useless string. The sun was low in a clear sky, across the hummock of the grassy field. The fox crouched and waited. The girl was slipping off the horse as it munched hay. The prince in a muddy tunic was tying straw as if his life depended on it. And a young man, even more mud-covered, was crawling out of a ditch.

'Toby!'

That sharpened his ears. He saw a kneeling figure, black with mud, arms waving. And at once forgave him for yelling a forbidden name.

Chapter 26

'I saw them coming from a distance,' said Far. 'Soldiers on horseback. And was able to crawl to the ditch. Just in time.' He shivered. 'I'm frozen to the quick. Got any food?'

Toby shook his head. 'None.' He indicated the girl now lying on straw on the ground. 'I don't know why I went back for her.'

'She still breathing?'

'Just about.'

The sun was sagging in the clear sky. The midday warmth was going quickly. Far was caked in wet mud, from head to toe. Toby helped him wipe it off with the hay. At least it thinned the mud and spread it. Far took off his leggings and jacket, and wrung them out. He put them back on and then stuffed hay inside his clothes. In his chest, down his leggings. It would give him some warmth, and hold the wet clothes off his body.

'It'll be a chilly night,' said Far, looking at the sky. 'Clear ones are the coldest.'

'I can't walk another step,' said Toby. He was as weary as winter, as worn out as an old shoe. 'I've got aches on aches. I could eat this horse – if I could cook her.'

'I ate a toad in the ditch,' said Far.

'What was it like?'

'Like jelly. Lots of bones to spit out. Some nasty bits. Don't know what they were.' He shrugged. 'Don't care.'

Toby rose stiffly. 'Best move on. Don't want to die here.'

'How much further?'

'I don't speak fox.'

'Hey – you're speaking better!'

Toby managed a grin. 'I've been practising. I'm Ned.' Then he remembered Far's earlier transgression. 'For heaven's sake – don't yell 'Toby' at me. I'm Ned.'

'Sorry, Ned.'

'And who's your Lord of the Manor? She asked me.'

'Earl Gomm,' said Far.

'Well would you believe it,' said Toby grimly. 'Do you know who she is?'

'No.'

'Lady Orly Gomm. And she is the haughtiest cow I have ever come across.'

Far sucked in a breath. 'The company I keep. Princes, ladies. Mum and Dad would've been proud.' He flapped an arm helplessly. 'You know, you look just like one of us.'

'I shall have you whipped for that, boy!'

Far searched him closely to make sure it was a joke.

Toby said, 'It's only fair. She's going to have me whipped.'

'Who by?'

'By my master.'

'Her dad – that would be. Earl Gomm. Not that he'd do it himself of course.'

Toby shook his head. 'No one left on her estate can hold a whip.' He stood over the girl. 'She tries so hard to stay the lady.'

'I bet she's a real stinker. Run here, fetch that,' said Far resentfully. 'I keep out of their way. Her sort.'

'My sort.'

'You never come to give us money,' said Far. 'My Dad says...' He quickly corrected himself. 'Said. They... your lot... come for taxes, blood and sweat.'

'I'm not asking for your blood now,' said Toby wearily. 'And you haven't got any money. Keep your sweat, and let's get away from here.'

Toby lifted the girl onto the horse, laying her onto the neck as before, then covering her with the blanket. He helped Far sit behind. It would now be his job to hold her on. Toby led the horse.

And so they went.

Out of the field and along a track, which went in the direction of a forest, some way off. Toby assumed they were heading that way. Sly kept ahead, keeping well into the hedgerow, just as anxious as they were at being out in the open. There were a few distant cottages, cows and sheep in some of the fields, but no people. It reminded Toby of Earl Gomm's estate. No one around in the fields, the stables, the kitchen... until he'd come to the front of the house. And found them all.

They passed two dead bodies on the road, a boy and an old woman. Perhaps granny and grandson, thought Toby, flies buzzing around them. He halted to examine them, though heaven knows what he would have done if they weren't dead. The boy had the top of his head hacked off, the old woman had her throat cut.

Neither spoke as they moved on. This was a land of death.

A couple of dogs, guarding sheep in a field, scented Sly. Shaggy, wolf-like animals, they came barking over. Sly immediately headed off across a meadow and they gave chase. Toby had no doubt she would lose them. And then be back. In the meantime they headed for the forest, now no more than half a mile ahead. Sly might even be waiting there for them when they arrived.

They came to a cottage on the side of the track. Smoke issued from the chimney, the shutters were closed.

'Ask them for bread,' said Far.

Toby hesitated. Begging doesn't come easy to princes.

'They can only say no,' insisted Far.

Toby rapped on the door. He could hear footsteps inside, and someone saying, 'Sh, sh,' but no one came out. He rapped once more. This time there was simply silence.

'Scared,' said Far.

This irritated Toby. It was so obvious. But he bit his tongue, knowing it was hunger making him peevish. They moved on. A cool wind was blowing and they were heading into it. He had no collar to turn up. He wished he had a cloak and hat. Though he might find a body soon to strip. He glanced at the girl, lying against the horse's neck, held in place by Far, and tucked in her blanket. Her face bluish white, she reminded him of a fish on a slab. How much closer could she be to death without being dead? The last sparks, the final splutter of a wet fire.

They rounded a bend and walked into the riders. There were perhaps a dozen of them on foot, by a stream watering their horses. A smoky fire was burning. Sly would have smelt them and warned Toby, but Sly was way over the hills, defending her own life. Swords were being drawn and in a very few seconds they were surrounded.

The men were mud-splattered from hard riding and living rough. And mingled in the mud were streaks of red, splashed on the swords, on the hands holding them, and rubbed into grubby faces. The grip of their swords was purposeful, their faces set. One more chore before they could eat.

A man grabbed Toby by the throat and shook him.

'What you doing out?'

He had one eye, the empty socket knotted inside. His face was grizzled in a blood-crusted beard.

Far answered quickly. 'Going somewhere safe, master.'

Another man, as bloody and as grizzled, dragged Far off the horse into the mud.

'Who asked you?'

He kicked Far in the face. Far yelled out as the girl rolled round the horse's neck and slipped onto the ground. Toby could barely breathe, his throat held so hard. He thought, this is it. It has come at last.

The one-eyed man gave another squeeze. 'I asked you a question.'

Toby staggered, the blood swimming before his eyes. He fought for breath. The man let go and gave him a push. He too fell to the ground, the men above them like malevolent trees.

'Looking for somewhere safe,' he rasped.

A few men laughed. The one-eyed man inspected his captives, like a slaughterman picking out sheep. He spat into the mud. 'I cannot understand you thick heads. No one is to be out. You would think that would be clear.'

'Kill 'em and be done with,' said someone.

'My Mum and Dad were killed, master,' sniffed Far, holding the bloody side of his face. 'I ran for my life.'

'Not far enough,' said a man.

'Who's she?' barked the one-eyed man to Toby, indicating the girl. She was lying on her side in the mud, pale-faced, eyes closed, the blanket half round her.

'That one's a lady,' said a man.

'I said who is she?' snarled the one-eyed man smacking Toby round the face.

His head swung. In the pain and confusion he didn't know the answer to the question. Tell them and what? Don't tell them and what?

Dead either way.

He said in a bloody lip, 'Lady Orly Gomm. Her family have been killed. I found her.'

The man got down on his knees and held the girl's face in his hands. And looked close.

'It's her alright.' He turned to Toby. 'You bloody fool.'

With his face aching, his throat constricted, he was whatever the man said.

The one-eyed man looked around his men. He spat. 'Let 'em go.'

Bewilderment, all around.

'What?'

'Take half a minute.'

'Get back to your grub,' ordered the one-eyed man. He held his blade at them. 'You heard.'

The fence of soldiers broke up, and retreated resentfully. The one-eyed man watched them amble back to their fire and horses.

On his haunches, he said quietly, 'I'm one of Gomm's men. My dad runs his stable.'

Toby thought, your dad's dead, but didn't say it. It wouldn't be wise to be the messenger. Instead he said, 'She's the last of the family.'

'Poor kid. I used to get her horse out. Good rider,' said the man sucking his lip. 'Where you going?' He waved a hand. 'Best not tell me.'

'Who are you?' said Toby.

'We're a gang of Zeke's raiders. I'm captain of this riff raff. Now get going. My men might just mutiny.'

'Got any grub?' said Far.

The man strode into a group of soldiers crouched down by a small fire. He grabbed a loaf of bread and came halfway back. He threw it across.

Toby just caught it.

'Clear off, quick.'

Chapter 27

The night came down quickly, almost as soon as they had entered the forest. It began to rain, and as it grew colder, the rain became sleet. Toby gave up speaking, his lip had swollen and his throat constricted. All adding to his awful weariness. He plodded like a sack. Ahead was Sly. She'd been waiting at the forest edge. There was no sign of the dogs.

The bread they'd been given was stale and hard. Toby broke a bit off and had to suck it in his mouth for several minutes to soften. Then he couldn't swallow it, his throat was so painful. He spat out the pulpy bits.

Behind him, Far was groaning. He had taken a blow to the face, his feet were hurting and he was aching from hours on the horse. Toby had no words of comfort. What was there to say? That there are no killers on the road, the sun will come out soon and a table will appear covered in hot food... The last thought amused him slightly and enabled him to cover a further ten paces.

The truth was his father was dead, he was the enemy of every man, hell had broken out in the Kingdom, he was bruised, exhausted, hungry and cold. Should he try a happy song?

He didn't know any.

The sleet soaked into them, working its way through their clothes to their skin like chewing worms. Cold and so weary, Toby knew if he stopped he would not start again. Only by moving could he keep moving.

Stop and die.

They had to cross a stream in the dark. The water was fierce and fast. Toby slipped on a stone. The water was icy, but coming out he was not a lot colder. Or wetter. Just as miserable, just as tired. He wanted to scream at the fox – where are we headed, when the hell is all this going to end? But it made as much sense as yelling at the stream for soaking him.

He thought it couldn't get worse.

But then they began to climb.

At first through forest, but then it was gone. Hacked down for firewood or houses. He tried to imagine it one big fire, glowing round the horizon and hot enough to fry his feet. Please! The track was rockier and had narrowed. And still they were climbing. The wind was biting cold, scouring any bare flesh and eating their clothes. It began to snow and settled very quickly. The flurries came in blasts of circling wind. Toby's frozen hands were pulled into his sleeves, his chin was icing up. He could feel the horse shivering beside him. He glanced at the girl. One side of her hair was covered in snow, he wiped some off her face with his sleeve but it settled again. Far had stopped groaning. He felt the youth's hand, it was icy cold. His arm was stiff.

Was he even alive?

Toby found his face, shook it and slapped it. A weary groan issued. A little life still. Oh this cold! And it was up to him; the very thought exhausted him. He was so tired, so beaten.

He stumbled on, and wept with the pain of the cold. His feet were lumps of ice, his ears were stuck with pins. He had no warmth at all to fight. All strength had been sapped from him; he had been through too much. All I have to do is lie down, he told himself. It won't take long. Very soon the life in him would give up. Surrender. Fighting was madness.

It was then he saw the man. At first it seemed just a dark rock ahead, but then through the blizzard, as they drew closer, it took the shape of a cloaked man with an arm held up. And within the hood a bearded face, long-haired.

He thought, why can I see him in this dark? There is a light around him...

He peered ahead. The snow was so fierce into his face. He heard his name surely. On the wind. And then again it came.

'Toby! I'm here.'

It was his father. That must mean that he was dead himself. He had been walking so long through the cold that he had died. But why did it still hurt so? Why was he still so weary?

'Father! Father!' he called.

And he ran, and stumbled, fighting the blast. He left the horse and his companions – and ran to the one who beckoned. He who would give him shelter, he who would give him warmth...

He fell on a rock. And when he lifted himself slowly to his knees the figure was gone. There was the cold, there was the biting snow, there was the darkness.

And there was no one but himself.

For a little while he lay like a wounded animal, waiting for the kill. And when he did not die, he half crawled and half stumbled back to the horse. And at its feet he stopped.

And surrendered.

Chapter 28

Toby's first sensation was warmth. He didn't want to move, the warmth was so beautiful. It cocooned and cuddled him. His aching body demanded no action.

He must not think.

There were only awful things to think. Just feel. Take in the wondrous heat.

He must not open his eyes. Out there was the dreadful world. He wanted to not know, to stay in unknowing, to melt in the warmth. Something had taken over from him, some mothering force, that he wanted to go on and on, without any obligation from him. And if he looked, and if he knew, he would be dragged into struggling on.

Spare him.

Some traitorous part disobeyed. Or perhaps babies never know what they really want. He opened his eyes.

He engaged.

Above him was a roof of rough white rock, flickering with shadow. He could see no more without sitting up, which he didn't want to do. That would be to reveal himself to whoever possessed the roof.

Over him were two rough blankets with stitched edges which he ran his fingers along. He was on a narrow bed, soft underneath. There was a sweetish, warm smell which curdled his stomach. And it was that which sat him up.

He was starving.

And in a large cavern, nearly the size of his father's hall. There were shelves around the cavern, and on them in one area bottles of all shapes and sizes, green and blue and white glass, stoppered with cork, jugs, and two mortars and pestles. On another set of shelves were books and scrolls. Some books were very large and lay on their side; smaller ones had other books as bookends. In the middle of the cavern was a large wooden table, on it were a number of basins, spoons and an assortment of herbs, leaves and bottles. There were three other beds in the space, two of them occupied. In one he could make out Orly's hair, the other head was under a blanket. Two lanterns were attached to the walls but most of the light came from a brightly burning fire. The wall behind was charred, the ceiling low above the fire where a hole drew the smoke. Sly lay by the stones around the fire, for all the world like a domestic cat, watching him watching her. And tending to it, his back to him, was a bald man, grey hair fringing his dome like seaweed round an exposed rock. He was wearing a long, brown cloak which came below his knees, and baggy, black leggings with holes at the back of both knees.

'Good morning, Toby.' The man spun round, a wooden spoon in his hand. And Toby knew him at once from the toothy smile and the folds of his face. He must be Maeg's son. The likeness was astounding.

Toby didn't know what question to begin with. They were piled on each other like stones on a cairn. But like his mother the man knew the priorities.

'Soup, Toby?'

And almost before he had assented, it was coming with bread.

He ate it in bed and the taste made him more certain this was Maeg's son. The same flavour of carrot and cabbage and parsnips, the same soothing effect in his hands and feet. And the same result when he had finished. More was offered.

'Your mother's recipe?' said Toby between mouthfuls.

'Sharp young fellow.' He tapped his nose, his mother's too. 'Your companions are asleep. The young man is exhausted. He was very cold, but he's tough. I've put ointment on his feet and they should heal quite quickly. The girl...' He sucked in a breath. 'She is low. Barely alive when she arrived. Ice cold, lots of bleeding. Though I think the cold might have saved her. But now she must be warmed again and the poisons purged from her blood. I am making preparations.'

'How did you know we were out there?'

The man indicated Sly by the fire. 'She came on her own. You were only a few hundred yards away. I took the others in by the horse. Then came back for you.'

Toby looked around the cavern. There was a noted absence. 'Where is the horse?' he said.

'I fed and watered her. And then let her go when the blizzard ceased. She has an army brand on her which could only cause us trouble. Don't worry. She'll end up back with the army. These days no one would dare to steal an army horse.'

'May I know your name, sir?'

'I am Erdy, son of Maeg. My mother, of course, did not say where Sly was taking you.'

'No.'

'I am sorry for that. It must have been a troubling and difficult journey. But if you were caught and tortured, you could not betray me.'

'We were caught too many times.'

Erdy shook his head and sighed. 'There are soldiers everywhere. They are seeking Tobards, they say.'

'There are no Tobards,' interrupted Toby.

'They are a fiction,' said Erdy nodding in agreement. 'Convenient to the Queen. But it's why you are alive.'

'She let me escape,' said Toby.

'I think she did.' He was sitting on a stool watching Toby eat with some satisfaction.

'Does it matter?' said Toby. 'She might as well have beheaded me.'

'I think not,' said Erdy, pulling at his chin. 'Indeed not.'

Toby was full, the little left in the bowl he could not manage. He was sitting on the side of the little bed, wearing a long bedshirt that came below his knees. He vaguely wondered about the whereabouts of his clothes, but did it really matter?

Erdy was rubbing his fingers in and out of each other. 'She can kill anyone and blame you. Take estates and say the owners were Tobards. Any rebellion, resistance. Tobards. They are everywhere. Under the bed, in the trees, along the footpaths.' He stopped catching Toby's eye. 'Yes, she helped you escape. She needed you alive.'

'The soldiers could easily have killed me,' said Toby.

'She can't be everywhere. Can't explain the subtlety of her plan to mere soldiers. They have been told to kill Tobards, and anyone who might be a Tobard, anyone they are not sure of. She would like to kill you secretly and claim you are still alive. Conspiring against her, organizing bands that she can then murder.'

Toby barely heard the last words as his eyes closed. As his head fell on his chest, he saw marauding bands yelling 'Tobard!' and ridding down helpless people, blades swinging. He was amongst them, standing still waiting, arms by his side, while all around him people ran in terror to be hacked down and trodden into the bloody mud. The soup bowl fell out of his hands, and he startled himself awake.

'I'm sorry, sir, but I am terribly tired.'

Erdy nodded. 'I have put some herbs in your soup to put you to sleep. When you awake, your body will be repaired. Rest now. There is much to be done, but not in this state.'

Toby could not even take this much in and dozed where he was, sitting on the side of the bed. Erdy rolled the youth, without waking him, into the bed and pulled the blankets over him.

Across the cavern, Far was stirring.

Chapter 29

Orly was propped on four pillows, her long hair tied back in a ribbon, draped over one shoulder. She had eaten a little soup, and to follow Erdy had given her a preparation from a small bottle. The grimace after swallowing was still on her face. Her paleness at once said she was an invalid – and so this might have to be a short conversation. Toby and Far, back in their everyday tunics and leggings, were seated on stools by the bed. Far's feet were heavily bound, a wooden crutch lay on the floor beside him. Seated at the end of the bed was Erdy.

'If the boy is to be present...' began Orly.

'I'm as old as you are,' mumbled Far.

'Don't speak until you are spoken to,' snapped Orly. She turned to the others. 'You see the way he already treats us? As equals.'

Toby was uncomfortable. He had made a promise to Far, rather rashly. That 'brothers' stuff, when plainly they weren't and never could be.

'I am a lady, you are a prince and he is...' she turned to look at him loftily, not unkindly, but Far knew the expression and gazed at his nails. 'A peasant,' she went on. 'No worse for that. The world needs peasants. But in the fields.'

'I'll go sit by the fire,' said Far awkwardly. He gathered up his crutch and began pulling himself to his feet.

'Stay,' said Erdy.

Far half looked up, first to the lady and then to Erdy.

'You talk, masters. You don't need me.'

'Stay,' said Erdy. And then added. 'Sit down please.'

Far sat down.

Orly sighed. 'I must insist.'

'And so must I,' said Erdy.

Toby said, 'He can sit with us, but be silent.'

'In my house,' said Orly, 'servants are summoned. They are given their duties. And then they go.'

'You are not in your house,' said Erdy quietly.

He could have added much more: the Queen had Orly's house and her servants were dead, but had no need as Orly's eyes welled with tears. She fought to hold them back, but they seeped out and rolled down her cheeks. Her lips pressed as she worked to hold in her crying.

'But a lady is a lady,' said Toby defensively. 'It is birth, not simply estates.'

'Then Far and I will sit by the fire,' said Erdy, turning from them.

'I didn't mean you...' pleaded Orly.

'No, not you,' agreed Toby, 'but position must be preserved. Otherwise what is a king or a prince or a lady?'

Far was picking the dirt under his nails with a splinter of wood. Not that his nails were dirty. He was cleaner than he'd been in weeks. But he could not argue the place of peasants. Those who tried to were severely punished.

'I live up here,' said Erdy, 'because I need bow my head only to storm clouds. My only King is the mountain. But you have come from down there, and it seems need kings and princes and their serfs. And if that has to be so,' he said with a sigh, 'then I shall be King up here. It is not a role I want, but otherwise you will squabble us to death.' He turned to Toby. 'You are a prince.'

'Yes,' said Toby.

'And she is a princess,' went on Erdy.

'She is not!' exclaimed Toby.

'Don't disobey your King,' said Erdy. He turned to Far. 'And you are a prince.'

'I don't want to be a prince,' mumbled Far.

'And I don't want to be a King. How unhappy we all are.' He sat down at the end of the bed. 'And it is because of that we must talk. All of us.'

'Not with that boy,' said Orly stubbornly.

Erdy rose. 'Come, Far. We'll sit by the fire.'

He left the bedside and crossed to the fire. Far took up his crutch and he stumbled after him. Halfway he had to stop, as his feet still hurt him. Then gritting his teeth he made the remaining steps. Once there, he crouched by the fire and stroked Sly who still watched the two at the bed.

'We must not give in to this equality,' said Orly, keeping her voice low. 'Otherwise who are we?'

Toby was uncomfortable. He wanted to be with Far and Erdy who were talking by the fireside, but knew too the sick girl needed his support.

'Erdy saved our lives,' he said.

'I grant he is noble,' said Orly.

'He isn't,' said Toby. 'I have seen his mother's cottage. She is hardly above a peasant.'

'I am a lady,' said Orly defiantly. 'I must be treated as a lady. Or else I am nobody.'

Toby suspected she might be nobody. As he was. But said nothing.

'I will not talk in the boy's company,' she added. Tired, she subsided on her pillows, breathing rapidly.

'Don't talk,' said Toby.

'We must treat our peasants well,' she continued, working hard to get out the words. 'I accept that. But we are not peasants.' She coughed, but painfully continued. 'Nor is it by accident we are highborn. We have a duty to be what we are. If we admit to equality – they will hang us.'

She stopped in a fit of small coughs.

'Enough for now,' said Toby.

All that anger in one so sick. She lay back now on her pillow breathing rapidly. All those words she must say. He wiped her brow with the damp flannel next to her pillow. She was so hot. He wondered how many of the words belonged to her father. As they could have belonged to his own. But he wondered too about her talk of hanging. Or rather who was the hangman. It hadn't been the peasants who had killed her family. Or his father for that matter. Though he didn't doubt they could.

She had subsided into sleep. And Toby crept gratefully over to the fire where Far and Erdy were talking quietly.

'I had to stay with her even though...' said Toby. His confused thought halted him.

'You did,' said Erdy. He indicated a space at his side. 'Sit down.'

Toby did so.

'My mother said three things to you,' went on Erdy. 'Do you remember what they were?'

Toby thought a while. Only a few days ago but so long.

He at last said, 'She said – I will rescue someone who lies with the dead. I will walk with the dead. I will destroy the secret of life.'

Erdy nodded. Then said, 'You have done the first.'

He knew he had, by saving Orly.

'And the second?' he said.

'You must go and see your father.'

'My father is dead.'

Erdy nodded. 'He is. But he must speak to you.'

'How do you know?'

'I have read it in your soup.'

Toby was bewildered and searched the man's face. Erdy's eyes were almost closed. He spoke in whispers, as if the dead might hear.

'There is something he must say to you.'

'How can I get to the dead?'

'You must go to the Underworld.'

'How?'

'There is a way through. Not far. Can you climb?'

Toby nodded.

'This journey will test the truth of it,' said Erdy. 'Take this.' From a pocket he took out a thin metal bracelet. 'Wear it always.'

'What will it do?'

'It will give strength to your hands and arms.'

'Is it magic?'

'Yes.'

'When must I go?'

'In the morning. By first light. Your father demands it. He is calling even now. He has some secret that can be told only to you. And on it depends the fate of your Kingdom. You must go. When you return, your friends will be ready.'

Chapter 30

The sun dazzled on the white mountain, the snow crackled underfoot. Toby wore woollen leg warmers, mittens and a hat with earflaps. Erdy was bound round and round in a scarf, which covered his neck, his mouth and nose and ended in a woolly hat, all in one connection like a serpent. Toby had to strain to hear him as his words too were muffled in wool.

He was surprised they were still climbing. It was the wrong direction for the Underworld. Way below were the fields of the countryside. There was no snow down there. The sun sparkled off a winding river. It seemed peaceful, untroubled, beautiful; they were too high to hear the screams.

No wonder Erdy chose to live up here.

'How do you make your living?' he said, breathing heavily from the climb.

'A miller brings me up a sack of flour every month,' he said in a voice muffled but with little sign of exertion. 'I saved his daughter two winters ago. A shepherd gives me wool. And I spin and I knit my clothes. Your hat and mittens, my scarf. I knit and I sing. I haven't much of a voice. But who cares? And every so often I go down,' said Erdy. 'I sell my potions in the market. I tell fortunes, I cure the rich for money. I cure the poor for a meal if they have it. I'd rather stay here on the mountain – but I must eat. And I'm curious about what is happening in the world.'

'It's so lonely here,' said Toby.

'Solitude is not the same as loneliness.'

Tears welled in Toby. He was as lonely as a flagpole.

'I have no one to argue with but myself,' went on Erdy. 'And no soldiers with hacking swords come this way.'

'Why not?' said Toby wiping his eyes with the back of a glove.

Erdy had stopped. 'It is too hard for the horses. And I have cured some of their masters. Besides, they are afraid of me.'

'What can you do?'

'I have some magic. And if I don't say what – it makes men careful.'

He was standing by a rock the size of a sheep which rested against a rocky side, too steep to hold snow.

'Move that, Toby.'

Toby was unsure he was in earnest. But there could be nothing else Erdy referred to. The instant he gripped the rock, he felt the power in his arms, hands and wrists from the band he wore. He swung it out as easy as a door. And that's indeed what it was. For behind was a hole, disappearing into darkness. Just large enough to take a person.

'That is Hell's Chimney,' said Erdy. 'It is narrow to begin with. Then it widens out. Beneath is a cavern. And then a river... And after that – I don't know.'

'How dangerous is it?'

'The climb is dangerous. There are the ravens. They'll have your eyes if they see them. After that I can't help. I only know of one man who ever went that way. One live man that is. And he never came back.'

'Why must I go if it is so dangerous?'

'Your father must speak with you. He would not call for you if he did not have something of great importance to tell you.'

'But I may not come back.'

'It is possible.' Erdy placed his hands on his shoulders. He said quietly. 'You do not have to go, Toby. It is not fixed.'

Toby thought, but it is fixed. Or his father would call for him forever. In every waking moment, in every dream.

'I have no food or drink,' he said.

Erdy held him in his dark eyes. 'No one eats or drinks there.'

Of course, thought Toby. He steeled himself.

'Take good care of Far and Orly,' he said.

Erdy turned away. Was he hiding tears? Without looking back, he said, 'Take off your woollens. Whatever dangers there are, cold is not one of them.'

Toby removed his hat, gloves and leg warmers.

'Thank you for everything,' he said, handing over the bundle. Yes, there were tears in Erdy's eyes, and the remnants in his own. The cold was nipping at his fingertips.

He had so much to say. He had nothing to say. This might be the last living man he saw. He clenched his fist. Then so be it.

'We shall be waiting for you, my son,' said Erdy as Toby slid into the hole.

Part Two

The Underworld

Chapter 31

The chimney began as a narrow passageway. More of a crawl than a climb. He went down feet first, as he knew the slope would increase and he might not have room to turn round later. For a little way he watched the circle of light shrink, the patch of sky, the crust of snow round the edge. It was the last help that Erdy could give him. Soon he would replace the rock.

The surface was hard, with no dust or soil, as if a giant had drilled this out with an auger and then blown away any powder. He turned a corner and the slope downward increased, but it was easy enough to hold himself against the edge and continue. The light up top was oozing away, as he edged downwards. The hole of sky had gone when he'd turned the bend, and, with another bend, he was close to darkness. He heard a crunching from above, surprisingly loud, and then it was dark. Erdy had put back the rock.

He had a moment of terror in the solid black. Could he get out? Suppose he changed his mind, could he push back the rock?

He stopped. Let himself breathe.

Yes, he could.

He continued. The slope continued to grow steeper. And in a little while it was obvious why it was called a chimney. The passage was barely bigger than his body and he was heading straight down into the mountain. Though, with his feet and knees pressed against the sides, and hands and elbows at the top, it was easy enough to support himself. He had no fear of falling; fear of the darkness, yes, of getting stuck – but of falling, no. It was almost impossible to with the bumps and lumps sticking out, easy hand and footholds and the grip of the sides.

Quickly he lost his sense of time in the darkness. Erdy was right, he was warm enough. And he found it better to keep moving. The sound of his breath and his scraping was some comfort in the total blackness. When he stopped he could imagine anything coming up from the land of the dead.

The tube became tighter. This was his dread, fear of getting stuck. He was now squeezed so tight at the hips, he could barely move forward. Toby stopped. What should he do? He might push himself in so hard he would not be able to get out. Neither go up or down. And be stuck till kingdom come.

And yet he had to get through.

He pushed on, slow inch by inch as if in the body of a great beast. One final squeeze and he'd be in as tight as a plug. His tunic rasped against the tight rock. Never had he been so frightened, so closed in. In the heart of the mountain, he felt like a foot in a wet boot. No room to turn his head, legs pressed against each other, arms fixed against his side as if he were stuffed in a sack.

He was sweating, trembling, as fixed as a bolt. His tunic had rucked up and he stuck fast. He could not move down. Wedged like a cork in a bottle. Toby tried pulling upwards. He would not go. Up or down.

He felt sickness. He felt panic. He would die packed in this tube. Shut in this coffin. He fought desperately like a worm in a bird's beak. As if he could crack the mountain... and find daylight and space.

Exhausted, he rested, breathing heavily. Time he had plenty of. He had got down this far, it must be possible to get back up. Below him, he had no idea. Except that at least one other had come this way and he hadn't found his jammed body.

Yet.

With a great effort, he inched his way upwards. Once up a foot, it was easier, and then further up. Until he had space enough. Or just about. He worked to take off his tunic. It was simple enough pulling it up his body, but difficult getting it off his arms which were over his head. At last it came away, and he dragged it behind him, as back he went, back down.

He hoped it was enough, shaving the thickness of the tunic off his body. Back into the tightness. Into the vice. Rapidly, it gripped again, but then he was past where he'd been. He was as hot as a lamp, sweating with fear and exertion. His body scraped the rock, each move was painful as if he were a nail pushing into wood, iron and timber fighting for space. Except he was flesh. And when flesh scraped rock there was only one winner.

Oh Mother, help me now!

No mother, no father. Only a squeeze of rock. If before he was lonely, this was its extremity. Packed in a tube, darker than midnight. Erdy had said he didn't have to go. That had been his chance. To say No to this. To death in the rock.

Yet still he wriggled forward. Going on and on, until there is no going on.

His legs were in air. There was a pale luminescence slipping past. He had not been aware of it earlier as his eyes had been closed in his exertion. But now with his legs free, he had opened them. The light was faintly greenish, the colour of grass under a rock. He eased his body to meet his legs and found himself on a ledge.

With intense relief, he realised he had come through the chimney. He was in a vast cavern, chiselled out of a dark rock, made visible in the greenish light. There were no shadows, the light seemed to come from everywhere. He was still high up; way below was a sea of rock, its wave-blown face frozen. And beyond, way beyond, was a river that snaked away to a distant horizon.

That was the one to cross.

He peered over the edge of the ledge. The face was sheer. But as he looked longer, he could see it was creased here and there. No giant had planed it flat. There were little handholds, footholds, at least where he could see. And so there should be others beyond.

This he could deal with. He was out in the open again. He shuddered at the thought of Hell's Chimney. At having to go back up again. But he dismissed the thought. Who knew what could happen before then?

Toby took up his tunic. He was about to put it back on, when he thought, no need. He was warm enough and the climb would make him warmer. Underclothes were decent enough. And who was here to judge? He dropped the tunic over the edge, and it flapped down like a bird. He marked out the spot at the bottom. He'd pick it up when he got there.

If.

Toby eased over the edge, holding himself on the ledge by his palms. He was so strong, he could support himself on just his hands, probably his fingers. His left foot found a cleft, and then his right. With one hand still on the ledge, he searched for one lower. And found a finger hold, eased the other hand down and searched for another grip. And once there, he was on the face of rock.

He had climbed many times down the castle wall. Going from handhold to handhold. This was much higher. That mattered little. Imagine it as twenty castle walls, one on the other. The height didn't worry him, but the difficulty. No windows for support. Just tiny clefts for hands and feet.

But he had a new strength. Erdy's gift.

And this was its element.

There was no rush. He could be as slow as he wished. There was no cold wind to freeze him. He found that he could support himself at three points easily. And even on two, if one of those was a hand. Take it calmly, take it logically. Release a hand, find a lower one, release a foot, search lower.

Several times he was stuck for maybe five minutes, and then having to go down on three points, a leg swinging, hoping to find something. And a couple of times on two, having even to go to one hand and hope there was something to grip on, with a hand or foot.

There was.

He would get there, he was pretty sure. It was simply a question of patience, logic and strength. And some luck. He was certainly afraid, but more excited. This was climbing. This was him and the rock.

He was no longer lonely.

Toby was perhaps halfway down the face when the ravens came.

Chapter 32

He hadn't seen them coming as he was fixed on the rock, searching for hand and footholds. Completely concentrated on tiny clefts and bumps, shifting his weight and strength here, there – as if there were no world at all beyond this face. Or beyond, even, the tiny bit he held on to.

They swooped on him shrieking, wings flapping fiercely. They snapped and gouged at him. Toby flapped one hand ineffectually at them. Their beaks dug and pierced, their claws scraped. They would strip him to the bone, here on the face. Or he would fall to his death. And there, they would consume him.

There were claws in his face, blood was dripping down his cheek. He closed his eyes and grabbed at the feet. He had one in his grip, the legs trying to pull away, the bird's wings beating in savage panic against his hand. He smashed the raven into the cliff face, and nearly swung himself off. But the bird was still. He had broken its head – and he let it fall.

The racket was still around him, the shrieking and rage, the beating of wings. There was one on his head, its claws digging in, its beak pecking at his forehead as if trying to crack a nut. He grabbed it by a wing. Feathers snapped in his grip. It was like holding a struggling fish, the pulling and fighting, the thrashing. He held fast. And hammered the bird into the rock face. The flapping ceased and he dropped the corpse. Purposefully, he reached out with his hand, grabbed a head, its beak pressing into him. His fingers jammed into its eyes and he squeezed it like a plum, the brains oozing out of his fist.

As this one fell, he felt the birds give up. Three dead were enough. He held still on the cliff face, eyes closed, and listening intensely as their flapping and shrieking died away. For perhaps a minute, he held himself this way. Then opened his eyes. They were gone. He searched about for them, in case they should come back and he could be better prepared. And at last saw them, three clusters on the ground. They were eating the meat of their dead fellows.

Toby wiped his hands as well as he could. He was oozing blood in various places but could do little to stem it. He must get down as quickly as possible. The birds feared him now but how quickly might they forget? Or others might come.

But speed was not a possibility. He was not running down steps, but going from tiny hold to tiny hold, searching them out in the rock face. He had but one pace, and that was a careful one. Erdy had warned him of the ravens.

Would they come again?

Pressed against the rock, Toby made his slow way down. There was no resting place. It was an effort to even stay still, pressing into the minute holds. At times, he seemed to be making no progress, going sideways even, but the strength of his hands meant he could make the most of the slightest cleft.

The birds did come again. But less sure this time, as if they held some of the memory of his early carnage – but could not resist the lone figure on the cliff, dripping with blood. Such tantalising meat.

He was ready for them. And smashed two against the cliff as soon as they swooped in. That was enough. Frantically, they flew off. A little later, he saw them below, on the ground, fighting each other at their cannibal feast.

At length he reached the bottom. Unsteady and bloodied, but on terra firma.

Chapter 33

The black rock under his feet was shiny and sharp, like glass. There were jagged points and bits cleaved into cutting edges. It was hard on his feet, but harder still on his hands, as he kept falling and had to heave himself over the glassy rock.

He stopped. And ripped off a sleeve. And taking that between his strong hands, he tore it in two pieces. Toby wrapped the sleeve halves around his hands. He continued his scrambling along the rock. The sleeve pieces protected his hands, but made it harder to grip. But better that then have his hands torn to shreds.

At one point, he turned to look back at the face he had climbed down and marvelled. From here, it seemed unclimbable, and would have been, if not for the bracelet given him by Erdy. He twisted its slim, silvery metal gratefully. Without it, he would have fallen. Either from the climb or from the attack of the ravens.

There seemed no day or night in the cavern. The green light was constant, unwavering, with no cloud or horizon to hide it. And yet no obvious source. Could it come from the rocks itself? Toby took a tiny piece and held it in gloom of his tunic. It glowed. And even felt a little warm in his palm.

Remarkably, considering his exertions, he felt no hunger. Erdy had told him of this. One blessing, as the rocks were completely barren. Nothing grew in the pale light. Nothing crept forth from the rocks. The ravens had gone to wherever they went. He was alone on the sharp rocks, scrambling, falling, rising and going on. He would have liked to have rested but in all the sharpness there was not a place to sit. He must continue, through weariness and pain, until he reached the river. The boundary between the living and the dead.

Chapter 34

As Toby approached the river, he wondered how he was going to cross it. It was perhaps a quarter of a mile wide. A long swim but he thought he could manage it. He was still on the glassy rock which was a little above the river, and would be there in a few minutes. Although its distance was deceptive. For a long time it seemed he wasn't getting closer. But now he could see clearly the dark placid water.

Any thoughts of swimming were swept from his head when a monstrous head and body broke though the water. The head was horned, with large teeth and bulging eyes, held up by a long narrow neck which disappeared into the water like a sunken tree on the swollen island of its body. The monster was staring at him, neck and head swaying. It took a great gulp of air and let out a roar, which echoed round the cavern, coming back in lesser and lesser echoes.

Toby turned and turned about, watching the places of echo in the sides of the cavern as it reverberated round and round. When he looked back to the river, the monster had gone. How deep was that water to hide such a creature? What else swam in its depths?

And how would he cross?

Toby had come to the edge of the rocks. About six feet down was black sand, in a long strip of beach about fifty feet wide by the side of the river. But just ahead was a short wooden jetty protruding a little way into the water. And alongside a rowing boat. Within the boat was a person. Man or woman, he could not tell, as it had its back to him and its head was covered in a hood.

Toby climbed over the rocks and let himself down to the beach. The sand was black as coal, but it too glowed when he held a handful within the dark of his tunic. The water was once again completely still. No monster or wind disturbed it. Toby walked up the jetty, and although his footsteps could be heard on the wooden planking, the person in the boat did not turn or stir.

Toby was at the end of the jetty. The man in the cowl, for it was a man, was leaning forward, back bowed, on the plank of the boat, hands held together. His face was bony with deep hollow eyes, and lifeless grey hair like cotton threads upon his head.

'Will you row me across, sir?' said Toby.

The boatman did not move.

Toby repeated his question and still received no response.

'Sir,' he began again, 'I am a stranger here. I would be grateful if you would row me across the river.'

The boatman did not move.

Toby considered. And then stepped warily into the boat.

The boatman took up the oars which were still in the rowlocks. He turned the boat skilfully with one oar, until it faced the far bank, and began to slowly row across the river.

Toby was seated facing the boatman. They were looking at each other, but for all the interest the man had in him – he might not have been there at all. The man's lips were pressed together, his deep eyes staring but Toby wondered at what.

'Have you a name?' said Toby to break the silence.

The man bit his lower lip and said hoarsely, 'Yes.'

'What is it?'

The boatman closed his eyes for a second as pulled the oars out of the water.

'I don't remember.'

Toby was unsure about the next question but had to ask it.

'Are you dead?'

The boatman gave a weary sigh.

'I don't know.'

This irritated Toby. It was stupid. He held back his anger.

'You must know whether you are alive or dead?'

The man shook his head.

'Too many questions.'

In exasperation Toby turned away from the boatman, who rowed in a slow, effortless rhythm that made the only ripples on the flat, black water. He looked to his right hand side, along the river to the far horizon. He could just make out movement. He screwed his eyes, held his hand at his brow. Could it be…? Yes, there was another boatman. He looked to the left and peered again. And once more, just on the horizon was a tiny boat. Of course, he thought, there can't just be one boatman to carry all the dead. He could imagine a chain of them, each with another to the right and left on the horizon, going all the way round the world.

But how did the dead get here? They couldn't come the way he came. They died, and then something took them over. And they began their journey. He turned, and looked behind the boat, its gentle wake sliding back over the water. There at the end of the jetty was a figure. Man or woman, he couldn't tell, but it seemed to be watching them. Presumably, the next passenger, waiting his or her turn. Old, young – he couldn't see. Just a figure, and most likely dead. He thought of all the boats along the river, all in transit, and all with someone waiting.

'How do they get here?' he said out loud.

The man shrugged.

'Why do you row them?' said Toby.

'I don't know.'

'Did you do something bad?'

The man nodded.

'What?'

'I can't remember.'

'How long must you stay?'

The man sighed, a long weary sigh.

'Too many questions.'

His hands were thin, the knuckles white where he gripped the oars. His movement was like the swing of a pendulum, slow, seemingly without effort, as if his arms were part of the oars. Almost it seemed as if he were a toy, and the movement of the oars pulled him backwards and forwards.

'Is this the only land of the dead?'

The man shrugged. 'I don't know.'

'How long will you have to do this job?'

The man sighed. 'Why do you ask so many questions?'

'I need to know,' said Toby.

'Why?'

Toby didn't answer. He realised the boatman didn't care what he replied. He had been doing the job so long, every question, every answer was the same to him. All without meaning.

They were almost across now. Without having to turn to see where he was going, the boatman was heading towards a small jetty, the mirror image of the one on the other side. Except no one waited there.

The man slipped the oars and the boat pulled in. He tied up to a ring on the side of the jetty.

Toby rose to get out. The man held him by the leg.

'Pay me.'

He looked down into the boatman's hollow eyes. 'I have no money.'

The boatman grasped his wrist. 'Give me that bracelet then.'

Toby pulled it away. 'No.'

'Pay me.'

The man was still holding his leg.

'I have nothing to give you,' said Toby.

'Give me your tunic.'

Toby hesitated. Then slipped it off over his head. He held out the bundle to the boatman.

The boatman went to grasp it – and Toby pulled it away and jumped on to the jetty.

'Pay me,' yelled the boatman, his bony hand outstretched.

Toby raced along the jetty. The man remained in his boat, and shouted after him in a voice filled with anger and pain.

'Pay me.'

Toby ran up the beach and clambered up the rocks, his tunic under his arm.

'Pay me.'

On he scrambled across the rocks, as if he were being chased, but the boatman remained standing in his boat with his arm outstretched. Toby pressed his fingers in his ears.

'Pay me!'

Chapter 35

Far was seated at the table on a high stool with a mortar and pestle. To one side were herbs and twigs, and little mounds of rock granules. It was Far's task to grind them and put them altogether into the large bowl in front of him. He had no idea what was to be made. He was simply obeying Erdy's instructions. Erdy had put out the ingredients and the vessels, showed Far how to use a mortar and pestle, and then left him to go down the mountainside to gather more herbs.

Far was grateful to be useful. His feet were still bandaged but less so. He used the crutch but hardly needed it. It took some pressure off his feet, though Erdy had said that from tomorrow he should go without.

Orly approached cautiously, her hands in the deep pockets of the tunic and leggings she wore, the same as Far. She had resisted giving up her black dress. It was the remnant of her ladyhood. And while she was still ill, Erdy had let her be. But once he felt her recovered enough, he had burnt it, just the day before. How she had raged at this. But by the time she knew, half of it had gone.

Erdy had told her that he could not have a lady in his cavern for all their sakes. She had taken this wrongly, believing he was somehow demoting her. And she sulked and harangued, while Erdy tried explaining that he was, in fact, protecting them all, as a lady on the mountainside could bring about their slaughter.

Reluctantly attired, she sat down at the stool, watching Far grind red lumps of rock in the mortar. Far knew of her presence, but concentrated on the rock, pressing it hard into the side of the bowl to break it down to powder, relentlessly pursuing the smaller pieces.

'You may talk to me,' said Orly.

Her elbows were on the table. Her hair had been cut short. Erdy had asked her permission to do this, which she at first refused, but he was able to persuade her that peasant girls did not wear their hair long. It had to go. But she shivered now like a shorn lamb.

'Are you going to talk to me?' said Orly.

Far did not look up, holding the bowl firm as he ground with the pestle.

'It is difficult to talk when you are given permission,' he said.

She watched him in the silence, sighing with boredom.

'I don't know who I am,' she said. 'My dress gone, my hair gone, my family gone.'

'My family is gone too,' said Far.

'Yes,' said Orly, 'I know that. And I am sorry. But peasants die all the time.'

'Everyone dies,' said Far.

'You know what I mean,' said Orly. 'Peasants are more used to death, what with wars and disease and bad food. You don't feel as much. Do you?'

Far stopped grinding and stared at her.

'How do you know how much I feel?' he said.

'My mother said...' she began.

Far interrupted her. 'Your mother knew no more than you.'

Orly's eyes filled with tears.

Trying hard to control them, she said, 'Please don't speak that way about my mother.'

'Was she a peasant?' said Far.

'Of course not.'

'Then what did she know about us?'

'What everybody knows...' she began and stopped, unsure of what everybody knows. The world had gone mad. Who on earth was she? Before her was a peasant boy, not simply speaking to her – well, she had given him permission for that, but chastising her.

With no one to whip him.

'Everyone's gone,' said Far bitterly, putting some herbs and twigs into the bowl. 'Mum, Dad, my big brother Tom, little Ellie. I didn't get on with my dad. Sometimes I wished him dead. He used to beat me with a birch pole. Last time, he said I gave the chickens too much feed. And I knew I hadn't. There just wasn't enough. Mum didn't try to stop him. She'd get it too. He beat her enough. I'd get out the way when that was happening, run off into the fields. But Tom would stop him. My big brother. He was as big as Dad – and if Dad tried to beat him then he'd know what he'd get. When Tom was about then Dad wouldn't hit any of us. Not me, not Mum. I miss him alright. And little Ellie. She was a funny little thing.' He sniffed and wiped an eye with the back of his hand. 'She used to run after me when I left in the morning. And when I came back from the fields, she was always so pleased to see me, with a smile as big as the moon. I'd pick her up and throw her over my shoulder…' He stopped, eyes closed, tears streaming down his cheeks. 'They're rats, the men that killed her. Lower than rats. Rats wouldn't do that. I get a pain in my chest just thinking about it.' He faced Orly, the pestle in one hand, eyes blazing. 'Who got 'em to do that killing? Your lot!'

'Not my lot,' said Orly. 'My lot were killed.'

Far sucked his lip. 'Yeh, sorry. Not your lot. I shouldn't have said that. It's just sometimes hard to tell one from the other.'

Neither spoke for a while.

At last she said, 'I didn't know you were so unhappy, Far.'

He'd gone back to grinding the sticks and herbs.

'Well now you know.'

'So am I,' she said.

'I know you are.'

She said, 'But I didn't know about you.'

They didn't speak for a while. Far continued grinding the herbs and rocks in the mortar and pestle while she watched, her fingers feeling her unfamiliar hair.

'Can I help?' she said.

Far looked up at her, unsure she meant it, but then what did it matter if she didn't?

'There's a mortar and pestle on that shelf.'

When Erdy returned about an hour later, both were working at the table with their mortar and pestles. They were talking intermittently, no longer about their families, but about the task in front of them.

Chapter 36

A desert of white sand. Or was it pale green? There was no way of telling. The river was some way behind. Toby had at last lost the sound of the boatman. He shuddered. What on earth would the man do with payment anyway? What was the standard fare?

He was not the only one on the sand. There were many others, all coming in, as if walking along the spokes of a wheel, to the hub. And that was a gate between high rocks. Men, women, children were coming. All the walking ages of humanity. What happened to babies, he thought? Or toddlers. There was no one crawling. Some little children, but old enough to walk on their own. And none carried or pushed. Toby was the only one curious, turning about to see who was here. Everyone else walked face front. All by themselves, about twenty feet behind the one in front. None making any attempt to catch up. Toby adjusted his pace. There was an old woman in front of him. Her back was bowed, and she wore a headscarf. Behind him was a young boy. Toby waved to him, but the boy either did not see or ignored the gesture.

Toby knew these were the dead. He had crossed the river. Recently dead, he assumed, though how they got here and how long it took them he could not guess. They might have been travelling for years for all he knew. Or it could be they were yesterday's dead.

He decided to slow up so that the boy behind would catch up, and then he could ask him his questions. And likely get more out of him than the taciturn boatman who either had forgotten everything or had no wish to speak.

But it didn't work. The boy slowed up as he did. And behind him, all those in his line also slowed. Toby stopped. The boy stopped. Everyone in the line stopped. And no one said a word. He thought, I could stand here forever – and so would they.

He sped up, trying to catch the woman in front. Those behind began again. Toby got to the point where he was twenty feet behind the old woman. And then found that no matter how fast he went he could get no closer. He was running, she was plodding – and the distance between them stayed the same, as if the ground was being stretched out the faster he went.

No matter how fast he went, his speed stayed the same. Why run, then? Out of breath, he slowed to an easy walk. And, like all the others, strolled towards the gate. The gate had two high stone pillars against the rocks on either side. Attached to the pillars were gates of iron, opened outwards against the rocks. The gates had no design on them, simply consisting of upright bars held top and bottom. At one side stood a sentry and at his side a three-headed dog.

The dead walked straight through. The guard did not acknowledge them in any way. The dog similarly ignored them. Toby could not understand why there was a guard at all. Did the dead need ceremony? The guard was a stocky man, bulging with muscles, threatening to burst out of the short leather tunic he wore. His arms were bare and tattooed from wrist to shoulder. In his hand he held a chain, attached to the huge three-headed dog that sat docile by his side.

For no apparent reason the dog began to bark. All three heads growled and threatened. The dog was off his haunches straining at the chain. The guard struggled to hold him back. He pulled, the dog pulled, the chain stretched to its limit.

Still the dead walked through unhindered. The dog was not interested in them. And as Toby approached, it was obvious that the dog wanted him. The three heads snarled, jaws slobbering, full of foaming, white teeth. The dog was wrenching with all its fury, its solid muscle fighting to be off its leash. The guard strained with every fibre to hold it, slowly slipping forward in the sand.

Toby stopped in terror, perhaps six paces from the guard and his dog. He had no doubt what would happen if the guard lost his battle. In a second, he'd be ripped to pieces in the sand, the three heads tearing him limb from limb.

The guard had both hands on the chain handle, his muscles bulging with effort, breath hissing through his pressed teeth, while his feet ploughed forward.

'No live meat this way,' he managed to say. 'Clear off.'

'I must come in,' said Toby, unable to take his eyes off the snarling horror.

'I can't hold them much longer,' gasped the man. 'Scram!'

'Is there another way?'

The guard was bursting with strain, his body at an impossible angle. Should he fall, the dog would lunge. The three heads were wild with fury, snapping and snarling, and intent on pulling away from their tiring keeper. There stood live meat – and they would not be held back from it.

'Through the Hall of Dead Babies,' screamed the guard. 'To your right. Run!'

Toby needed no second bidding. He was off. Fear speeding his run: an image of the charging dog pounding him to the ground, and teeth meeting teeth through his bleeding flesh. His terror was boundless, and didn't need the spear of barking and growling to press him on. He was panic on legs.

He had run perhaps fifty yards at full sprint, when he noticed the barking had stopped. He turned briefly. And there was the three-headed dog, once again docile by his master.

But that didn't stop his run.

Chapter 37

He entered a cave in the rocky cliffs, high enough to stand upright, which proved to be a passageway into a large chamber that he could see, about twenty paces ahead of him. From the chamber came an ear-splitting racket which he at first thought was made by seagulls. And having rejected that as too unlikely, realised the sound came from a vast number of crying babies, echoed and re-echoed on the walls and ceiling of the chamber.

At the end of the passageway he found himself on a balcony, one storey in height above an immense floor in a hall of rock. The floor was packed with babies. Each was wrapped in a white blanket with just head and arms showing, a foot or two from its neighbour. The arms were frantic, the fingers wriggling like desperate tentacles. And the infants were bawling, as only they can, with every ounce of their being.

Toby pressed his hands to his ears, the sound was agonising. Not simply the volume, but the pain expressed by the tiny bodies. Some were very small, some a fair bit bigger, a number of these with hats. It was like a great baby farm. As if they had been planted, and these were the crops, like marrows, growing out of the rocky floor.

In this field of babies, he saw a number of girls, all with long dark hair, aged perhaps twelve or so. A number of them had babies in their arms. At first he thought it was they who brought the babies, but then he saw it was the reverse. They were picking them up, then stepping carefully over the floor so as not to tread on any tots, and carrying their charges down the hallway to an entrance at the far end of the hall.

There was a girl just below him. She was going for a particular baby, ignoring all the crying and pleading hands she was stepping over. And then she stopped. The one she stood over was the only one in that group who was not crying. She stooped and lifted the baby onto her shoulder. She patted it on the back to comfort it. It was then Toby saw the girl's face. It was old and gaunt, with none of the freshness of youth – as if age had pounced on her like a wild cat clawing at her cheeks.

And then for some reason, the baby she was holding began to cry. And to Toby's surprise, the girl put the baby down again. And with the baby now as frantic as its neighbours, she walked away from it. A little later, he noted she picked up another. This one was not crying. She held it over her shoulder and patted it on the back in the same way as the first. The second baby did not cry and she carried it down the hallway. Toby watched her a while and hoped the mite she held would stay silent. Or it would be abandoned like the first.

There was only one way out of the hall, and that was the far end where the girls were going. Toby too must head that way. And hoped from there he could somehow find his father. There were no stairs or path down from his balcony. He looked directly below the low balustrade. It would be easy enough to drop to the ground, except there were babies against the wall. Dead to be sure, but he still didn't want to drop on to a baby, dead or not.

He would have to climb down.

Toby kneeled on the balustrade and, gripping the top with his hands, lowered himself down the wall. It was only about three feet to drop then – but there were the babies underneath. The climb down, he had no trouble with. He stepped into the space between two babies. And each of them latched onto his right foot with their hands, like crabs onto a stick. He lifted them off, their grip was slight enough. And found his left foot had three babies holding on. He removed them, immediately found a stepping place for this foot, and felt his right foot encumbered again.

He thought he would just walk, and carry the load as far as he could. He had gone no more than ten feet when he had about six babies on each leg, bundled over each other like small sacks. As he went to remove them, they grabbed his arms, and other babies took their place on the leg.

With great effort he was able to free himself. But not for long. Perhaps it was his warmth they detected, some property of a living body. But for Toby, it was like walking across the heaviest of ploughed fields; the babies were the clay mounted on clay adhering to his boots. He was exasperated, and quickly exhausted, by the sheer effort of walking with the weight and the constant plucking them off. The crying threatened to burst his head, and in spite of their screwed-up, contorted faces, he lost all sympathy for them.

He was getting nowhere across the hall. Babies held him back as if in a swamp. They grasped him, clutched at him like cleavers. But it wasn't even as if they stopped crying once they had a grip; if anything it was worse, afraid they'd be taken off, which of course they were. He had no comfort for them.

And was any possible?

With three babies on each leg, a couple on each arm, he contemplated of going back to the balcony. At least there he had his own space. In desperation, he even considered risking the three-headed dog. This quagmire was useless. He was working like mad and getting nowhere. Weary, Toby stopped and watched. At first almost in fascination, as if they were alien creatures, watching them grip him like hydra, and then others grip the first on board. The bigger ones climbing over the little ones, like maggots in a box. In horror he realised that if he did nothing, observed them like a naturalist, then he would simply become a hill of babies.

They would smother him.

As rapidly as he could, he removed them. In panic throwing them off, not caring where they landed. He thought he was losing; there were more coming than he could remove. He tossed them away; they are dead, he thought – what does it matter? Trying desperately to create a space around him. A little island of safety.

And when at last he had done it, he collapsed with exhaustion. He was in the centre of a space about six feet in diameter, the circumference – a tangle of pleading hands. He couldn't be more than twenty feet from the balcony. It would take him an age to even get back there but infinity to cross the hall. No wonder the entrance to the Hall of Dead Babies had no need for a three-headed guard dog. Who on earth could ever cross this space?

The girls.

In wonder, he watched one a little way off, homing in on a silent baby. The infants ignored her. It was as if she were invisible to them. What did she have, that they did not feel her presence? That hardly needed answering. The babies still wanted to live; that was their misery. They hoped by hanging onto the one living thing here, they might be given life themselves.

She was picking up the baby as Toby leapt in. He felt softness under his foot, he did not care to look at what he had crushed. It is dead, he told himself. I cannot kill what is already dead. He stood behind the girl, as tight as a shadow. And in her wake, no babies clutched at him. She put the baby over her shoulder and patted its back. Toby put his hands on her shoulder; she didn't seem to mind, perhaps didn't feel him at all. She began her journey. To stay so close he had to take small steps in tune with hers, and watch the ground carefully to stay off the infants.

They ignored him.

With her he could cross. Toby made sure his hands stayed firmly on her shoulders and his feet stayed off the babies. He had no idea how far there was to go; he dared not look up from the ground.

The girl walked on steadily.

And suddenly, he was through the entrance on the far side. Out of the Hall of Dead Babies. For a little while he held onto her shoulders, then realised there was no need. And released her, and watched her continue at the same pace down the corridor, where on one side a line of girls were walking into the far distance, each with a baby over her shoulder. And on the other side was a row approaching him, all with aged faces, walking, about twenty paces apart, to the hall. There to separate the silent ones from their noisy companions.

Chapter 38

'Can I help you, sir?'

An extremely thin man approached him. He was tall and lanky, dressed in a green shirt and leggings. His bony feet were bare. He had a concerned look on his face, as if he really cared. Toby, though, was wary.

'I am lost,' he said.

The man nodded as if this were a regular occurrence.

'If you'd just show me your ticket...' he said.

Toby didn't reply. He didn't want to give himself away.

'Lost it?' said the man.

'Yes,' said Toby quickly.

The man touched him in the shoulder, with perhaps a suggestion of a smile.

'I'll take you back to get another,' he said and turned about.

Toby took a step after him and tapped the man on the shoulder. 'Please,' he said. 'I never had a ticket.'

The man turned and looked at him quizzically. He was completely bald, his eyes large and unblinking. But there was a sorrow in him, a remnant of feeling.

'Are you alive?' he said.

There was little point denying it. No ticket, lost. And he badly needed help.

'I am,' said Toby.

'That is most unusual,' said the man sucking his thin lips. 'I haven't come across one of you... for ooh...' said the man grasping at a figure, then giving up. 'In I don't know how long. Once. It was such a long time ago. A young man he was, looking for his lover. What was his name? Played such beautiful music.' He stopped and shook his head sadly. 'There's not much gets through to anyone down here, but that music. It's the only time I have seen the dead weep.'

'Don't the babies weep?'

The man shook his head. 'That's not weeping. That's rage. The poor mites have been denied life. But I'm forgetting myself. Where were we? Ah yes.' The man patted him on the shoulder. 'Yes, that's warmth alright. You are alive. Why have you come?'

'My father wishes to speak to me.'

The man raised his eyebrows. 'And how did he make contact?'

'Through Erdy. He's a healer, a fortune teller, a magician I think.'

'All of those. I've heard of him.' Then the man added quietly, 'His sort, they're not very popular down here. They interfere. Mind you, we could do with some interfering...'

'You seem...' said Toby, searching for the right words, 'well, more alive than the others I've met.'

The man sighed. 'That's my trouble. I should have moved on hundreds of years ago. But I keep asking questions. And you mustn't do that. I shall have to give it up, then I can go on. But you see – it's a bad habit with me. I can't help asking questions. It's quite stupid. I rarely get any answers. But forgive me, I am talking on, but I so rarely get the chance for a conversation. I shall be your guide. My name is Nom. Sometimes called Nom the Talker, or Nom the Questioner. But I'm also Nom the Guide. And pleased to be at your service. I hope you don't mind me going on so.'

'I love it,' said Toby with relief. 'Talk all you please. You're the first one I've met who wants to say anything. Speak all you like. And I'm Toby.'

'Pleased to meet you, Toby.'

'I'm searching for my father as I've said. He was a King. Murdered.'

Nom wrinkled his face. 'That's easy. We need the Hall of Deposed Kings.'

'Is there a whole hall of them?'

'Oh yes. Kings. Always getting murdered. Dying in battle. Kingship seems to guarantee you a short life. I wonder anyone takes it on. The seduction of power I suppose. Each one thinks they are going to beat the odds. Are you going to be King?'

'I was. But I am a deposed Prince.'

'Still alive though. Not to be sniffed at. Let's go find your father. I hope you are not in a rush.'

Toby thought he should be, but didn't feel that way, experiencing for the first time in the Underworld safety in someone's company.

'Take your time,' he said.

'Just as well. No one rushes down here. Time is something we have plenty of. Not much else – but we are plagued with time.' He rubbed his chin. 'Now let me think. Yes, let's go this way.'

And he led the way down the cavern.

Chapter 39

They had climbed onto the ridge of a mountain. It was misty. Not cold at all, but still the mist hung. Nothing grew on the bare rock. No moss, lichen, or a single blade of grass. No birds flew. But there were people about. Men and women who suddenly appeared out of the mist and then disappeared back into it.

'What is this place?' said Toby. 'Who are these people?'

'This,' said Nom, 'is the Mountain of Sighs.'

A young man came out of the mist before them, reading a poetry book out loud. He passed Nom and Toby without seeing them and disappeared into the haze.

'Those who died for love are here,' said Nom.

They passed a young woman sitting on a rock, her face hidden in her hands, her elbows on her knees. Her blonde hair reached to the ground. Toby looked back at her as he and Nom wandered on, until she disappeared in the mist.

'How long do they stay?' said Toby.

'Until they forget their beloved. I was here once, when I first came.'

'Have you forgotten your beloved?'

'Totally. I can't recall her name or face or even whether she was female at all.'

'That's so sad.'

Nom shrugged. 'It might be. It might not be.'

A woman came by gazing into a locket. Her face was white with suffering. She suddenly stopped and threw the locket over the mountainside.

'She can't go on like that,' said Nom.

'Sh! She'll hear.'

Nom shook his head. 'She can hear nothing but her own sighs.'

The woman was crying.

'I thought you said no one weeps here,' Toby whispered.

'She has no tears,' said Nom. 'That's simulation. She is doing what she thinks she should do. After all, she died for love. She feels the need to justify herself. But all she is doing is playing a part.'

Toby watched the woman. He could not see tears, but her chest heaved and the piteous sound she made convinced him.

'Are you sure?' he said.

'No.'

'Look out!' yelled Toby. He pushed Nom. From above where the mist was thin, a man was falling, his cloak splayed out like a bat.

'Mary!' he was screaming, his arms and legs flailing.

The man hit the ground a little way from them.

Toby rushed over, but before he got there the man had risen. He brushed himself down, sad it seemed that he was still in one piece, and then ran back up the mountainside declaiming, 'Mary! My love!'

'The dead can't kill themselves,' said Nom. 'But he'll keep trying. Until he forgets who Mary is.'

Perhaps not a bad thing, thought Toby.

They had come to a fast stream, the water gurgling out of the rocks and rushing down and disappearing below.

'You must soak yourself here,' said Nom.

'Why?'

'Because you are alive. And it will become very hot.'

Toby stepped into the cold water and shivered.

'Freezing.'

'Soak yourself to the bone,' ordered Nom.

'I'll die of cold.'

He was sitting on the stony bottom, teeth chattering. Nom splashed him over the top of his tunic and head.

Cold as he was, Toby was suddenly aware he had not eaten or drunk since coming down to the Underworld. Somehow the need for these basic necessities was suspended. Even in the stream he had no wish to drink.

Nom grabbed him by the hair and dragged his head under.

Toby yelled and gurgled and spluttered.

'You're drowning me!'

Nom released him.

'Let's go,' said Nom. 'While you are cold and wet.'

They crossed a hillock, and the mist was suddenly gone. As if it and the sighing lovers knew they shouldn't go here. And, as Nom had warned, the ground was hot. For a while Toby was able to walk over it, his feet steaming, but then it began to burn through his shoes.

'Get on my shoulders,' said Nom.

He knelt down and Toby climbed onto his shoulders. Nom stood up straight. He might have been thin but he was strong, and had no problem lifting and walking with Toby on his shoulders. Down into the valley he went. And as he walked the rocks became still hotter. Toby felt the fierce heat even on Nom's shoulders. His tunic and hair steamed.

The rocks were beetroot red with the heat, then bright red, then glowing, molten and white. Nom walked right through. He did not burn, even as his feet sank into a stream of lava to his ankles.

'You cannot die twice,' he said.

He slipped to his waist in molten rock. Toby had to lift his feet to keep them away from the white heat. He was roasting and choking in the sulphurous fumes. Any wetness from the stream had boiled away. He was cooking in the heat. He closed his eyes. He was in an oven with the door shut, baking with the bread.

'I will die,' he moaned.

It was as hot as a furnace. As hot as the centre of the sun. He was the only living being in the land of the dead – and soon, very soon, there would be no living beings. He would toast, he would scorch. He would burn to a cinder.

And then he was cold. And hot and cold. And water sizzled all about him.

He opened his eyes and he was lying in the snow. Or rather sinking into it as his hot body melted him further into the snowdrift. Snow was all around. The lava had gone. He was in a valley of snow.

'There,' said Nom indicating an opening in the rock face, almost obscured by snow. 'That is the entrance to the Hall of Deposed Kings.'

Chapter 40

The hall was vast, a cavern gouged out of the rock with, it seemed, just a thin ceiling of mountainside above. Within it were men only.

'Is there a Hall for Deposed Queens?' asked Toby.

'There is,' said Nom. 'Smaller.'

They had just come through the entrance; the snow was melting off their shoulders. Toby noted all the men were singular, none spoke to any other. They each had a small rock on the ground. Some were seated on it, others standing nearby. But none far off it, as if they were afraid this very last bit of their kingdom would be stolen too.

Nearby was a man in armour. Toby presumed he had died in battle. Another in bed clothes. Poisoned or stabbed in bed.

'None have their wounds,' he said.

'It would be unfair to have to wander in the Underworld,' said Nom, 'headless, legless or with half a body. It's enough to lose a kingdom.'

More than enough. The cavern quaked with despair. Something he could recognise. He had been a prince. The chosen of his kingdom. And had it all ripped away. None of these men knew who they were.

'I must find my father,' he said.

Nom left him to it. Toby's search was like wandering through a graveyard staring at the stones, seeking the right one. Those with their backs to him, he had to walk round to see their faces. Those seated on rocks, their heads in their hands, he had to peer at closely to make sure. Most seemed not to care about his presence as he wandered between them, so long as he stayed off their territory. A foot in the wrong place gave him a malevolent scowl, reminding him of dogs barking off intruders.

None wore crowns, nor any regalia. No gold chains, sceptres, orbs, in fact no jewellery of any sort. Not even rings or brooches. Their clothes were well made, in fine colours, some with gold thread. But without attendants and regalia – they were simply men. Some short, some tall, some medium height – the full range of men. And quite unremarkable. Toby had seen much despair in the Underworld, and a cavernful certainly belittled it.

So what had made these men kings at all?

Birth, Toby knew. But that wasn't enough. A king had to stay a king. He needed an army, castles, ships.

Good fortune.

Should he ever become king, would he end up here with these miserable souls? All killed so some other could have the throne. And would that other not come here too? Deposed as he had himself deposed. Part of that long chain of murder that kept living kings awake in their beds.

Chapter 41

His father was strolling round his rock, as if on a small island in the sea. Toby was able to watch him unobserved as his father paced round his rock. Nothing outside his space was of any interest to him. He could have been out in the garden, thought Toby, walking round a shrub, planning affairs of state. He wore the clothes Toby had last seen him in at that fateful dinner: a long green tunic with yellow leggings. The sleeves of the tunic were short, and under it was a white undershirt which could be seen about the throat and down to his wrists. What on earth was he thinking in these relentless circuits, thought Toby. Of him? Of his step-mother? Of nothing at all? His hair was down to his shoulders and he had a full grey beard, which he pulled at as he walked round and round.

'Father,' called Toby.

His father stopped and turned his head, startled out of his thought. And looked long at Toby, who was perhaps four paces away. His back had been bowed in his walk, but now he stood upright. And went to straighten his chain – which was not there.

'Why have you been so long?' he complained.

'I came as quickly as I could,' said Toby, coming in closer.

'You call this quick!' shouted his father, his face contorted in rage. An expression that Toby knew well, but no longer had the same effect on him. For though it was his father shouting, it was not his king.

'As soon as I knew, I came, Father.'

'You lie, boy!'

Toby felt the same impulse that had sent him charging out of the room, those few weeks ago. If he'd had a horse he would have run to it. Realising, though, the foolishness of that impulse (hadn't it caused him trouble enough?) he stood his ground.

'I am not lying, Father. And it's unfair of you to yell at me like this.'

His father strode to within a couple of feet of Toby, boiling with rage. He went to strike Toby around the head but Toby caught his wrist.

'Let go of me, boy. I am your father. I am your king,' he exclaimed as he struggled to release himself.

Toby let go of him.

'You are not my king. And a poor father you have been.'

His father stepped back, his eyes blazing, clutching his wrist. Toby had forgotten the strength of his hands. But he had the advantage and did not wish to lose it.

'I was thrown in the dungeon after your murder, accused by your foul Queen and her son of being the murderer. I was to be executed on the block. I have been on the run, chased by dogs and soldiers after my blood. And all brought about by that bitch's leavings you dared bring to replace my mother.'

This subdued his father. He bowed his head and paced round his rock.

'She murdered me,' he said through clenched teeth. 'Her and her son... what's his name? I forget things here.'

'Pig's snout,' said Toby. 'Called Zeke by some.'

'They came to my chamber. He stabbed me in the back then she in the front.'

'And blamed me for it.'

His father stopped his pacing and faced him.

'I know.'

'How?' said Toby.

His father waved a hand. 'Down here we see, we are told – and can do little.' He stopped, and almost pleading said, 'Why have you been so long?'

Toby clutched at the air. 'I have told you, I came as quick as I could.'

'The journey is swift,' said his father.

'Perhaps when you are dead,' said Toby, 'but for the living it is long and it is dangerous. I have come down Hell's Chimney, climbed down a cliff of ravens, evaded a three-headed dog and crossed molten lava. I could have died many times. And then, if I had died, been with you as quick as you wished.'

'I am sure you could have come more quickly.'

If Toby had any doubts this was his father, then he had them no longer. Here he stood, dead, without a throne, and as stubborn and as stupid as he had been in life.

'I could not have.'

His father turned away. Toby turned away. And for some minutes they did not speak. Toby thought of his step-mother, her petulance and temper. And her recourse to his father, who always saw only her side. Banished him to his room, forbade him riding and meals. Left him to the scorn of Zeke. Yet still, even after his murder, his father must maintain his rectitude. Here in this cavern of stripped monarchs he imagined he still had authority over more than just his little rock.

Toby burned with anger.

And yet what was the point of argument? Toby had come all this way because his father had something to tell him. Surely, something more important than that he could have come more quickly? There were times he and his father argued, there were times they got on well. The switch could come in an instant. But if Toby had his father's temper, Toby had also learnt, in the last few weeks, that there were times to curb it.

He faced his father and said as calmly as he could, 'I am sorry, Father.'

Its generality had the desired effect.

His father said quietly, 'My boy, I am glad you have come. And I have something of great importance to tell you.'

Toby listened while his father strode round his rock, his arms behind his back.

'My queen – I admit your judgement of her was correct. I was swayed by her beauty...'

'And her lies,' interjected Toby.

'And her lies.' He raised a hand briefly in admission. 'I was a fool. I was her path to power – so had to be removed. You, too...'

'She was in no hurry to kill me,' said Toby, 'but couldn't explain the complexity to her soldiers.'

His father nodded.

'You know she is a witch?' he said.

'No,' said Toby, more startled by this information than he should have been.

'She has some guardian creatures. I can't help you with those as I know little of them. But down here I have discovered that she is not as she appeared.' He stopped pacing and faced Toby. 'She told me she was thirty-six years old.' He shook his head. 'But she is not. Oh, most certainly not. She is in fact 297 years old.'

'How is that possible?'

'The stone she wears round her neck. The yellow one – you must know it. She never removes it. Not even in bed. It is the Stone of Oull. And gives its wearer eternal life. You must take it from her and smash it. And she will die.'

'That won't be easy. To get the stone.'

'No,' said his father. 'But you got down here, even if you took your time. Smash the stone! Smash the stone!'

The thought took him over. He paced wildly round the rock uttering the same incantation. Toby tried to intervene, but it was as if a wall was surrounding his father. He left him waving his arms, repeating angrily, 'Smash the stone!'

Chapter 42

He was depressed when he met again with Nom in the passageway outside the Hall. He felt, again, that ache of dismissal. His father had no concern for his journey, no concern for his troubles in the living world. Simply his own demands.

'He gave me not one kind word.'

'He will not learn kindness down here,' said Nom.

'I will never see him again,' said Toby, 'and I am dismissed with his orders. No embrace, no goodbye, no hopes for a safe journey. Just the commands of a king who isn't a king. I am thinking – is that all my father is?'

'It is all he is now,' said Nom. 'And he will be even less. But it is not who he was. And that's what you need to remember. Coming down to the Underworld can never renew feelings. He is but a shadow of what he was. Your interview had to end in disappointment.'

Toby nodded reluctantly. And wondered what he'd been expecting. A coming together, a proper parting. Forgiveness, an admission that his father was wrong. But above all, comfort. Someone to tell him it would all come right. Someone who believed in him, rather than someone who yelled at him for being late.

He closed his eyes and sighed. This was where he was. Not some dreamy world of wishing, but the land of the dead. And he knew what he had to do. But he ached with renewed loss, as if his father had just died.

'I must go back to the living world at once,' he said wearily. 'I've had too much of the Underworld.'

'I can see that,' said Nom. 'This is no place for living men.' He indicated a narrow tunnel off the passageway. 'Let's go this way. It's a shorter way to the river.'

They turned into it, and were just able to walk side by side. The tunnel was gloomy, lit by an occasional fire torch. Toby was reminded of the dungeon hallway outside the cells – and how he had made his escape. He thought of Far, Orly and Erdy and how he wanted to be with them. With real people who had needs like his own.

He must accept the death of his father. He had spoken to a man who looked like his father. Who had some of the attributes. But he was dead. And the dead aren't the living. Can never be. Will never be.

My father is gone, he said to himself.

And I have work to do.

He must get over the pain of the meeting. And of the parting. It would be hard. But he must take away only the knowledge he needed. Not renew the suffering he had felt with his father the King and his Queen.

The passageway opened into a well-lit, large hall. All about the floor were scruffy children, mostly seated or crouching, in small groups. Quite a few were playing a game with stones he did not know. There was laughter even. This amazed him. In the Hall of Deposed Kings there had been only despair and anger. But here, well, he would almost describe it as happiness.

'Where are we?' he said.

'This is the Hall of Dead Street Children.'

Some of the children were small, just beyond toddlers. Others almost as old as himself. Boys and girls, dirty-faced, torn clothes. The hall was full of chatter that echoed in the walls, the clicking of stones, and yes – laughter.

'Why are they so content?'

'These children,' said Nom, 'lived on the street. They begged for food, they fought for it, they stole it. Here, there is no need for food. They were abused, beaten, despised. Who is here to do that to them? They were frozen and wracked by disease. That too is over.'

Toby shook his head. Something was wrong. It came to him.

'Why are they not fighting?'

'Because they cannot hurt each other. They can kick and scratch and bounce on a child's head – and make not the slightest dent. Why then fight?'

Why indeed, thought Toby. Every fight he'd ever had was to hurt someone or defend himself from hurt. So why fight without that? It becomes like tumbling or dancing.

'There are boys and girls,' said Toby. 'Do they not...?'

'Death ends all sexual feeling,' said Nom.

And ends another reason to fight and abuse, thought Toby. These children had had the worst of everything. No wonder they could enjoy the simple pleasure of sitting. Without cold, without hunger, without abuse.

'It's awful,' he said, 'that they are happier here than in their lives.'

'Who cares about street children?' said Nom.

He did not answer, as his reply would do him no credit. He had cared little. Often his father had decreed the streets be swept clear of them. And how they suffered, because of that, had not concerned him.

They continued through the hall. The children ignored them, intent in their own play. Or simply sat. They did not have toys or even bats and balls. Chips of rock served.

'They do not stay here long,' said Nom.

'Where do they go?'

'I do not know.'

They were at the far side. Toby took one last look back. This hall was such a contrast to the one where his father paced round his rock. He should have been glad for the happiness of these street children. But he was not. They had been murdered or died of disease or cold in his own world. And life should not be hell for anyone.

They came out onto a hillside.

'There is your river,' pointed out Nom.

And there it lay, just at the bottom of the valley. Here once again was the green light that shone in the hinterland of the Underworld. And there, rowing across the river, was the boatman with a passenger.

'Thank you, Nom, for all your help. I don't know what I would have done without you.'

'Please don't thank me. Before our meeting, I had not had a conversation for over a hundred years. No one had asked me a question or enquired about me. Until you came. And if my answers have been less than adequate, then I apologise. There are things I never knew, there are things I have forgotten.' He stopped and bowed his head. 'Thank you, Toby, for letting me be your guide.'

Toby's eyes welled. This, from a stranger. When his father could not find a good word.

He took Nom by the hand. It was cold. He did not mind, as it meant his own was warm – and Nom would feel it.

'Goodbye, my friend,' he said. 'And good luck.'

And they parted. Nom went back into the caveway. And Toby set off down the hill to the jetty.

Chapter 43

He stepped into the boat. The boatman, deep in his cowl, looked up. It was the same man as before. The same bony face, the skin so tight it was almost a skeleton, the deep hollow eyes.

He said, 'You did not pay me.'

So much had happened, that Toby had forgotten how he had run off and cheated the boatman. And now he was back demanding a ride again. But, he thought, the boatman must go back. His passengers are on the other side. Toby had got in as an old woman had got out; normally there would be no-one here. The boatman must row to the other side. All Toby need do was sit it out.

'You did not pay me,' said the boatman.

'I am sorry,' said Toby.

'Now you must pay double.' The boatman held out a bony hand.

'I don't have any money,' said Toby, wishing he had remembered all this earlier. He was sure Nom would have helped him.

'Then you must row,' said the boatman. And he stood up in the boat.

Well, yes, he could do that. It wasn't far across the river. There was no current. It would be easy enough.

'Very well,' he said, standing up himself. 'I will row.'

They changed positions, causing the boat to rock. The boatman sat himself in the passenger seat. And Toby sat in his place with the oars.

It was at once plain the boatman intended giving him no help. Toby had trouble getting the oars correctly in the rowlocks. He had often been in a rowing boat, but he had never rowed. Princes don't row. His father would not allow him to do such things. 'Why do we have servants?' he would say.

Turning the boat round to face the far jetty was a chore. He began by using the wrong oar and crashed into the jetty. The boatman did not say a word. Nor did he smile. His face was empty. With much splashing, Toby got the boat facing the right way.

Then he began to row with the two oars as he had seen rowers row. At first he dug them too deep into the water and they came up with a splash, then too shallow, barely skimming the top so that they gave little forward motion. It wasn't tiring for Toby, simply awkward. He was strong enough but lacked any skill. In fact, rather too strong, with the effect of his bracelet; and much of that strength went into splashing and wasted motion. But in a little while, he adjusted, and thought he was doing quite well. He had a rhythm going. Pull and stretch, lift the oars, forward. And felt quite pleased with himself.

But then he noted that he was quite out of line with the jetty he was facing, the one he had left. And so must be out of line with the one he was going to. He glanced behind. That was true enough. And someone was waiting.

With one oar he circled the boat until it was aiming for the jetty, then rowed in. Every so often he had to turn round and pull with one oar to keep heading for the jetty. Rowing was more difficult than it looked. And he admired the skill of the boatman. But then he'd been doing it for hundreds of years. And this was Toby's first attempt.

He was glad the boatman did not speak or laugh. Even when Toby splashed him, as he did often enough. And the only other watching was the dead man on the jetty, who did not bother Toby. The dead don't care, he had learnt.

He had trouble pulling the boat into the jetty, taking several tries and bumping badly. But at last he tied up.

'We have arrived,' he said with relief.

At which the boatman jumped up, and stepped out on to the jetty. He ran down to the end of the jetty, onto the beach, and continued his run along the sand.

Toby watched him scamper off. He wondered where he was going. There was nothing up the beach but more beach. Did the boatman even know? But the boatman did not look back and continued running along the black sand.

There will be one less boatman, thought Toby, as he went to step on to the jetty. But he found he could not. It was as if there was some wall there – and he could not get through it. He was unable to put a foot onto the jetty. He pushed, he exerted, until at last streaming with sweat, he sat down on the seat.

And the dead man, who was waiting on the jetty, stepped into the boat.

Chapter 44

Toby rowed the man across the river, thinking that perhaps he could get off there. And then go up the beach to the next boatman for his ride back.

Except he couldn't get off.

The same wall held him. Try as he might, Toby could not get through it. His passenger left him, and Toby rowed back, hoping that whatever force held him would now let him go.

An old woman was waiting. And, once more, Toby could not get out of the boat.

He rowed her across. And tried again to get out, with the same result.

By the time Toby had rowed six passengers across, back and forth six times, he had given up hope of getting out of the boat. His rowing had considerably improved, but he was stuck. He realised the only way out was to get someone else to take the oars.

And who on earth would do that?

As he rowed from jetty to jetty, he began telling his story to the passengers he ferried, hoping one of them would be touched. And then would agree to take over the oars. But the dead did not say a word; they stared at him with their glassy eyes. Had any of them even heard a word of his tale? He did not know.

On he rowed, back and forth, picking up the dead and taking them across. Toby had become the ferryman. But

Toby was alive. The last boatman had been here so long that he could not remember how long.

Was that to be his own fate?

Chapter 45

With the coming of Spring, the weather warmed on the mountain. Far and Orly had fully recovered. They awaited Toby. Without him they were on their own, simply surviving. With him they would have purpose.

Erdy had begun to teach them healing. Whatever happened, he said, it would be useful. He had always found it a good way of earning a living. And with the kingdom in its present state, the wounded and sick abounded.

Far took to it at once. He had a keen eye for plants, and for the slight difference that was so important in the healing arts. Orly was rather lazy, reluctant to accept that she would ever need to earn a living. But she did take it on, otherwise what on earth was there to do on the mountain? And she began to enjoy the walks to collect the plants they needed. Up the mountain to find alpine plants in the high meadow, and down into the forests and along riverbanks to find the varieties that grew in those environments. At the lower levels they had to be more cautious, keeping to the curfew, and doing as everyone else did: avoiding the military and keeping their counsel.

Orly learned to talk like Far with the accent of a peasant. Her story was that she was his sister; the two of them had left their homestead when their parents died. An increasingly likely story in a land full of orphans.

One day when they had come back from the high meadow, Far said to Orly, 'Will you teach me to read?'

'Why all of a sudden?' she said.

'Because I can be only half a healer if I can't read or write,' he said. 'I need to know what's in those books.'

'I may not be a good teacher,' she said.

'It's you or Erdy,' said Far. 'And he's too busy. So I'll take who I can get. Will you?'

'Yes,' she said, and was actually pleased he had asked. She had grown increasingly fond of Far. He was good with animals and she liked his sense of humour. She knew he loved the books and would flick through them looking for pictures of the increasing number of plants that he knew.

She began with the alphabet, the capital letters. And then in a few days the little ones. Then first words: 'Far' of course. And he was so happy to write his name. Very spidery but readable. And then Orly and Erdy and Toby.

Where was Toby? He had been months.

Erdy said, 'Time is different in the Underworld.'

'Will he be any older?' said Orly.

'I don't know. I have never met anyone who has come back.'

Far said then what they'd all been thinking.

'Suppose he doesn't come back?'

They were round the fire having eaten their supper, cooked by Far and Orly. A chore begun at first reluctantly by Orly. Peeling vegetables and washing up were not done by girls of her class. And the more she did such things, the more she feared losing what she considered her real place. A thought she knew was a dream from a lost time, a lost place – but she could not help having it.

Until one day she burst the barrier.

She said, 'I don't know what I may need. I may yet go back and be a lady, I may have to be someone else. In the meantime, I will cook and clean and learn to be a healer with good grace. I can't just wait and hope for something that may never happen.'

And Far made her a celebration cake.

She became a much better healer and a good cook. She enjoyed getting her hands dirty when they planted herbs.

And now she poked the fire, delighted they had enjoyed her apple cake and custard.

'Suppose he doesn't come back?' repeated Far.

Erdy sighed and his hand ran absently round his bald crown. 'Then we go on as we are. You earn your living, I earn mine. And we stay alive, and hope for better times.'

'And live under the Queen?' hissed Orly.

'I hate her,' declared Far.

'Would you kill her?' said Erdy.

'Yes,' they said together.

'And Zeke?'

'Him too,' said Far.

'And then who rules?'

Both were silenced. Who? The big question, because if there were no one – then there would be civil war. A fight for the crown, and heaven help those caught between.

'Come back, Toby,' exclaimed Orly. 'And you shall be King.'

Chapter 46

Toby continued to tell his tale. Old men, old women, young people, children – to everyone he ferried, he told his story. He had perhaps ten minutes from when the passenger stepped into the boat until they left at the far side. And he could tell a lot in that time. But all he received in return was an empty stare. And a penny. For each and everyone gave him one. Where they got them from he could not fathom. But each knew the price and each paid him without question.

He collected them in tens on the small shelf at the prow of the boat. And by the time he had ten piles, he prided himself on not disturbing the coins. His rowing was as smooth as the last boatman's. He could turn the boat easily with one oar, and could row into the far jetty without looking back at all.

When he had a hundred piles, the space was full. And he wondered what to do with them? The last boatman didn't seem to have any coins, when he should by rights have a boatful. And if he couldn't leave the boat like Toby, then there was only one thing he could have been doing with them.

At the centre of the river, on his way back, Toby threw them all in the water. The river bottom must be full of them, but the water was so black he could not see any at all. Each coin he threw in quickly disappeared in the dark depths. From then on, every time he was given a coin, he dropped it into the water on the way back. He no longer wanted to keep count of his endless trips.

He lost any sense of time. There was no day or night here, simply the endless pale green light. And a passenger always waiting for him on his way back from the land of the dead. And a tale he had to tell, told now so automatically, that he barely knew he was saying the words as he rowed his silent passengers across the river.

One day a young man got on the boat. He was as dead as the rest, as blank-eyed and as pale. Toby had lost any curiosity about their former lives. There were so many and none would speak to him. But out of the most hopeless of hopes, he continued telling his tale. Knowing that once he stopped, he would have admitted to himself that he could be here forever, rowing the dead across this black river.

Toby could not remember what he had just said when the young man leaned forward and touched his wrist. It was a gesture so unusual that he ceased rowing and the boat came to a halt in the middle of the lake.

'Did you say Orly?' said the young man.

'Yes,' said Toby, not actually remembering but he had done often enough.

'Is she alive?'

'I rescued her,' said Toby.

'How?'

And Toby told him of the day he had gone to the big house, and gone out to the front and found the heap of bodies, amongst them Orly. He told how he had rescued her and taken her by wheelbarrow and horse to Erdy's cave where she had recovered.

The young man winced with pain in the telling. When Toby has finished, he was silent for a short while.

At last he said, 'I am her brother, Martin.'

'Why have you taken so long to get here?' asked Toby.

'I stayed awhile, haunting our house, waiting for Orly to return as her body was not with ours. But as she never did, I thought she must have died elsewhere. And now the Queen has our estate.'

'But Orly is alive.'

'I am so grateful to you for saving her,' said the young man.

And Toby saw this was his chance. Perhaps his only one, ever.

'I have a mission to defeat the Queen,' he said. 'Will you take the oars?'

'Gladly,' said Martin.

'You may be here for a very long time, as you cannot leave until someone takes the oars from you.'

'You rescued my sister,' said Martin. 'I am so grateful. I don't care if I am here for a thousand years. And should you take revenge on the woman who murdered my family and stole my estate – then I will gladly stay here forever.'

'It is possible,' said Toby carefully.

'Then so be it,' said Martin, rising from his seat.

Toby rose from his and they exchanged places. Martin took the oars without hesitation, and at once Toby felt a heaviness fly off him. Martin turned the boat with one oar, much better than he had first done. A little lower in rank, it seemed, allowed him to do a little more.

Martin rowed back to the jetty, and tied up.

Toby took his hand. 'Thank you.'

Martin shook his head. 'My thousand thanks to you, Toby. Tell my sister I am happy she is alive. And throw the Queen into a pit of scorpions.'

Toby rose, somewhat unsure. He had tried this many times, and each time failed. This could be a dreadful disappointment. But there was not to be one. He stepped on to the jetty. Solid ground at last. An old man waited there, but Toby walked past him.

He was free.

When next he turned, halfway up the beach, the old man was in the boat, and Martin had already begun to row him across the river.

Chapter 47

Far and Orly were preparing for the market at Errlop. This was to be their test. Erdy was sending them on their own.

'It's a big market,' he said, 'lasting three days. I always do well there. It's time for you to show you have learnt your lessons.'

And Far and Orly knew he was not simply thinking of the lessons in healing, but also the lessons in staying alive in a dangerous countryside. They must travel slowly, they must know who they are – and take every precaution to avoid trouble.

They loaded three wheelbarrows. Not that the wheelbarrow was their means of transport, but the wagon and horse were at a farm at the foot of the mountain. It wasn't possible to drive up the narrow, rocky track to the cavern. So they must wheelbarrow everything down and transfer it. In the days before, they made up preparations of herbs in small bags, bottles of lotion and liniment. And they put into the barrows larger bags and bottles of herbs and various ingredients, so they could make up preparations on the spot. They took two sets of scales, two mortar and pestles, dishes and bowls, spoons and stirrers, charcoal for a fire – everything they would need for a busy healers' stall.

One wheelbarrow had things for daily living, like pots and pans, plates, knives and forks, blankets, soap, clothing and a little food to start them off. The aim was to earn enough to keep themselves going.

'If you starve,' laughed Erdy, 'it'll be your own fault.'

It was all rather exciting, and fearful. They had done small trips with Erdy to neighbouring villages. But he was always the master and they did what they were told. From time to time, he let them serve a customer. Then, he would listen in with half an ear, and put them right if needs be.

But this trip they would be on their own.

Far kept a book, very precious to him now, in which he wrote down the recipes for preparations and any difficulties in making them. He wrote notes about plants, their leaves, their berries, their roots, stems and bark. The first writing was very childlike and badly spelled, but over the months he had improved considerably. He would spend hours copying out of big books in the cavern, asking Erdy or Orly what this word was, and that one. Until it got to the point when he rarely had to anymore.

Orly too kept a book, but there was far less in it. She, after all, wasn't using it to teach herself to read and write. Though when it came to preparing for this expedition she wished she had written more. The book wouldn't simply be a primer but an important tool of the trade.

She must work tonight by lamplight. Get down in her book as much as she could. This would be her last chance as tomorrow they would be on the road, treated as healers and expected to be healers. And there was so much to know. And so much to get wrong.

The thought terrified her.

A few berries, just the right number for the body size and the patient recovered. A few more and they died in agony. The human body could be so delicate, so different, and so the same.

After their supper, and after their period of study, Far and Erdy went to bed. Orly sat at the big table on a high stool, almost hidden in books and scrolls. Hers was the sole lantern, close to her notebook, throwing flickering shadows on the walls and ceiling of the cavern, barely reaching the entrance which was almost in darkness. She was in a state of panic, made worse by her tiredness. She could hardly keep her eyes open but there was so much she didn't know. Some preparations and illnesses she had never heard of. And yet she would be expected to treat them. The fire was almost out with just a few glowing embers. Sly lay flat out before it like a rug. Erdy was snoring and Far was buried under his blanket. Dare she wake them? She had read a fact in one book about a root extract and its efficacy for whooping cough, and the complete opposite in another. Or was she just confused in her sleepiness? She couldn't find one of the books. This was madness. She couldn't learn healing overnight. She must sleep. But knew she couldn't. Her head was a muddle of preparations, potions, restrictions and warnings of the direst consequences of mixing this and that, while giving it in certain doses, but on the other hand...

'Orly!'

And then she didn't want to sleep. Or even need to. And she could wake Far and Erdy and they would not say a word against it.

Toby was back.

Part Three

The Secret Of Life

Chapter 48

There was no sleep at all that night. The three were eager for his news, but Toby was eager for food. And he was filthy and bloody. Ravens, he said, referring to the cuts, scratches and dried blood in the muck on his forehead and arms. Erdy forbade him to talk. They had waited long enough, they could wait a little longer. Far made him a bath, while Erdy concocted a preparation for his cuts and scratches and Orly prepared food over the fire.

His clothes were rags and Erdy said they should be thrown away. While he bathed, clean clothing was gathered up. And, before he put them on, Erdy rubbed ointment into his wounds and dosed him with a foul-tasting tonic. How they pampered him! Waited on him, hand and foot – like the special guest he most surely was. Food, drink, another cushion, a footstool – they couldn't be more willing to welcome him home.

And Toby could eat. And eat.

They refilled his bowls and his plates and he consumed them like ten men.

'I haven't eaten since I have been away,' he said between mouthfuls. 'How long has that been?'

'Sixteen months,' said Erdy

He gasped at the time. Yet shouldn't have been surprised, looking around at the three of them, his feet on a stool, cushioned in an easy chair. Erdy was much the same, but the other two had changed considerably.

'You have a beard, Far.'

Far shrugged, a little embarrassed as he scratched the fuzz on his chin. 'I shall shave in the morning.'

'And you, Orly. You were such a disagreeable invalid when I left.'

She smiled at him, allowing the tease. 'I hope I have changed for the better.'

'You're...' he hesitated before going on, 'a woman now.'

That had been obvious to him when he first saw her behind the pile of books. For a second or two he had not recognised her. True her hair was shorter, true she wore a shapeless tunic – but she had filled out, rounded. Jumped instantly in his picture of her from girl to woman.

'And you were so long,' she said. 'We had almost given up on you.'

'I am so happy to see you,' exclaimed Far. 'After a year I thought, Toby's not coming back. And here you are, eating like an army.'

'It's wonderful to wear clean clothes,' sighed Toby, stretching out his stiff limbs.

'So long since you went down Hell's Chimney and disappeared from my sight,' said Erdy. 'Did my bracelet work for you?'

Toby held up his wrist showing the silver band. 'Without it, I'd be amongst the dead.'

'Tell us!' declared Orly. 'No more bits and pieces, clean clothes and how we've all changed. Tell us everything!'

And Toby began.

He told them about Hell's Chimney, climbing in the dark through its tight passage. And then down the cliff, attacked by the ravens. He told them of his journey across the glassy rocks to the black river where the boatman waited. And how he had to run off at the other side with the boatman screaming 'Pay me!' He told them of the three-headed dog held back by the guard while the animal slobbered for the only living being. They listened open-mouthed while he told them of the Hall of Dead Babies who latched onto him like leeches, and how he had to follow in the wake of a girl to get through. He told them of his luck in meeting Nom, who helped him make a little sense of the World of the Dead. And how Nom had taken him through the Valley of Sighs where dead lovers learned to abandon their love. And then over the molten lava with Nom walking through it as if it had been a cool stream, and at last into the Hall of Deposed Kings, with the depressing vista of kings who ruled no more than a rock, and were as jealous of it as if it were their kingdom. And he told them of the conversation with his father. The shell of his father... He told them of the Stone of Oull worn by the Queen around her neck, her age and her vulnerability.

'I wondered what had become of the Stone,' said Erdy thoughtfully. 'I should have guessed as much. Her history is rather vague. She seems to have come from nowhere. I wonder who she has been.'

'297 years old,' said Far shaking his head. 'Not that I have ever seen her.'

'I have,' said Orly. 'She came to our house. She was so beautiful, oh so charming... The King was with her. They'd only been married a few months. He was everywhere with her. Out riding, boating. We had archery in the big field, and he let her win...' Tears were streaming down Orly's face. 'And a year later she sent her men. Oh yes, she remembered our beautiful estate – and now it's hers.'

Far put his arm round Orly, and she leaned against him, still weeping. Looking at the pair, Toby wondered what had been going on since he'd been away. She, a lady, now so friendly with a peasant... The same Orly who called Far 'boy' and would not speak with him present, now rested on him for comfort.

Were they lovers?

Toby did not comment, but instead went on with his tale, forgetting the pair for a while in his narration, but every so often his eyes were involuntarily drawn to the two of them to see how familiar they had become.

He told them of his journey back through the Hall of Dead Street Children, a surprising place of happiness in that dismal country. And he told them of his return across the river. How he'd been trapped in the boat, becoming the ferryman, telling each passenger his tale, hoping that one would pity his plight and take over. Endlessly rowing to and fro across the black river dividing the living from the dead, until Martin came and took over his oars.

Here he stopped and looked to Orly, expecting more tears. But although her eyes glistened, she smiled faintly.

'Oh, my lovely brother,' she sighed.

And when she leaned into Far, he felt a stab in his ribs.

Chapter 49

They sat long around the fire, throwing in the odd log to give them warmth and light while their shadows flickered against the rocky walls of the cavern. There was so much to take in. Toby's arrival had changed everything. Especially, his news of the Queen's vulnerability. They spoke too of the Queen's guardian creatures. Who or what were they?

'I've heard tell of a dragon,' said Erdy. 'It has been seen but has not yet attacked.'

'What's its purpose?' said Far.

'I believe it is after Toby.'

'And I've been in the Underworld,' said Toby with a wry smile.

'Here, under my protection,' added Erdy, 'it cannot detect you here – but once off my mountain...' He turned over his empty hands.

'We must get the Queen,' declared Orly. 'That was your promise to my brother.'

Toby nodded. 'It was.'

'We have the permit to travel to Errlop,' said Far. 'Can we not get another one to the castle?'

'We'll get one,' said Orly angrily. 'Or we won't. But we'll go to the castle, and smash her stone.'

Erdy was rubbing his chin, gazing into the fire, his face red in the heat.

'We have two healers going to Errlop,' he said. He turned to Toby. 'You must be their servant.'

'Their servant!' he exclaimed.

'What other role can you play?' asked Erdy. 'Can you heal?'

'No,' he said quietly.

'I have been teaching Far and Orly these past sixteen months. They know enough for the marketplace. You are ignorant of the healing arts, and so they must be your masters for the journey.'

Toby did not reply. And the others left him to struggle. How things had changed! He had brought them to the cavern. But they had moved on while he had been in the Underworld. It was a bitter pill; to play servant, especially to a serf for heaven's sake. But he thought of the purpose and hardened himself. He must get to the castle. Toby clenched his fist. To be killed on the road would be useless.

'I'll do my best,' he said at last.

Erdy nodded and put his hands on his shoulder. 'I have faith in you.'

He turned to the others.

'I can give you all one piece of magic each. No more. I cannot go with you. I have been cursed, years past, and can only go so far.'

This was a story none of them had heard, but it was not the time to ask.

Erdy continued, 'Toby already has his bracelet. He will need it yet.' He drew something small from the pocket of his gown. 'Orly, I give you this earring of invisibility. When you twist it, then no one can see you. I shall put it in your ear before you leave.' He turned to Far. 'And to you, I give the Voice.' He took a neck chain from his pocket. 'With this, you will be able to speak to Toby and Orly from afar.'

'Can they speak back to me?'

Erdy shook his head. 'No. But whenever you grip the chain they will hear your thoughts or the words you speak.'

'Let me have that one,' said Toby attempting to grasp the chain as Erdy pulled it away.

'Why?'

'It gives him too much power.' He glared round at them all in the firelight. 'I am to be a mere servant. That's humiliation enough. And then to hear the voice of a...' He fought against the word but had to say it. 'Of a serf. That I cannot even reply to.' He shook his head vehemently. 'It's too much.'

'No,' said Erdy, handing the chain to Far.

'Then give me the earring. Let me have some power.'

'No,' said Erdy.

Toby kicked a log in the fire and sparks flew. 'Who is the prince here? Him?' He pointed at Far. 'Her?' He stood up and held his head in anguish. 'I am to be in the company of this loving couple. And be their helpless servant. This lacks any fairness.'

Orly rose. She pulled his hands away from his head.

'We will work together,' she said. 'My magic is your magic.'

Toby shook his head.

'We want the same thing,' said Far. 'My magic is your magic.'

Toby sank back into his chair. 'I did not expect to come back to this.' His body rocked back and forth. 'I am to be the least. The one left out.'

'You will be what you will be,' said Erdy angrily. 'One piece of magic each is my gift. And that is now set. You must work together or you will die together.'

Toby in his misery did not reply.

Chapter 50

They set off a few hours later down the mountainside with their three wheelbarrows. Erdy accompanied them. All were tired, Toby most of all, but they could not delay. They had their permit to travel – and they must obey the times given to them.

They were healers setting off today to journey to Errlop for the market. Two days there, the permit said, a day in the town and two days to get back. They must pick up on sleep when they could.

At the farm at the foot of the mountain, Far took their horse out of the barn. Erdy had a deal with the farmer. He would keep the farmer's family in good health, and they would feed and care for the horse and give space for the wagon.

The horse was a sturdy, obedient animal, mostly brown with a white streak running down its head between the eyes to its nostrils, with a white underbelly, and white too in the lower leg with a tuft of white hair coming from the fetlock. Far harnessed it to the cart. Toby watched carefully, determined that he would do this job in future. He would not be useless.

He knew too that his tantrum was part tiredness, from his climb up the chimney. But not simply that. Perhaps too his own stupidity, expecting everything to be the same as when he left. As if all they had done was wait for him.

Once they had loaded up the wagon, he apologised to Erdy who clasped him to him. A warmth he needed. Far too embraced him, making him wonder for an instant about Far's new confidence, but realising too that he needed a companion in this venture, not a serf. Orly too embraced Erdy. As Toby watched, he knew that she would give him a different difficulty.

And could he stand it?

Not without sleep. They agreed he could slumber at the back of the wagon. Far took the reins. Orly sat beside him, as with a crack of the whip the horse began its slow tramp onwards.

Chapter 51

It was cold and misty to begin with, but the spring sun gradually lifted the mist, revealing a cloudless, pale blue sky. The road was rutted from wagon wheels, and pitted with animal tracks from the herds of the drovers. It was a bumpy ride for Toby and he could not sleep. His pillow was a bag of herbs, and he had a blanket on top, but the hard planking of the wagon added to his restlessness.

A little later, Orly, seeing him twisting and turning, found him a sleeping draught. And in a while it worked, and Toby was out to the world.

The road was quite busy, with other wagons up ahead, and some coming towards them. From time to time the way would be flooded with sheep – and all they could do was stop, and let them by. And once, hundreds of honking geese, making such a racket you would think it would wake the dead – but not Toby. He had sleep enough to catch up on.

'He's going to be difficult,' said Far, indicating the snoozing Toby.

'I think so,' nodded Orly.

'He thinks he's still a prince. And can't get away from it,' sighed Far. 'He called me brother once, but was quick enough to change his mind.'

'Better not order him about,' said Orly.

Far flicked the whip, not at the horse but at the flies buzzing above the horse's head.

'You have to shout at servants,' said Far. 'You must have done yourself.'

'Plenty of times. Only Toby will get resentful and be even more difficult.'

'If we don't treat him like a servant then no one will believe he is one.'

Orly laughed.

'What's so funny?'

'You. I believe you'd be as bad as he is – if you were a prince.'

'Lucky me. I'm not. Never will be.'

She laughed again. 'Oh, it's such a lovely day,' she said. 'Who would believe the terror of this kingdom?'

'It's easy to forget,' he said. 'Not even the Queen can stop the sun shining.'

'She stopped it for me, for a long time,' said Orly.

'Then maybe she can. Maybe she did. When your head is chopped off you don't care whether the sun is shining or not.'

'I'd a hundred times rather sit here in the rain and have my family back.'

'We always get miserable, don't we?'

'I wouldn't trust you if you were happy all the time,' she said.

He gripped her arm urgently. Up ahead were a couple of soldiers and they were stopping the various travellers.

'Got the permit?' she said.

'Yes,' nodded Far. 'Shall we wake Toby?'

'Let him sleep this one out,' she said.

'Right.' He stiffened. 'Remember who you are.'

'Lily, your sister. And Lord Haskett is my lord. And we are going to the market at Errlop.'

Their wagon went forward in fits and starts, in tune with the traffic ahead. There were a few pedestrians and one wagon in front of them.

'I hope Toby, I mean Ned, doesn't wake,' hissed Orly.

'They scare me soppy, these soldiers,' whispered Far. 'Cross fingers.'

It was their turn. Far held out the permit. One of the soldiers took it, glanced at it, looked them both over and said, 'Who's the one in the back?'

'Our servant,' said Far.

'Just says two healers here,' said the soldier indicating the permit.

'Aren't we allowed a servant?' said Orly.

'Not if it's not on your papers. Let's have those reins, sonny. You'd better come with me.'

Far tried to control his nerves. Orly clutched his hand as the soldier led them on. They did not dare speak; the soldier was too close and the other was watching them go. Their soldier walked a little ahead, directing them along the road.

'You can't say two and carry three,' he said. 'Won't you people ever learn?'

Orly put a finger to her lips; her other hand went to the ring in her ear. She twisted it through. And disappeared. A second or two later Far felt his hand being held once more, telling him Orly was definitely still there, if unseen.

Far was most unsure about this, but could say nothing with the soldier so close. How would the soldier react to seeing just two when there had been three? Could they have talked their way out of it and simply got the permit adjusted? Was Orly just adding to their danger?

Far looked behind at the other soldier, but he was now busy examining the permit of a man on a cart. At least he hadn't seen Orly go.

They were being led towards a gate where a guard with a spear stood. Far couldn't see what was within, as trees at the entrance blocked his view.

'You've been warned,' said their soldier. 'And if you don't listen, you get what you deserve.'

And what was that? thought Far. Surely things had improved? It wasn't summary execution still. His heart jumped in his chest. Should he run? Take his chance. But there were soldiers on the other side of the road, stopping wagons in that direction. How far would he get?

It was already too late.

The horse was halted at the entrance. Within the field beyond Far could see a number of wooden huts forming three sides of a square. Some soldiers were drilling in the centre. To one side, a blacksmith was hammering on an anvil. Horses were tethered. And three bodies were slowly spinning from the branch of a high oak tree.

Had they had a problem with their permits – or some other crime?

The soldier said to the guard, 'Three more.'

'You've only got two,' said the guard.

The soldier swivelled round. He scratched his head. 'There were three, I swear it. Couple of healers and an extra.'

'Then you lost one.'

The soldier let go off the horse's halter and strode back to the wagon. He chucked about bags of herbs and clothes. The figure asleep in the blanket was plain enough. He searched his way through the wagon, looking for another.

'There were three, I'm dead certain. A servant and two healers...'

'Either you miscounted, mate,' said the guard slowly, 'or you're in big trouble.'

The soldier was trembling, having given up on the wagon, he was desperately scouring the road. 'Maybe there were just two,' he managed to say. 'Yes, two. I don't know what I'm up to.'

'Then they'd better move on,' said the guard. 'Quick.'

The soldier hurriedly began to turn the horse.

At that moment, a soldier from within the camp walked up to the gate. Both soldiers saluted as he approached.

'What's the problem here, guard?'

'No problem, sir. This wagon, er... they were asking directions, sir.'

The officer gazed at Far quizzically. Then inside the wagon with the supplies and where Toby was sleeping under a blanket.

'Show me their permit,' said the officer.

The soldier handed it over, his hand shaking.

The officer read the permit. He looked again at Far.

'You're young to be a healer.'

'I'm Erdy's apprentice,' he said.

'Erdy eh? That's some recommendation.' He indicated the sleeping form in the wagon. 'That your sister?'

'Yes, sir.'

What else could he say? It was all on the permit: sister and brother, names, purpose of journey... Oh, stay under the blanket, Toby!

The officer sucked in his breath. 'Erdy eh? If you're half as good as he is...' He flicked his fingers at the soldier. 'Put the wagon over there. Come with me, young man.'

'Yes sir.'

Far jumped off the wagon, and followed the officer. Orly remained with the wagon, where she had been all along. She watched the two of them walk across the square to the central hut, which had a veranda across the front. When Far and the officer were close to the hut, a man stood up and came off the veranda to meet them. Orly knew him at once.

It was Prince Zeke.

Chapter 52

Inside the hut was a made bed, a table covered in maps, and a smaller table by a sofa with a number of stools round it. On the small table was the remnants of a card game with half filled cups of wine. Zeke had gone in first, stumbling and coughing. Far had followed the officer. When the officer told him whom he had to treat, he was terrified but remembered Erdy's prime stricture: half of healing is confidence in the healer.

He was barely over the hearth when Zeke turned on him.

'I'm sick as a dog. You make me sicker and I'll strangle you in your own guts.'

'I am a proficient healer, your highness.'

Zeke waved a hand dismissively. 'That's what they all say.'

'Tell me your symptoms, your highness.'

Zeke strode about the room, pushing a hand through his blond hair. His face was white and blotched, the scar across it showing out even more in bright pink.

'I've got streaming diarrhoea, a headache to kill a horse, and I can hardly move this arm.' He indicated his right arm.

'Thank you, your highness.'

He must be polite, he must be formal, he must show he knows what he is doing. Far turned to the officer who was still in the room, 'I'd like a bowl of hot water, sir.'

'Get it,' ordered Zeke.

'Right away, your highness.'

The officer hurried off.

'Your highness, I must go to my wagon to get my preparations. I'd be obliged if in the meantime you remove your shirt.'

But Zeke was not letting him leave the hothouse so easily.

'So what have I got, healer?'

'If it was dysentery you wouldn't be standing up. Probably food poisoning...'

Heavens, he'd omitted 'your highness'. Too late to add it.

'I did eat some muck yesterday,' said Zeke. 'What about this bitch of a headache?'

There were empty wine bottles lying around the floor. It would not be a good idea to mention those, even if they fitted the symptoms.

'I need to look at the wound on your arm, your highness. See your tongue. Examine you for fever...'

Zeke sank onto the sofa and clutched his head with his good arm.

'Do you think it's the Tobards, young fellow?'

'I don't understand, your highness.'

'Gave me this headache. The diarrhoea.' He laughed then winced at the pain it gave him. 'They do everything else round here.'

'I think your highness has killed most of them,' said Far cautiously.

'Damn right. Except one. The chief dog.' He wagged his finger directly at Far. 'You know who that one is?'

'Yes sir. I mean your highness. Prince Toby.'

Zeke was at once on his feet and lunged at Far, grasping him by the nose.

'How dare you call that dung bag a prince?'

Far reeled in pain as Zeke twisted.

'Sorry, your highness. I didn't mean it. He used to be...'

Zeke let go. And spat in Far's face. Half in his eye, half down the cheek.

Far let the spit lay. He would have liked to arrange his nose but Zeke was demanding his attention.

'He is called Traitor Toby. Not Prince. I am a Prince, so how can he be one? Traitor Toby. Get me, boy.'

'Traitor Toby, your highness.'

'Do you know what I'd do to him if I had him?'

The spit was dripping down Far's cheek, over the side of his mouth. His nose was stinging.

'Torture and kill him, your highness.'

'I'd make him eat his own eyeballs. Toasted. Then his tongue. The last Tobard in his own stew.' He threw his arms wide and then yelled in pain, 'Get your bloody preparations, healer. Cure me, or I'll hang you by your big toe.'

Far rushed out.

Chapter 53

'It's Prince Zeke, isn't it?' whispered Orly.

She was still invisible by the wagon which Far was searching through.

'It most certainly is,' said Far. 'And he'll kill me if I'm not back pretty soon.'

He was breathing heavily, his nose still hurting. He had wiped the spit off his cheek.

'He knows Toby well,' said Orly.

'Sh!' said Far, 'the guard by the gate is watching us.' He clutched the band around his neck, and his thoughts came through to her. *Keep Toby asleep if you can. If he wakes, tell him what's going on, so he can pretend to still be asleep. I'll do my best to keep Zeke inside. But he's an animal.*

Orly nodded, then realised an invisible nod was quite useless to anyone.

Far picked up his sack of herbs and preparations.

I must get back.

'Be careful,' she whispered.

He nodded and began his way back. His voice still came to her.

I hope I can cure Prince Zeke. And get him to keep his temper long enough so we can get away in one piece.

She wanted to reply, to say something hopeful but he had the only power. All she could do was watch him cross the parade ground, the sack over his shoulder. He did not turn. Nor should he. To anyone else, she was not there.

A groan came from Toby. It was likely he'd wake soon, she thought. His head was out of the blanket. Anyone, who looked at all closely, would see he was no sister.

She felt rather useless. Was there anything she could do herself? She could go in and see Zeke. Though what would be the point to that? She couldn't help Far. He was a better healer than she was anyway. And it would simply leave Toby unattended. And if he woke up, then sat up – that would be enough. Invisible, she'd be the one to get away; but Toby and Far would be dead meat.

Toby was definitely stirring. Perhaps she should move him quicker.

Within the wagon, she tipped a flask of water onto a piece of cloth. Carefully she wiped it over Toby's face. His eyes opened. Putting her lips right next to his ear she whispered to him.

'This is Orly. I am invisible. Don't speak. Just listen. Keep lying there. Whatever you do, don't sit up. We are in a soldiers' camp. Prince Zeke is here.'

'Zeke!' exclaimed Toby.

She put a finger to his lips. 'Sh! They think you are Far's sister. There's only two on the permit to travel. Far and his sister. Stay under the blanket. And shut up.'

Toby nodded.

With relief she realised he had taken it in. An awful lot when she came to think of it. How much did he in fact understand? An invisible person telling you that you are someone's sister in an army camp with your enemy in shouting distance – had he got all that? Some, all, what part?

Toby felt around and gripped her hand. He pulled it further towards him. She thought of resisting but gathered there was some point to this. Then he followed up her arm to her head. He felt around her head, squashing her nose. He found an ear and, as gently as he could – not that gently – pulled it down to his level.

'Get in the wagon,' he whispered.

To talk more easily, she thought, as it was quite painful bending her head over the wagon board. She took his hand away and climbed in. Then lay by his side.

'Well?' she said.

'Give me the earring,' he said.

This angered her. Toby even now, dangerous as it was, was determined to take her magic.

'No.'

'Don't you see?' he whispered. 'You must be the sister. Visible. It's me who shouldn't be seen.'

She couldn't deny that. Of course. If Toby were the invisible one, then there would be a male and female as on the permit. The rat, she thought; he was going to get her earring as he'd wanted. Reluctantly, she twisted it out of her ear. And, as she did so, form flooded into her.

'Good to see you, Orly.'

'Pig,' she grimaced, and handed him the earring.

'How do I get it in my ear?' he whispered, ignoring the insult.

She took it back with a sniff of disdain. 'I'll have to force it,' she said almost gleefully. 'It'll hurt.'

'Do it.'

'Bite your sleeve,' she said.

He bit his cuff. And she pushed the prong of the earring into his ear. It was like forcing a nail through. The skin stretched and reddened. Toby winced and moaned. She continued pushing. And suddenly it was through in a burst of blood.

'I feel like a stuck pig,' groaned Toby.

'Shut up,' she hissed.

Orly twisted the earring. Then back again. The tips of her fingers were covered in blood.

'It's not working,' she whispered. In spite of everything, part of her was glad.

'Let me have a go.'

He took it and twisted it back and forth himself, several times. And he stayed persistently there. Visible.

'It only works for you,' he said, giving up.

She took it out of his ear and put it back in her own. But she didn't twist it, instead considering matters a while.

At last she said, 'I'm staying visible. I'm Far's sister, Lily. I have to be here. You're not here. You must hide under the herbs and our clothes.'

Toby thought about this. Then nodded.

'Help me hide.'

He rolled into a corner of the wagon. Still lying down, to keep out of sight, Orly placed clothing and sacks of herbs over him.

'You must stay absolutely still,' she whispered. 'I'm now going to wake up.'

And she stretched her arms and sat up in the wagon.

Chapter 54

Far was still in the hut. Orly thought of going in to see how he was getting on. He might be captured, and she could have some go at rescuing him. He might be dead, and that would be as well to know too.

'Hurry up and cure the bastard,' hissed Toby from under his cover.

'Sh!'

'I'm stiff as a board.'

'Shut up, or you'll be dead as one.'

The guard had virtually forgotten about her. She was the girl on the permit, and he knew nothing of the other passenger. She had tidied up the wagon, she had eaten and given Toby a crust and some water. She had thought of watering the horse, but that would mean leaving Toby. And if she was here, then if needs be she could distract whoever came. Besides, it wasn't clever for her to walk around. Zeke might well recognize her. Admittedly it was a couple of years ago, she was better dressed then and younger – but why add to the risk?

A young man and woman were being brought in by a soldier. Both had their heads bowed. The soldier had his sword out and was walking behind them, harrying them across the parade ground. More incorrect papers, thought Orly. She crossed her fingers for them as they went into one of the huts. The door was open but it was too dark to see in from this distance. A little later she heard a man yelling. It was followed by screaming, from a man and then a woman.

Orly covered her ears, she felt sick and terrified. Life here was as cheap as firewood.

She still had her hands over her ears when Far came out of the central hut. The officer was accompanying him. They were chatting, laughing even. They at last parted, the officer went to the gate and Far to the wagon.

Far saw Orly and was puzzled for a second. She indicated the wagon with her head and he nodded.

At the wagon, he climbed at once onto the front board.

'Let's get away while we are winning,' he said.

'You've cured him?' she said.

'Let's get away.'

He took the reins and turned the horse to face the gate. He directed the animal forward. It lumbered slowly to the entrance. The officer was talking to the guard.

As they came through the officer said to Orly, 'Had a good sleep, Miss?'

'Yes, thank you,' she said.

'Your brother has done a first class job.'

'He's the best,' she said.

'Pleased to do my duty,' said Far.

And they were through. Far turned the horse back on to the road. Orly was eager to hear what he'd done but Far would not speak. So they settled into silence, part of the slow traffic of the road. It was a little cooler than it had been; the day had clouded over. There was a drover in front, going their way with a herd of sheep. After perhaps half a mile the drover turned off. There was another wagon a few hundred yards ahead, and one as far behind.

'I cured him,' said Far.

'How?' said Orly.

'I gave him willow bark for the headache.'

'I could have done that,' said Orly.

Toby was listening in the back, sitting up and stretching.

'Chalk and dog's parsley for the stomach ache.'

'Even I knew that.'

'I said the diarrhoea would go away and he shouldn't eat until it did.'

'Why did he think you were so wonderful?' exclaimed Orly. 'I could have done any of that.'

'I washed his shoulder wound, bathed it with nettle and beeswax infusion, and then bandaged it in sphagnum moss.'

'Alright,' she admitted, 'a bit better than I would have done. But not much.'

'Then I gave him tonic number 3.'

Orly burst out laughing. 'Oh you didn't!'

'What's so funny about tonic number 3?' said Toby.

'It contains the laughing mushroom,' said Orly. 'Erdy says it won't cure anything but will make you feel better. And by the time you realise – you might well be.'

A driver of a wagon, piled high with turnips, coming the other way raised his hand to them. Orly raised hers in greeting.

'He offered me a job,' said Far. 'As his personal healer.'

'What did you say?' said Toby.

'I said I'd take it up on the way back.'

Orly laughed. Toby laughed too. They knew their journey was one way. Either they would change the regime. Or they would be dead.

'And then,' said Far. 'I killed him.'

Orly looked at Far to see if this was a joke. He was holding the reins lightly, a slight smile on his face. So maybe it was a trick of sorts.

'What do you mean 'I killed him'?' she said.

'I mean I killed him.'

Toby was leaning between the two of them. Far had little to do as the horse plodded on. The road ran in a slight rise to the horizon.

'You can't have,' exclaimed Toby standing over him. 'They wouldn't have let us go. We'd be dead.'

'I did,' said Far.

'Please make sense,' said Orly.

'I made him up an infusion of Dark Angel.'

Toby looked to Orly. She shrugged, not understanding.

'I put honey in it and mint,' went on Far. 'It tastes delicious. But Dark Angel is very poisonous, slow acting with no antidote. He'll be dead in ten hours.'

'Are you certain?' exclaimed Toby.

'As certain as I can be. A couple of weeks ago I talked about it with Erdy, I've read it up. And I put in double the dose.'

They were silent for a while. The only sound was sheep bleating in the field, the squeaking of the wagon wheels and the clip clop of the horse on the hard ground.

'Suppose he dies...' said Toby.

'He will.'

'They'll be after us.'

'They won't be sure it's me,' said Far.

'But think it pretty likely,' insisted Orly.

Far nodded.

'We can't go to Errlop,' she said.

'No,' said Far. 'A change of plan is needed.'

'How are we going to eat?' said Orly. 'We're healers. We were to sell our remedies at the market to make money to keep ourselves.'

'I don't care,' yelled Toby, suddenly ablaze. 'Zeke is dead.'

He stood up and did a jig in the back of the wagon, his hands high in the air.

'Zeke is dead!'

He stopped and sank to his knees, leaned forward and kissed Far on the cheek.

'You have made me happier than I have been in two years. Bless you, Far. Meeting you was my lucky day!'

Orly laughed and clapped her hands.

'Oh Far,' she exclaimed, 'your first proper job at healing – and you have killed the patient. Well done!'

And she kissed him on the other cheek.

'And here's a promise for you, Far,' said Toby. 'May Orly be my witness. Should I ever become King then I will make you a Lord for what you have done today.'

Chapter 55

Everything was now changed. Or rather, it would be soon enough. When Zeke finally died the soldiers would be after them. And would catch them quickly in this lumbering wagon.

'We're going to have to dump it,' said Far.

'Can we sell the horse?' said Toby.

'I doubt it,' said Far. 'We need a market. And we can't go to the one at Errlop where we would be able to sell it, because it'll be too late.'

'What about all this gear?' said Orly, indicating their packed wagon.

'We'll have to abandon most of it,' said Far.

They were still on the road, meeting other wagons, drovers and their animals and some on foot. In other times the road would have been busier, but the necessity for every traveller to have a permit cut back the numbers severely. No one travelled for trivial reasons.

They had a few hours yet – but had to make the most of them. All were agreed on the necessity of abandoning the wagon. The problem was where. If they simply stopped on the road, took out what they could and left the rest, then the soldiers would find it at once. And would know where they had left the road.

They would have liked to have waited until dark. Easier then to lose the wagon and disappear across the fields and back roads. But they couldn't delay that long.

'We must get up to the High Ridge,' said Toby.

He and Orly were in the back of the wagon looking at a map. It wasn't a particularly good one, but at least had the main features and towns. The High Ridge coursed across the country. No roads crossed it, although there were paths here and there. Its difficulty was their advantage. It couldn't be travelled on horseback.

They pulled into a field surrounded by a high hedge. They drew the wagon hard against the hedge in one corner, hoping it would not be seen from the road. And then began to unload what they needed.

'All the food,' said Orly.

'There's not much of it anyway,' said Toby.

They sorted out in three heaps what they thought they needed. It was still too much and they cut back.

'Absolute necessities,' said Far.

Toby was holding a long length of rope. It was heavy, but who knew what they might meet on the High Ridge? He bound it round his waist. Blankets of course, a cooking pot, flint and tinder, a plate between them, a knife each, a water jug. Make it two.

Hammer and nails?

Toby had decided on the hammer and was counting out nails – when there was a shout across the field. All looked up and saw a man running towards them gesticulating. Their gear lay scattered on the ground. If they ran off, they would have nothing.

They waited. Toby gripped his knife.

The man was middle-aged, stocky. His arms were bare and thick and he was shaking his fists as he ran down the hill towards them.

'Say as little as possible,' hissed Toby.

'What you doing in my field?' yelled the man.

He was on them now, breathing hard.

'Just tidying the load, master,' said Far quietly, trying to calm the man down.

The man looked at all the gear on the ground, at the three heaps.

'You've got a strange way of loading,' he said. He looked from one to the other. 'This stolen?'

'No, master,' said Toby.

'So why have you come right into this corner? Why not at the gate?'

He stood hands on hips, challenging, disbelieving. Toby thought, he's strong. Can we rush him?

'You illegals?'

They did not reply.

'Show me your permit to travel.'

Far took it out, hoping the man couldn't read. The man snatched it.

'It says two. There's three of you.'

'Yes,' said Far, 'that's why we had to get off the road. The soldiers...'

'But you're dumping this gear. What's going on?'

There was no answer they could give. They would have to jump him, thought Toby. Maybe kill him.

The man rounded on Orly.

'Alright, Miss. Tell me – are you Tobards?'

Orly hesitated. Too long.

Toby drew his knife. 'Yes, we're Tobards.'

The man laughed. 'You're the first I've heard admit it before torture.' From inside his coat he drew out a bill-hook. He wetted a finger and ran it down the long sharp blade, all the time looking at Toby with narrowed eyes. 'I don't know how good you are with that.'

'Do we need to find out?' said Orly. 'You go, and we'll go.'

The man spat.

'I've no reason to love the Queen,' he said. 'But you can't be too careful.' Then he stuck the bill-hook in his belt. 'Zeke's raiders killed my two sons.'

'He's after us,' said Far. 'We have to get off the road.'

The man nodded. 'Makes sense.' He glanced at the horse and wagon and the bags and jetsam lying about. 'So what you doing with everything?'

Toby put his knife away, sensing the danger had passed. 'Dumping it. Taking just what we can carry.'

The man pulled at his chin.

'Don't know what you done. Doesn't have to be much these days.' He held up his open hands. 'Don't tell me. But I'll buy your horse. Can't afford your wagon.'

'It's yours,' said Far.

'Let's go up to the house,' said the man.

Chapter 56

An hour later they were away. They had taken the horse and cart to the farmer's house. There the farmer had unharnessed the horse and mixed it with the half a dozen he had already. Much of the gear in the wagon they burnt, the herbs, the sacks, the clothing. The rest, knives, plates, bottles he simply mixed with his own. None of it was at all special. As for the wagon, the farmer planned to swap the wheels with another of his.

His wife made them some food which they ate on the way: bread, cheese, some apples. And gave them a loaf for the journey. The farmer paid them for the horse in small coin.

'Much easier to spend,' he said.

They wrapped their gear in blankets and tied them to their backs with rope. And then they left. The farmer led them across his land, which increased in slope as they made their way towards the High Ridge.

At last by a stile, he stopped and shook their hands.

'Tell me nothing more,' he said. 'But I wish you all the luck in the world.'

They thanked him profusely, but he waved away their thanks. He pointed out the way up to the Ridge. And they parted.

The farmer walked back down the valley. And they continued upwards. The sun was setting, the climbing was stiff.

'Has he died yet?' said Orly, stopping for a few seconds to adjust her straps.

'I do hope so,' said Toby.

'He is at least dying,' said Far. 'And painfully.'

'If that's so, then his men may already be after us,' said Toby. 'We must get as far as we can before it's too dark.'

Quite soon they were scrambling up scree. Up so high, the sun held out a little longer for them. But soon it set. A chilly wind scoured the rocks. There remained sufficient daylight for them to go on a while longer, but by the time they reached the High Ridge, it was completely dark. And too dangerous to continue. It would be too easy to break an ankle or fall over an edge.

In the shelter of some large rocks, they settled down for the night.

Chapter 57

They slept badly. The rock was hard on their backs, and the cold nibbled through their blankets. At first light they set off and ate a little food as they walked. They were grateful for the morning mist, even though it was chilly. It seemed to keep the world away. In a while though, the mist cleared with the warming sun and then the bells began.

At first from one distant spire, but then they began to sound from here and there in the valley below as if there were a contagion of bells. Deep sounding bells, high bells. Every church it seemed was ringing its bells to a different tune. A cacophony of chimes from every village and town.

'What's going on?' exclaimed Orly.

'At least while they're ringing, they're not chasing us,' said Toby.

'Every church, every bell everywhere,' said Orly looking over the valley.

'I know what it is,' said Far.

They turned to him.

'Someone has died. Someone important.'

And no more needed to be said. But it gave an urgency to their march. They tried to keep to the middle of the Ridge, less likelihood of them being spotted from below, thought it was not always possible, and then, at the edge, they stooped low.

Toby wondered who would be mourning. The country might wear black, and priests might intone Zeke's princely virtues from the pulpit. Choirs might sing and crowds line the way as his coffin went by. But amongst all those bowed heads, amongst the profusion of wreaths and flowers, there would only be one true mourner. A woman with a yellow jewel about her neck.

She would howl. And heaven help anyone who caught her eye.

From their high vantage point they could see a number of roads. And dust clouds flowing down them. And knew there were riders, carrying terror from town to town. Hunting two healers, and a word, a nervous glance could cause a head to leave a neck.

'What would they do if they caught us?' said Orly with a shiver.

'Every torture you can imagine. And then some you can't,' said Toby.

At times they had to scramble, at other times they found a path for part of the way. And sometimes had to climb up and down the rocks that stuck out of the ridge like the teeth of a monster. Early afternoon Far dropped a jug that held half their water. It shattered on the rock. There was nothing that could be done; they would have to carry on with just the one jug. But a few hours later, they ran out of water. They shared the last few drops and sat down to rest and consider what they might do.

On either side of them was a sheer drop. There was water, they could see it several hundred feet below – and the difficulty getting it was certainly one of the reasons why there were no others on the High Ridge.

But they must have it. And Toby was the climber.

He tied the empty jug around his neck, and set off down the face. There were no ravens here, and the climb down was easy enough with the power of his bracelet. His fingers and wrists relished the challenge of hanging in the tiniest fissure. Once down at the stream, he drank himself and then filled the jug, and set off back up. He could see Orly and Far looking down on him. He waved, they waved back. The sun was shining brightly. He would enjoy the climb back to them.

True, there were no ravens, and the sun shone out of the bluest sky. But a half-crazed heart had sent her creature. Toby was about halfway up the rock face, when the dragon came.

Chapter 58

It was perhaps fifty feet long with wide thrashing wings. Purple with a white underbelly, and spikes that began just behind the head and increased in size along the mid back, dying off near the tail. The front paws were short with three toes and talons the length of a short sword and as sharp. The head was elongated like a horse's, scaly with red bulbous eyes below two straight horns. Its tearing teeth left no doubt as to its carnivorous nature. And the smoke issuing from its nose and between its teeth left the impression that it often grilled its food before eating it. But in spite of its size, the dragon could be remarkably silent, soaring in on Toby on an air current, wings at full stretch to make the most of the updraught.

So silent was its coming that Toby was unaware of it. His total attention was on the cliff face, finding the slight indents for fingers and toes to hold himself as he slowly rose upwards, in a fashion that was ridiculed in the flight of the creature that had him in its sights. If he had turned, he would have seen it homing in, its throat swelling as it built up the spurt of fire that would begin and end its attack.

Not that Toby could have done much if he had seen it. He needed three points to hold him to the cliff face, and what could a knife do against thick scales, ignoring the talons and its mouthful of knives? True, he had a quart of water – but it would be better to drink it himself then attempt to quench the dragon's fire. On the ground, the best thing to do would be to run. Find shelter. On a cliff face he was not offered that possibility. Toby was a hundred feet up and if he let go he'd smash into the rocks below. Should he survive, a remote possibility, with every bone broken – he could only wait helplessly for one possible end. A dragon's meal.

A voice in his head said, '*Toby, a dragon coming, from below.*'

Far was using the Voice.

And Toby looked for the first time at his adversary. And shuddered with fear. It was a few hundred feet away, a little less high than he was, and drifting in on a current of air which shortly would take it close to the cliff face. And to Toby.

A couple of small rocks flew over the cliff face. Orly and Far were throwing them. Toby knew they were useless; even if they hit the dragon, it would barely notice. Quickly Toby rejected his own options. Forget the knife, forget the water.

His hands through were strong, and if he had any chance, then it would be them that would save him. He watched the creature, and hoped it would treat him as a helpless thing, like a bird going for a caterpillar on a leaf.

Its throat was bulging, ready to blow. The great wings held steady, rippling slightly in the waves of air holding the giant up. The current was drawing it closer to the rock face. The creature was perhaps twenty feet below him, dark smoke issuing from its nostrils and running like twin ropes up the cliff. Toby held fast and waited. He would have but one chance.

The dragon was almost close enough to reach out with its talons. It opened its cavernous mouth, and took in a huge breath to blast its flame...

Toby dropped.

A torrent of fire and smoke shot out. The small plants on the cliff face charred and fizzled. Toby felt the heat of it, but was already below the blast as it came. And half a second later was on the dragon's wing.

He almost slipped off but was close enough to grab a back spike. He hung on, his body dangling down the dragon's side. And pulling hard, he drew himself up the back and into the saddle between two spikes. And clutched at the one before him for all he was worth.

The dragon knew he was there. It raged and roared, and tried to snatch at him with his claws. But Toby was just out of reach. Several times it tried, the talons coming within a couple of feet, but its front legs were just too short. Toby knew he was also safe from fire here. The dragon would not want to burn itself. But he knew too what else to expect.

The dragon would try to throw him off.

It began writhing and wriggling, bucking and throwing its body. Toby bumped up and down, his legs splayed out but he held fast, fingers entwined round the spike. The dragon was in a frenzy. And, like a horse trying to throw a rider, it thrashed and tossed, the great muscles of its body contorting it and throwing it up and down like an animated whip.

The thrashing came thick and fast. Toby had the strength to hold on, but the dragon was trying to unbalance him, catch him with the shock of a throw. The creature writhed like a hissing snake and Toby hung on for his life, for all the dragon's antics were high in the air, the cliff on one side and hard rock below.

The bucking stopped. Toby could feel the blood pumping through the dragon's body. It was tired but no less angry. And rage would make it try again. And again. While he had little choice but to hang on.

The dragon began to fly upwards, its great wings surging, thrusting the air behind to gain lift. Higher and higher until the Ridge was way below. Toby could just make out Orly and Far looking up at him like two tiny dolls.

And then came the dive.

This was far worse than the climb. The air screamed past his ears, the water whipped off his eyes, the blast stretched his arms to their fullness. And still the speed increased as the dragon zoomed into the rock of the High Ridge. Rushing towards him came the ground and his stomach threatened to fly from his body.

At the last moment, the dragon turned. Did a half circle and then flattened out. Toby was sick and weary but he knew the dragon was exhausted too. The blood was thumping through its arteries and torrents of smoke pouring from its mouth. It was wheezing and the creature's head was rolling. Badly in need of a rest before its next surge.

And there would be one. The beast would never give up.

Toby's arms ached, his legs were bruised. How much more could he take? A swift unexpected throw, and he'd be off. He was fairly close to the wing. Just below it, he could see a sinew that tied a muscle to the bone. If he could cut it. Then perhaps... He must get in closer. The dragon was resting on an updraught which made it easy for Toby to shuffle over a couple of spikes and get as close to the wing as he dared.

He examined the sinew. He would need to hack in as hard as he could in one blow, because as soon as the dragon felt him chopping then it would resist – and one glance of the wing could knock his head off.

There was also the problem of height. If it worked then the dragon would fall – but if from too great a height, then Toby would fall to his own death. It had to be judged finely. And without too much delay, as the dragon was renewing its strength to have another go at him.

Toby took out the knife and gazed keenly at the cutting point. There, one hack, where the muscle stretched from the bone. Choose the moment, and chop true and hard into the bite of the sinew.

The dragon drifted lower, still a little high, but he might not get a better chance. And he threw all his strength into a swinging chop. And then quickly pulled back.

Just in time, as the pain angered the dragon and the wings thrashed like a great sail in a hurricane. The dragon buckled and roared; flame spat from its mouth. And Toby thought – it hasn't worked, I've made him angry as a bee. He'll have me now. As the dragon writhed in pain and wild fury.

But then there was a snap, a crack like a tree just about to fall. And the wing he had worked on swung to the creature's side, useless. Toby hung on like mad. This was it. Nothing can fly on one wing, and down dropped the dragon like a rock.

Its massive body hit the ground with a thump. Toby was thrown back up, off its rubbery flesh. Down, then up again, as the thump echoed and re-echoed, throwing all the breath from his body. But the dragon's fleshy vastness had cushioned Toby. He lay still, the body underneath him not moving, splayed out flat on the top of the High Ridge.

Chapter 59

That night they stayed in a shallow cave. It was hardly longer than their bodies, and so low they could only kneel within it. But it kept the bitter wind off. The second jug had broken too. Now they had no water, nor anything to carry it in. They had a little food left, bread from the farmer, but without water they just nibbled a little.

Toby said he would go back down in the morning. He'd have to go to a village or farm and buy a jug and supplies. A dangerous thing to do, but there was no option.

Outside their low cave, perhaps twenty paces away, the great dragon lay slumped on the ground. And as it grew darker, its silhouette was like a mountain crest, with evenly spaced peaks along the rim.

In the middle of the night it rained heavily. There was a puddle just outside their cave. Orly went out to drink from it but it tasted of blood. And so did others all about. Obviously blood from the beast, contaminating the area around. They had no vessel to catch water, but caught it in their palms as it trickled off the outside of the cave. Quenched a little, they ate some more and then quenched themselves again.

Water ran into their cave. They could do nothing about it, glad at least they could not see its redness. They crouched at the back, arms round their knees, feet and backsides in water, shivering under their wet blankets.

It was a miserable, long night with sleep out of the question. The time had to be got over. There was nothing to be done but bear it. Toby ached with stiffness from his battle with the creature. He shuffled all night, making himself even wetter.

At first light they rose. It was a dawn of absolute redness; the red and orange of the sky and clouds, and the puddles of dragon's blood painting the rocks. Other colours battled in vain to be seen through the wash.

But once walking, they were quickly free of the bloody puddles. And glad, as the sun rose higher, to be in full sunlight. There was growing warmth in it and, with their movement, it stifled their shivering. They wrung out their blankets, swung their arms, their breath steaming in the morning air. They walked on, stopping occasionally to drink from puddles. Mid morning, they ate the last of their food. With the sun bright in a clear sky, the temperature was high enough to halt. They draped their blankets over rocks to dry.

And Toby went down to get supplies.

Chapter 60

It was a hard climb down. Toby was stiff and tired from his exertions with the dragon, and his muscles creaked. At one point, halfway down the cliff, he almost gave up and thought to himself – it would be so easy simply to drop off. He'd fall and smash himself on the rock below and it would all be over. The end of his tiredness, the end of his necessity to force himself on. His life would not end in the torture chamber or on the executioner's block. He would never again have to see Far and Orly making eyes... Rest, complete rest. It was not just body weariness, but the ache of living hand to mouth, fearing death, and humiliation.

Once on firm ground, he felt better. Tiredness and loneliness had depressed him – and death was so simple. But here in green fields, sheep were staring, then black and white cows who idly looked up then returned to their grazing. The round of life went on, the grass still grew... But he knew too that swordsmen were sweeping the land, that a Queen's anger had to be washed in blood – but could never be soothed. A lamb chased a butterfly among the cowslips of the meadow. Amazing there still could be such unknowing beauty, with the farmer perhaps coming to cut its throat.

Should he laugh or should he cry? Neither. But keep his wits about him. Danger was constant. One mistake and he was dead. He was not a baa lamb, and must retain that knowing – for life was precious. And if he must die then he must not do it carelessly.

Nevertheless, he sat down on a bank, laid back, chewing a grass stalk. And marvelled at the blue of the sky and the uncaring beauty of the clouds. The sun warmed his face and drew him to his purpose. A ewe might care for her lamb, but only human beings can understand love and hate. If they choose to.

Toby rose. Below was a farmhouse. There would be food and water.

And there would be risk.

His blanket was tied upon on his back, with a few items wrapped in it. He had to be a traveller with legitimate purpose. And must behave that way. He went over his story as he came through the fields to the habitation.

As he neared, a dog began to bark. Its fierceness worried him and he picked up a stick from the hedgerow. A walking stick for a traveller but also a cudgel to beat back the animal if needs be.

A large brown dog rushed out to him, baring its teeth as he approached the house. He held the stick up as a warning and continued more slowly. The dog was standing fast and snarling. Should he go or retreat?

He stopped and called out, 'Hello! Is anyone at home?'

The dog came no further forward, and neither did he. As if there was a line in the mud between them, once crossed he knew it would go for him. Toby wasn't unduly frightened. He had his stick, he had a knife in his belt, and, with his bracelet his fingers were strong enough to strangle the animal. But beating or killing a dog was no way to get provisions from the farmer.

Toby was about to walk away when the farm door opened. A white-haired man put his head out.

'Will you sell me provisions?' called Toby.

The man stepped out. He was stooped, wearing a drab, brown smock; he too had a stick. As he swung it, the dog ran. It was obvious the animal had felt it often enough. Toby walked in to the cottage. The dog was to one side watching, with a quieter growl.

The man waited, leaning on his stick. He had a deeply etched face and sunken eyes that stared hard at Toby as he approached.

'What d'you want?' said the man sucking his lower lip.

'Provisions,' said Toby.

'You said that,' said the man. 'Got money?'

Toby took out five shillings from his belt bag. From the man's greedy look he knew it was too much. But it was too late now.

'I smashed my jug,' said Toby. 'So I need something for water. Have you got a skin maybe? And I want food enough for a day or two.'

'You're not from round here,' said the man.

Toby was ready for this. Knew he'd be questioned.

'I'm a ferryman on the Blackwater.' He showed his open hands; they were callused enough from his stint on the River of the Dead. And the man nodded. 'Going to visit my parents,' added Toby.

The man, wide-eyed, waved his hands fiercely. 'Are you stupid? With Prince Zeke dead – only lepers and the mad are on the road.'

So it was confirmed, Zeke's death.

'I set off before,' Toby said. 'And then it was too late to head back.' While the man pondered this, he added, 'Do they know how he died?'

The man shrugged. 'They haven't told me. And I haven't asked.'

Leave it be, thought Toby.

'Where'd your parents live?' said the man.

Toby gave him the name of a village near the castle.

'Don't go there,' said the man. 'Unless you've a permit.'

Toby didn't reply.

'If they find you without one,' the man went on, 'they'll kill you.'

'What should I do then?'

The man smiled, showing a few black stumps. 'Go back to where you came from. And that's risk enough...' The man screwed up his eyes, and said quietly, 'Course you could join the army. They got a post in the village. They'd take a young man like you, no questions asked.'

'I might do that,' said Toby. 'But I need provisions.' And knew as soon as he said that the man knew he wouldn't. For why did you need provisions if you were about to join the army?

The old man said, 'Stay there.'

He went in the house. As soon as he did the dog crept in growling, testing him. Toby gripped his stick and watched the animal. He had lost his protector. The dog was perhaps five paces away, its jaw agape, a string of saliva linking the teeth. Toby swung the stick in a fierce arc. The animal stopped. Show it who's master, thought Toby. He ran towards it brandishing the stick and yelling 'Get away!' The animal backed off.

Toby shook his fist at it. 'Stay away!'

The man came back out. He was clutching a leather water bag. He had some bread and cheese and a couple of weary apples.

'Five shillings,' said the man.

Toby realised he was being cheated.

'Three,' he said.

'Five shillings,' said the man with a grin, clutching the goods like a child hanging on to her only doll.

'Too much,' said Toby but knew he was beaten. He would willingly pay five, but didn't want the man to know he was desperate. He didn't want to face another farmer or a shopkeeper.

He tried four but the man had got his measure. What does it matter? thought Toby. And he agreed on five and handed over the money. The man smiled pityingly and gave him the goods. The bag smelt of sour milk, the bread was hard, and the cheese past its best. But it would have to do.

Toby wrapped them in his blanket and made his farewell. He then purposely took a direction away from the

High Ridge. The man stood outside his door watching him off. Toby looked back from time to time but the man remained watching, until he turned along a stone wall – and could no longer see him.

When he'd gone about a mile, Toby circled back. And was just able to dip behind a hedge when he saw the man striding towards a collection of houses. Going where? thought Toby. To double his five shillings with reward from the army. He was certainly in haste. Maybe he always walked quickly.

Toby watched him out of sight, and then continued his journey. At a stream he washed out the water sack and filled it. He repacked his blanket. And headed back to the High Ridge.

Chapter 61

Far and Orly were in a windbreak on the High Ridge. A rock behind them, another to their side. They had watched Toby climb down and then disappear in the fields. How long would he be? The sun was warm on their faces. Far's eyes were closed.

'I am so tired,' he said.

Orly next to him, took his hand.

'I'm pretty weary too,' she said. 'Just drying out.' She gave a half laugh. 'If my mother could see the company I keep. One found guilty of killing a king and the other has just poisoned a prince.' She added with a grin, 'Must be my turn.'

They were silent a little while, their fingers interlocked. A lark was trilling overhead. And Far thought, I wish I could stay forever. No future, no past. Just here and now with Orly.

As if she'd been continuing the conversation in her head, she went on, 'I am not a very brave person at all, Far. I was enjoying life with Erdy. Then Toby comes back and our little world is smashed like an egg.'

Far was looking into the sun through his lids, his vision glowing red and warm.

'Are we are really off to kill a Queen?' he said lazily. 'On such a lovely day.'

'Perhaps Toby has killed her already,' said Orly squeezing his hand.

'That would save us some trouble,' said Far.

'You know,' she said with a laugh, 'I wish he'd never come back. That's mean of me – isn't it?' She paused, then added, 'If he were still rowing that boat... If my brother hadn't arrived... He could be rowing forever and ever.'

'But Martin did arrive, and Toby did come back.'

'And here we are all, we three, off to kill the Queen. Hey-ho...' She was quiet a while, stroking the hair on his arm.

Far was thinking, how is this possible, all in one place, sunlight, love, and murder. He wished he could still his head. Not think so much.

'He's jealous of you, Far,' she said. 'Wants me to be a lady again. He's worse than I was sixteen months ago.'

'I hate the way he watches us,' said Far.

He sat up and blinked in the bright sun. He had made himself angry. Orly leaned against him.

'Has he got anything to be jealous about?' said Orly.

'What d'you think?'

He turned to her.

Orly slowly smiled. 'I think he has.'

Far grinned back.

'I loved it on Erdy's mountain,' he said. 'I was so glad Toby wasn't there. I knew soon as he came back things would be different. I knew he wouldn't like me getting on with you. Erdy didn't care – did he? But Toby, I knew, would detest it.'

Orly took Far's face in both hands, and looked into his eyes. Far felt charged with her gaze and tried to turn away, but she held him firmly. And then he couldn't look away. Eyes held eyes. A whirlwind blew in his head, scattering his thoughts.

'Don't move,' she said gently. 'But answer me this. Suppose we do kill the Queen. What then?'

'I can't think about that.'

There was just her eyes and her.

'Think about it,' she insisted.

'Can't,' he said. And he held her hands away from his face. But eyes continued to hold eyes. Far shuddered with the force of it, as if nothing else existed. The world around had gone.

'Answer me, please. Suppose we kill the Queen. Tell me what will happen.'

Far sighed deeply. He let go of her hands. He blinked. Had he blinked before? She leaned back, blinking too. The moment had gone. But she hadn't gone. Waiting. The sun shone behind her hair.

'Alright,' he said, struggling to make words. 'Let's imagine.' The first syllables came. He wanted to touch her face but somehow went on. 'The Queen is dead. Don't ask me how. We did it. And Toby is the King. Hallelujah. And me? Who am I then? Faithful servant once more.'

'He said he'd make you a lord,' said Orly with a smile.

'Do you believe him?'

Orly sniffed. 'Toby blows hot, blows cold.'

'Doesn't he just. One minute it's brother. The next it's kiss my feet. You know – I never liked my dad, he was a bully, but I always remember what he used to say whenever things were going well: 'Always prepare for a kick in the teeth." He stopped, caught her eye. 'And whose boot would be on the foot? Toby's or yours.'

'I'll kick you alright,' she said in sudden anger, standing up and raising her foot over him, 'but not in the teeth.'

Far grabbed her ankle. She struggled and hopped about.

'Hey, I'm a lady,' she yelled in mock fear. 'Toby – come and save me!'

She collapsed onto Far. He wanted to kiss her but couldn't. She was forbidden. It went too deep.

And so she kissed him.

It was a long embrace. Compounded of fear and loneliness, and the time together on the mountain. Of late conversations in the cavern and the shadows flickering on the walls. Of gathering herbs on the hillside, and reading together. Compounded of all the time they had wanted to and hadn't.

Chapter 62

Toby returned. He was tired, and ached with the climb and his exertions of the day before. He crumpled in a heap, leaning against a rock, his legs outstretched. But in a little while, took out the water and food from his pack which they all shared. Once he was rested and eating with them, he saw the change in them. The way they looked at each other, shared bread, touched. And while they didn't freeze him out, it was difficult not to feel unwelcome.

'What you two been up to?' he said warily.

'Nothing,' said Orly lightly.

Far smiled.

'Nothing, I bet,' said Toby. 'I've been over two hours.'

'We had a chat,' said Far.

'Some chat,' said Toby. 'A peasant talking to a lady. I wonder what you have to say to each other.'

Neither of them replied. Toby looked both of them over, but they would not catch his eye. They are lovers, he thought. Playing me stupid. I'm the errand boy, climbing up and down the cliff and getting them food and water. The anger surged in him. He could have tipped Far off the cliff. And might have done, if he'd said a word.

But Far knew better.

Orly too knew. Toby was fuming. Nothing could be said to him in this state. Neither of them spoke, quenched by Toby. And in a little while he stood up, as tired as he was, packed the water and the remains of the food. And headed off.

Orly and Far followed.

The way was rugged but fairly flat. There were places where grass grew and the walking was easy, but other places where they had to scramble. Toby walked ahead stridently. His stiffness was beaten down by his temper. Orly and Far were content to let him go. With him well ahead, they could talk once more. Pretend he wasn't there.

The day was warm. The rain clouds had cleared and the sun was high. Toby was sweating in his angry march. He stopped to take some water, and looked back. The others were maybe two hundred yards behind. At least I have the water, he thought. He saw they were holding hands. And at once felt a weakness that almost caved his knees. What am I doing here with these two? How can I be their chaperon?

He took food out of his blanket. And laid food and water on a rock. Toby looked back once more. They were dawdling, holding hands, gazing at each other. This is the wrong place for me, he thought. I cannot bear it. Anywhere, anywhere else.

He turned away, tied his blanket firmly to his back. And headed for the edge. Quickly he was over and climbing down. In a minute or two they would find the food and water. And then look for him. And when they didn't see him ahead, search him out. Perhaps he shouldn't have left the provisions. But he knew he had to. It would make them see where the true power lay. Show them that they needed him much more than they needed each other.

And he didn't need them.

As he climbed down the face, he waited for the inevitable call. His stomach was hollow, his tongue dry. He ached to the core – but he must get away. Be no one's nurse. He concentrated on his handholds, his feet. There is just the rock face. Don't look up. Get as far down as possible before they realise...

'Toby!' called Orly, already faint on the wind.

He did not look up.

'Where are you going?'

Away, he thought. Miles away.

'We are in this together!' she cried.

Then he gazed upwards, in spite of himself. He saw two small heads, faces down at the cliff top. Two heads so close together, almost touching.

He did not look up again. And ignored the cries in his descent.

Chapter 63

Once at the bottom Toby crept into a shrubbery. He was utterly exhausted. His body was bruised as if it had been hammered. He slept a restless sleep. And when he woke up the sun was setting.

He was just as stiff, just as weary when he arose. He wondered what Far and Orly were doing. Tried to dismiss them but they kept returning. Why couldn't he be on his own?

He found a stream and washed himself. He drank. And felt better. It was when he lay down that he felt weak. Felt alone. He must walk. Keep going.

It was dark. And darkness was at least some protection. He couldn't be too far from the castle, and for lack of any other objective, he would go there. Before darkness fell, he had noted a village not too far away. He would go round that. But beyond that he had seen forest. It could be the forest just before the castle. It could be another. It didn't matter; forest was safer for him. He must stay away from people.

He plodded on, treading one weary limb before the other. Moving because he had to move. And this hurtful journey meant at least he only had bodily pain to concentrate on. He ached so much, if anyone came for him he'd be able to do little but surrender.

The night was clear and he had taken his bearing by the stars. Keep the Pole Star to his left to find the forest. That was all. A barking dog speeded him up. Two riders on horses caused him to halt, and hide tight behind a hedgerow until they trotted past. An owl hooted up ahead.

He came to the forest. And once within it, was quickly lost. Within its leafy canopy he could no longer see the stars and it was hard to follow a path even though a half moon had risen. He fought through thicket, he walked into streams in his blindness. He scratched himself on bramble and holly. Without any sense of direction, he stumbled on, barely able to make out the spectre of trees against the blackness of night. He was going nowhere, rambling like a drunken man thrown out of the inn.

He found himself a thick patch of leaves and lay down. Toby covered himself with his blanket and hoped for a few hours' sleep. But he rolled restlessly on the leaves. Around him he could hear creeping in the forest as if ghostly things, the creatures of his dreams, were out to hunt him down. The cold seeped in, from the air and the dampness underneath. The blanket was useless. After rolling restlessly, he sat up and pulled his knees to his chest, huddling to hold in any warmth. But he shivered, his teeth chattering, the chill wiping him over with icy hands. He thought of Far and Orly lying together, and was glad to be where he was. As miserable as he was, as lonely and cold as he was. He hated his petulance, his jealousy. Here there were only trees to scream at.

From outside the blanket, he felt a nuzzle distinctly. Something was out there. It brushed him on the thigh. Some animal. He thought wolf, he thought bear. Toby clutched at his knife and wished he could see whatever it was. Cautiously, he put his hand outside of his blanket and felt about. He felt softness. Fur. He moved along it and felt its warmth, blood pumping through. And then a smell he knew.

Sly!

He clutched at the animal. And she nuzzled him with her wet nose. He felt the bushy tail, and then cradled her to him. Pleased to grasp something alive that cared for him.

Warmth on a cold night. Hope. He nuzzled his face into the fur.

'However did you find me?' he said softly.

And she pulled out of his arms in a flurry of fur. For a second he felt abandoned, his hands empty of warmth. But realised what she was telling him. A message he had first translated more than a year ago.

He must follow her.

Chapter 64

Orly and Far watched him climb down. And watched him disappear. They waited for a few hours thinking he might yet come back. And when he didn't, they set off themselves. Slowly; they felt in no hurry to get wherever they were going.

'It's as if he's still here,' said Orly. 'We can't get away from him.'

'I expect he has the same problem,' said Far.

'We were rather obvious,' she said.

Far shrugged.

They were scrambling over rocks. Waiting for each other. There was no leader striding away from them.

Far sat down on a rock.

He said, 'I am a peasant. You are a lady. How do we release ourselves from that?'

'Up here, there are neither,' she said.

'Down there – there are both.'

She pursed her lips but did not reply. The world overwhelmed them.

'Where do you think he's gone?' she said at last.

'To beat the Queen. All by himself.'

Orly sprang up. 'Then we'd better help him.'

Far rose slowly. 'I don't really want to help him.'

'Neither do I,' she said. 'But I do want to beat the Queen.'

'Before she beats us,' said Far.

They continued walking throughout the day. Stopping to eat and drink, pleased to be with each other. And knowing that their time together might be short. Here, though, they were equal. No-one judged them. But below, every man and woman was a judge.

The day closed down on them. Before it got truly dark, they found themselves a ring of shoulder-high rock. It would keep the wind out and they must just hope it wouldn't rain.

'If only we could stay up here,' said Far.

'No food, no water,' said Orly.

Far smiled.

'Who needs to eat?'

That night they shared their two blankets. And kept each other warm. There was no Toby to tell them of their place. No anyone else in the broad, wide world.

They rose early. Ate and drank a little. The High Ridge, they knew, came down a few miles from the castle. And from a vantage point they could see it, above the surrounding villages, the sun rising over the walls. The towers had flags flying. They could just make out the guard on the battlements. The light glinted silver in the moat.

'It's not as close as it looks,' she said.

'I wish it was a hundred miles away,' he said.

She squeezed his hand.

He said, 'I could use the Voice. And tell Toby we are going to the castle.'

She shook her head. 'Don't bother.'

'Why not?'

'He doesn't want to hear from you.'

Far didn't reply. He had no wish to speak to Toby. Say what? That he was sorry – when he wasn't at all. If the King can be angry at the peasant, why can't the peasant be angry at the King? In normal times the peasant would lose his head, but these were not normal times. And he was angry. Toby expected him to crawl.

'What are we going to do?' she said.

He looked into the distance, at the banners flying from the towers. There was no way back.

'We have to go on to the castle,' he said.
'And then what?'
'Find the Queen. And kill her.'
Orly clapped her hands and laughed.
'Oh that's so easy.' She pulled him up. 'Come on, Far.'
The way was gentle for a while. And they were able to walk holding hands. They were losing height; it was becoming obvious to both that this was the slow climb down from the High Ridge.

Something was bothering Far. And when they came to the ravine, he was not at all surprised. There had to be a good reason why they had seen no-one else on the High Ridge. And there lay the cause, deep and stark before them, and at its foot a rushing river.

They walked along the edge of the ravine, looking over as they went, trying to find a place they could scramble down. Though how they would cross the river if they managed it – that they left to be worked out when they came to it.

It was as if the ravine had been cut with a knife. The sides were sheer. Toby could have managed it. Maybe they could, with his help. Or if they had ropes, then perhaps they might have managed the climb down. But Toby wasn't here, and the short lengths of rope binding their blankets to their shoulders were useless as climbing ropes.

If there were no way down, then they would have to go back the way they had come, along the ridge for two days or more. A depressing thought. They lay on the edge and looked down the sides, envious of the birds that nested in holes lower down. They ate the last of the food, musing on this unforeseen difficulty. The bread was hard to swallow; each bite had to be taken with a mouthful or two of water. The cheese was rancid. Far managed his but Orly could not stomach hers, and so he had hers too.

'Peasants eat what they are given,' he teased.
'Ladies don't have to.'

Below, the river racing over the rocks was music to their words. It danced white and wild, the restless energy invigorating them. They came to a place above a waterfall, the river bubbling over in a fierce curtain. Walking on, they found the water above the waterfall was quiet and fairly shallow. If they could get down, then there they could cross the river.

It was then they came to the bridge.

The sides were rope. The walkway was plank. Obvious too that this was a new bridge, the planks newly cut, the rope barely weathered. And it crossed from one side of the ravine to the other.

Far said, 'I don't like this.'

'It's too convenient,' agreed Orly.

But it was a bridge and there was a ravine to cross. They went one before the other, Far first. He looked to the other side. There was a rocky outcrop with a way between, and then woodland. It all seemed clear. The planks were shaky, and they kept a hand on both of the ropes as the bridge creaked and swayed beneath them. Far did not look down to the river below, his legs wobbly with vertigo. Instead he kept an eye to where he was going, and his hands firmly on the side ropes.

He thought, if this bridge should fall – could I climb up? And he imagined the far end collapsing, and him holding on for sheer life with Orly tumbling on top of him... their free end bashing into the cliff like a pendulum. But he was already at the middle and it seemed the bridge was well made, and although it wobbled, there was no sign of it detaching.

He made a half-turn to see how Orly was getting on. She grinned, took one hand off and gave him a wave. It seemed she was enjoying it more than he was. Breathe easily, he told himself. Keep putting one foot in front of the other, and don't look down...

At last Far stepped off the bridge, onto firm ground – and, in relief, turned to watch Orly complete the last few paces. But she was not there.

'Orly!' he called.

'Sh!' she hissed and touched him on the shoulder.

There – but invisible. And seeing what Far had not. For when he turned to the front, it was to face two soldiers a few paces ahead. Where had they come from? They were stern-faced, wearing tunics and carrying spears. He could see just beyond them a way through the rocky outcrop, and a little way along it a little wooden shack just sticking out of a recess. Obviously they were the guards of the bridge. Orly had been quick enough to use her gift. Far hoped he could somehow persuade the soldiers that his journey was lawful.

'So where you been, young fellow?' said one of the guards.

'On the High Ridge. Lovely morning for it,' said Far with a friendly smile, pointing behind him, though he hardly needed to. 'I've been looking for herbs. I'm a healer.'

The front guard turned to his mate who shook his head.

'A healer eh?' The guard poked his spear into Far's stomach.

The other guard quickly went behind.

'I like the early morning,' began Far, already feeling this was lost. The spear was steady against his belly.

'You're in trouble, son,' said the man behind his back.

Far could feel him binding his hands. He attempted resistance and his arm was twisted.

'Ah!'

'Then let my mate get on with his job,' said the front guard, with a dig of the spear.

Far let himself be tied.

'The Queen's got a thing against healers,' said the front guard with a wry grin. 'You might have heard. One of your crowd didn't do her son much good.'

Far began, 'I was only gathering herbs...' when the spear pressed into his belly. Deeper this time.

'Save the details for the executioner.'

A rope was thrown over his head and pulled close in to his neck. And he was led away like a pig to market.

Chapter 65

Toby was stretched out in the chair before the fire, drinking soup, that beautiful, healing soup. And opposite him, in the other chair, was Maeg smiling at him through her gapped teeth. The firelight flickered on her plump face. She wore the same red spotted headscarf that he recognised from his last visit, but her hair was whiter. In her features he clearly saw Erdy, her son. Earlier they had spoken of him, while she was washing away his soreness in the tub. Toby told her what he knew. And Sly pricked her ears up, and he could have sworn she understood – and, if the fox could speak, have added much more.

He was relaxed before the fire, enjoying the sensation of being warm and fed, the stiffness gone. The depression that had held him earlier had lifted, but he was left with a nagging pain.

'I have abandoned my friends,' he said.

Maeg nodded, pulling a long hair from her ear.

'You've had a hard time,' she said. 'Alone in the Underworld, rowing the ferry boat back and forth, with only the dead for company. And then once you return you are off again, still soft with suffering.'

'I should not have left them,' he said, shaking his head.

'Did you have any choice?' she said quietly.

He did not reply. Wondering what else he could have done. Could he really have stuck the company of lovers?

'Are you in love with the girl yourself?' asked Maeg.

He avoided her eyes. 'I haven't time for love.'

Maeg smiled, and said gently, 'I think though it has time for you.'

'I'm fond of her,' he said carefully. 'But love? I don't know what it means. Besides, I hardly know her. Before this trip, most of the time I was with her she was unconscious. I was wondering whether she was dead. And then there were only a couple of days in the cave before I left – mostly she was pretty groggy. After that I was away for sixteen months with plenty to keep me occupied.' He stopped for a second and then burst out, 'I am infuriated that she is so close to Far.' His eyes pleaded with the old woman. 'But then anyone of my rank would be.'

Maeg sucked her lips. 'So it's just rank, is it?'

'I think so. Yes,' he said uncomfortably. He wished she wouldn't stare so hard. He spooned some soup, looking into the bowl as if the cauliflower and carrot held some deep meaning.

'Are you jealous of Far?'

He did not look up, and stopped to think, as if he really needed to. 'No,' he said at last. Then added, 'Perhaps a little. Resentful. Is that the same as jealousy? Maybe. It's so unfair. I was down below – and Far was doing... what Far was doing.'

'Suppose it was reversed and you'd spent sixteen months with her? Would it be alright then?'

He looked up for an instant, then retreated to his soup. 'They are such an unsuitable couple. She's an orphan.' He stopped again, felt his face reddening. He'd never had conversations like this. 'Yes, I admit I feel excluded. I'd like to punch Far on the nose and slap her round the face. I don't know what I'm feeling half the time. That's why I had to leave.'

Maeg nodded.

For a minute they didn't speak, Maeg idly rubbing Sly's head.

'What should I do?' he said at last.

'What do you want to do?'

He put down the soup bowl and stood up. He leaned over the leaping fire, grasping the high mantelpiece.

'I can't abandon them.'

'You can't,' she agreed.

He turned to her. 'Anything could be happening. They could be dead. Captured. Tortured. I put them up to this. And then left them to it.' He clenched his fists and sighed. 'I would so love to stay here a few days.'

'I would love you to, Toby.'

'But I can't.'

She nodded and rose. The back of her hand wiped a watery eye.

'You must get there by cover of night,' she said.

And here he had second thoughts. Must he really give up warmth and safety for the cold of the night? For danger and maybe death. Must he? But there were friends out there, there was a promise to his father...

The choice wasn't his.

And Toby realised in that instant something of the pressure of being king. He was chosen. And there was no other way he could go. No matter how it weighed on him. He could do it badly, he could do it well – but he must do it. Or how could he live in the world?

The die was cast.

At the cottage door she embraced him. She had given him a water bottle, bread and cheese. He abandoned his blanket, kissed the old lady on the cheek...

And followed Sly into the night.

Chapter 66

Far paced, hit the wall and returned. Fading light came in through the high window, making an orange patch on the wall opposite. His legs ached with walking, he had tried sitting down in the straw but it stank of pee and sweat. It was crawling with bugs. Sooner or later though he would have to succumb. He couldn't walk all night.

He leaned against a damp wall and shivered. Was it to end here?

He'd gathered from the soldiers that the Queen had been killing healers. Any and every one of them. She had found them collectively guilty of the murder of her beloved son. To be a healer was to be complicit. You could say the Queen's plan had worked. In her trawl, she had at last caught the guilty one. Rather expensive in lives, but she'd got him.

But every healer? He shuddered at the thought. All those deaths... Soldiers bursting into workshops... If he'd known their fate, would he have still killed Zeke? Except he could not have known. And how many other lives did killing Zeke save? He couldn't answer that either. As Zeke couldn't kill them, he couldn't count them.

The gaoler had given him the good news; the executioner wouldn't be back till the morning. But then the backlog would be cleared. The Queen didn't believe in keeping prisoners. That way, said the gaoler, she didn't have to waste money feeding them.

He was impressed with the economics.

It was so cold. Far rubbed his shoulders and blew into his hands. The damp chill soaked through to his bones. At least Orly was safe. Invisibly, she had followed him down to the castle, with the guards. Even holding his hand part of the way. She was not able to get down to the dungeon. The door had shut too quickly. Just as well. What could she do in here?

He'd used the Voice to tell Orly that he was safe until the morning. And other more personal matters: his feelings for her, urging her to stay alive and not do anything stupid – but in reality it was rather late to be saying that. Every now and then he spoke to her, but it was painful and unsatis-fying, as he couldn't hear back. And so had no idea how she was faring.

They'd had their few hours on the mountain. Was that to be it? The end of their relationship. Peasants do not marry ladies. Love cannot break down walls. Or kill Queens.

Pray she was safe!

She had come here with the same mad idea as himself. In the castle, but not as a guest dining at the Queen's table. She was a fugitive. A mouse baiting the cat. Quite a one-sided contest. If caught she would take her place in the queue for the executioner's block. He might find all his friends there in the morning.

Toby too. Or was he somewhere else – still in a mood? Though he could be shivering in the cell next door. Well, he'd find out early tomorrow when he walked the last walk. Did princes take precedence on the block?

That one, at least, he'd willingly concede.

He shivered and took in the acrid smell. They hadn't emptied the soil bucket from the last occupants. More prison economics, why empty it if no prisoner stayed longer than overnight? He'd been forced to use it himself, sitting on it holding his nose, flapping away flies.

And that awful straw. How many had spent their last hours lying on it, crying into it, fouling it? Even as he yet would. But come the morning, one chop, one gurgled cry – and that would be that. Another severed head. Though he still hoped somebody out there would do something, so he could yet live and love. Surely it couldn't end like this?

But did all those others, brothers of the soil bucket, feel the same? Hoping against hope.

Oh it was cold.

He paced on, grasping his shoulders with crossed arms. Five paces wall to wall. Eighteen all the way round, not twenty as he first supposed, because of the width of his body. He tried it sideways, pressing himself against the wall. Nineteen paces.

If he could walk through walls... But all he could do was scratch at them, as others had done. Their epitaphs to futility. One had written in a low corner: *The Queen is the Devil.* Did the man get away with those brave words or was he tortured until he broke?

Might he too have been a healer?

A thought came to him. The castle must have a healer. And if the Queen was executing healers in her anger, then surely he'd have been one of the first to go. But his workshop must be here. With his herbs and mixtures...

He knew what he would do. He couldn't though. But perhaps she could.

Orly, he called, using the Voice. *Find the healer's workshop. He's probably been executed. I don't know what's there, I can't help you with that – but make a preparation for the Queen. Put it in her night-time drink. Do it tonight, and I might yet survive.*

And one more message. For another who might help.

Toby, wherever you are. I am in the castle dungeon, and will be executed in the morning. Orly too is in the castle. But she is free and invisible. And looking for the healer's workshop. She will make something for the Queen's night-time drink. Her last, I hope.

He had no wish to say more. To either of them. It would be only self-pity. How cold and afraid he was. Best be silent. Let them look after themselves. And leave him to walk round the damp walls.

Chapter 67

Orly had gone where she could in the castle. She'd followed a boy struggling with two buckets of water into the kitchen. And had to hide under the table in the peelings, it was so busy there. All the yelling and fury, with kitchen boys and serving girls running non-stop, big knives chopping vegetables, a pig roasting on the spit with a bare-chested boy, red as a strawberry, turning the spit and spooning fat over the browning animal. The long room was baking, steamy and foul with curses. The smells made her hungry. Orly worked her way under the lengthy table to a pyramid of hot rolls on a tray. She had taken a couple and the mountain had fallen. And a boy was whacked with a wooden spoon for it.

Leaving the kitchen, she'd wandered into the guardhouse by the gate. Three soldiers were playing cards, half a dozen more were sleeping in the straw. Another washing in a bucket. The room stank of sweat and beer.

At the stables she noted someone important had come back from a ride. Eight horses were being wiped down and watered by boys in leather aprons. As they were finished, a blanket was slapped over the animal's back and they were given an oat bag. A larger horse was being put into the shafts of a wagon.

Orly had been to the castle several years before. The last time was with her father; she had been a guest at a banquet held by the King and Queen. Before it, while her father had been busy on state business, a lady-in-waiting had taken her for a tour of the castle. And so now she was renewing her memory. She went again up to the battlements, and to the blacksmith's workshop in the middle of the courtyard where half-naked men hammered white-hot iron.

That time, years ago, she had been taken to the healer's workshop. A large room with drying herbs hanging from the ceiling, with bottles and pots on shelves, where an old man and his wife worked with an assistant. Something foul-smelling was being brewed – but she remembered them as a cheerful group, who bowed to her when she entered. The place had little meaning for her then; she forgot the names the man used for his remedies as soon as he had said them. But now after her time with Erdy the equipment and potions would make more sense to her.

And she must find the workshop once more. She had heard Far's message. Wished to hear more, or perhaps to hear less as she could give him no comfort in return. But at least his message meant he was alive and not being tortured.

She had thought of going down to the dungeons, doubted though that she could get him out, doubted whether she could get into his cell at all. But failing anything else – if she remained alive – then she would attempt to get into the dungeon for a last farewell. She rehearsed the words she would say. A reminder of happy times in the mountains, a promise to remember...

And shook off the melancholy. She was far from giving up. Far had said – defeat the Queen and he might well stay alive.

Her first attempt to find the workshop took her to the washhouse. There, five burly women with huge, pink arms were washing sheets in steaming tubs. They had a barrel of ale which they drank from freely. And their language was quite as foul as the cooks'.

It amazed Orly that everyday work could go on amidst all the terror of the kingdom. But then, she reflected, the Queen too must eat, her sheets and clothes be washed. And how often would the Queen go to the washhouse or the kitchen? So long as the women washed well they could drink their beer and tell their bawdy jokes. So long as they said nothing more.

Life had not been so fortunate for the healer. Orly came to the workshop through a small gateless arch. At the end of a short stone corridor were a number of doors, most of which were storerooms, but one was the healer's workshop.

Or rather had been.

The door hung off its hinges and was badly smashed. It was held in the entrance by two planks of wood, nailed to the walls across the door in a forbidding X. There was just space in the broken door for Orly to squeeze through and into the workshop.

It was nearly dark, but Orly had prepared for this. In her visit to the guardhouse she had left with an unlit lamp and flint. By keeping to the walls in the courtyard in the gloom, no-one had seen them move by themselves around the space.

Once in the workshop, Orly lit her lamp. And the devastation hit her like a bolt. Shelves had been pulled down, the bench turned over and smashed, the top upside-down and the legs splayed out helplessly. Glass bottles were broken, bowls shattered. She walked in tentatively. The floor was a carpet of scattered herbs, glass and clay shards, pages from books, torn scrolls, scale pans, cracked mortars, powders and unknown liquids. She could see, mirrored in the wreckage, the time the soldiers burst in and trashed the place before carting off the bewildered mild threesome.

It was so wicked. So senseless.

She sighed deeply. What on earth could she find amongst this debris?

She put the lamp in a corner, so that little light would spill out of the workshop. And then, down on her hands and knees, worked her way through the bits and pieces. Before the raid, everything had been ordered on the shelves and labelled. Now chaos reigned. Some of the dried herbs she recognised – but they were of little use to her. She didn't want to bring down a fever or cure a cold. Not cure anyone at all.

She was startled by a noise. A brown rat was in a corner, its ears twitching. Of course the animal could not see her, but could hear her well enough. She threw a pestle at it and the rat scuttled off into the debris.

She returned to searching. If only Far were here. If she had paid more attention to Erdy's teaching, read more. A broken bottle of hemlock infusion frustrated her. That would have done. But now it had soaked away into the boards.

Outside were footsteps. Her heart jumped in her chest. She stilled herself and shielded the lamp in a piece of cloth. The footsteps approached; light and shadow from a swinging lamp came through the broken door, and passed up the corridor. A cupboard was opened, there was some shuffling, the door was closed, and the footsteps and lamp went back the way they had come.

Orly waited a while, motionless. She must keep her wits about her. Make little noise, keep the light protected. She brought the lamp to her, and kept the cloth over most of it, just allowing a beam to play where she was looking. It meant she could cover the lamp quickly, if need be. Orly began one more looking through the remnants. A leather glove took her attention. She put it on, it was somewhat loose on her hand – but it would serve. There were unpleasant liquids and glass on the floor, and it was not her object to poison herself.

She turned up a tiny brown bottle. It was still corked and labelled, but the label meant nothing to her. She needed an Erdy or a book. And with pages scattered about the floor there was scant chance of finding the one she needed. With her teeth she withdrew the cork and sniffed at the contents. A memory seeped back. She had smelt it before. It was sweet and pear-like but sharp too. What was it? Oh, she knew it! But she had smelt so much in Erdy's workshop over the year. If she could think back when it had been. What was she doing? Oh, she knew it!

She sniffed again, closed her eyes and tried to picture the time.

And it came to her. When she had been ill, that was when. Erdy had given it to her to put her to sleep. And it had worked well enough. Yes, she was in the cavern, haughty to Far, calling him boy and peasant, refusing to confer with him. And Erdy had given her this draught.

Orly corked the bottle and put it in her pocket.

Chapter 68

Toby lay on the damp grass. Night had fallen. It was over-cast, without stars or moon. Difficult to see by, but difficult to be seen too. He was on the far side of the moat from the castle, gazing up at the battlements. He needed to know where the watch were.

He'd kept a good pace through the forest following Sly. And still had the heat of it in him, though it was becoming chilly. He was renewed during his time at Maeg's cottage: the hot, plentiful food, the soothing away of aches, physical and mental. And someone he could talk to without argu-ment.

One guard passed on the battlement. He must wait for the other, going the reverse way round. Far had told him that he was in the dungeon. Well, he'd have to stay there a while. And Orly was somewhere within those walls. He had no idea where, or what she was up to. Not the best way to do things. He blamed himself. They should have conferred, made a plan. Worked together.

Except they hadn't.

Or rather he hadn't. Next time he wouldn't choose lovers. Especially if...

He shook off the thought. What was the point of finding blame? He was where he was. And the other guard was coming. Toby lowered his head and listened. He could just hear the footfall on the battlements. He waited until it was in front of him, then counted twenty. That would be long enough. The first guard wouldn't be back round for a minute or so.

He crawled, legs first, down the bank. With a few feet to go, he turned on his front, then slipped down into the cold water lizard-fashion. He went under, hit the bottom and pushed up at an angle, staying below the surface. It was too dark to see where he was going; he swam blindly, holding his breath. His aim was no splashing, no ruffling of the surface water. He swam slowly, hoping he was going more or less straight to the wall. There was simply liquid blackness ahead.

It seemed an awfully long way.

Lungs bursting, his hand hit hardness. He felt along; it was the slime of the wall under water. Toby came to the surface and sucked in rapid breaths. Water rolled down his face as he looked up the stonework. A little out of position. He pulled himself along the wall, hand over hand, for a few yards. There.

And began looking above him for handholds.

Chapter 69

Orly was at the top of stone steps. She had entered the main door when the upstairs guard changed. They'd made it easy for her. The new guard was chatting with the two outside guards and holding the door open. How kind of him. She slipped under his arm and was inside.

She'd waited at the top of the steps, and a little later the new guard came past. He walked along the corridor to where the old guard was standing. They whispered a few words to each other and changed over. The old guard came along the corridor, past her and down the stairs.

Good. Now there was just one to deal with.

And surely, he was outside the Queen's room. She vaguely remembered it from her tour two years ago. Of course, the Queen might have changed rooms. She had changed just about everything else. But these were the royal rooms, she knew that. And the guard was in the red livery of the household guard. The leggings were red, the jacket too, but it had thin, well-spaced gold piping down the length, also in the soft flat hat. The man held a spear and was picking his nose, thinking no-one present.

Her father, she recalled, had told one off for leaning against a wall. Another he reprimanded for not wearing his hat straight. She had no intentions of delivering reprimands. Her task was to get by him, and inside the room that was his charge.

She must distract him. She might be invisible but she still had to go through doors, and so must get him away from the one he guarded. Orly had considered this beforehand, and had picked up a few pebbles from the courtyard as she came. Now she crept a little way down the corridor and threw one at him. It struck him in the midriff. The guard looked around, surprised. Then picked up the stone, his brow furrowed.

She threw another.

It hit him on the forehead. He stared in the direction of the throw, and scratched his head. Clearly he could see no one, for there was no one to see. He opened his mouth, thinking of shouting – then closed it, not wanting to appear an idiot. The two stones were in one hand which he kept gazing at to convince himself they were real, then he stared up the corridor hoping to catch whatever it was. Then back to the stones.

Orly went within a few yards of him and threw one at his face, hitting him on the cheek. He jerked back in astonishment and looked hard along the corridor. It was well lit, with a number of oil lamps along the wall. The stones in his pocket, the guard stalked up the hallway, spear before him, as if there might be a bear about to spring out at him.

Orly passed him and went to the door he'd stood by. She turned the handle. It was well greased and didn't squeak as it twisted. She pulled open the door a little way and squeezed inside, then closed the door behind her.

There was a click as it shut.

'Who's that?'

The Queen was sitting bolt upright in a four-poster bed. On the bedclothes before her was an untidy bundle of scrolls and documents, one of which she was holding. She was in her nightdress, worn under a black nightgown. Her face was white and smooth, a beauty like marble, her pigtails swinging about her neck – where hung, on a thin chain, the yellow jewel.

'Who is there, I say?' she called sharply.

Orly did not dare move. The Queen was bent over, looking at the door which was to one side of her. Her hand was on the long bell rope by the bed. She shook her head and shrugged, took her hand off the rope and returned to the document she was reading.

The bed was curtained, but they were open now that the weather was warmer. Not that the room was at all cold; a fire burned in the grate. Orly stood at the front of the bed. There lay the woman who had ordered the slaughter of her family. Reading. Such an ordinary task. Her own mother had sometimes gone over the household accounts in bed. But whose accounts were these? What estates? What lives to be paid? It made reading a dangerous task.

The Queen gave out a long sigh and wiped an eye with the back of her hand. There were dark rings under her eyes, and dried tears down her cheeks. Orly could almost feel sorry for her. She was in mourning for her son, even to the black nightgown, and black ribbons on her pigtails. She may have been a sham widow but these tears were true. The lady wept for him in the long night, tore her hair during the endless day.

Beware the mourning mother. She has little to lose – and plenty of pain to spare.

But beware, too, those you have orphaned.

On either side of the bed were two low wooden cabinets. On both of these were oil lamps, the only lighting in the room apart from the fire, illuminating the Queen in the theatre of her bed. On her right-hand side was a goblet. Orly crept round to this, hoping she was still drinking from it. In it was a dark liquid, with a lemony, raspberry smell, still warm. She uncorked her little bottle, and held it to the rim of the goblet, tipping it slightly so the liquid would pour in slowly, without sound.

Orly was recorking the bottle when the Queen absently stretched out and picked up the goblet. She sipped a little, then stopped and licked her lips. Had she detected the change of taste? Now what? She smiled, nodded her satisfaction – and drank some more.

It was a cunning little drug, thought Orly, disguised in some heavenly sweetness. Over five minutes the Queen drank all of it. And when it had gone, looked into the cup for more.

Would it work?

Orly sat in a chair a little way beyond the bed, as if she were the night nurse, keeping watch. As she was. Nothing seemed to be happening, the Queen was still reading. Orly's attention wandered. At the far end of the room, above the fire, was a picture she couldn't make out at first, as the light was mostly at the Queen's end. But growing more curious she went to look. It was Zeke, in heroic pose, on a white horse in armour and holding a lance. By the side, on a chest of drawers, were a pair of boots, black gauntlets, a number of rings, a velvet hat, and a white shirt with lace collar and cuffs forming a semi-circle around a tall vase of white lilies. This, she realised, was Zeke's shrine, where the Queen kneeled and wept, and kissed the remnants of her beloved son. And changed the flowers daily.

She was crying now, taking a handkerchief from her sleeve to bathe her eyes. In sudden exasperation, she swept the papers off the bed onto the floor. Then lay back on the pillow, a forearm over her eyes. Might the drug be working? Her chest was heaving, she was still weeping. But in a little while the heaving and weeping stopped, her breathing became shallower. And the hand over her eyes dropped away.

Give it a little longer, thought Orly. She knew she must go for the jewel around the Queen's neck. And for that she must be truly asleep before Orly could attempt to lift it off. Or be caught in the act.

There was scratching at the window. A bird, she thought. She hoped not a jackdaw, as that was the bird of bad luck. Her mother had said that such signs should not be dismissed. Gently she stepped behind the curtains, and at first she could see nothing out the window, but could still hear the scratching. She opened the curtains slightly so a little lamplight would assist her to see. And then could make out a figure. It was only in shadow; she could not see the face or clothing.

But she knew at once it was Toby.

And he couldn't get in as the window was shut on him. Did she want to let him in? Proud, sneering Toby. If the Queen was now asleep, Orly thought, she could do this herself. Finish off the monster who had massacred her family. Gladly she would. Who had stolen her estates. Killed every servant and cowhand. She would walk over hot coals to do it.

Toby had deserted them. But she knew, too, he had been hurt. And had left them his food in spite of it, and had come here. For that she must forgive him. He too wanted what she wanted. And who was to say it would be so easy? The Queen might be asleep, but sleepers wake. And if Orly's only help was locked outside...?

She was persuaded.

Orly pulled the bolt and pushed the window out. The casement hit Toby on the chest. He gasped his surprise. She stretched out her hand to touch his.

'Toby,' she hissed. 'Come in quietly.'

The phantom nodded. And began climbing in through the window. Orly backed out of the curtains to get out of his way. Toby came into the room dripping wet, the lamplight glistening in his plastered hair.

Orly crept to his ear. She whispered, 'Please, no noise. She has just fallen asleep.'

Toby nodded. He had already spotted the Queen and was watching her closely. Orly knew his thoughts. She was thinking much the same. How light was her sleep? Could it be done now?

And then Toby strode to the bed. The Queen was lying on her back, her arms splayed out over the bed covering. Toby grasped the yellow jewel. His knuckle was white. Let it cut her neck like a cheese wire for all he cared. And he tore at the chain.

It ripped away in his hand and he was propelled backwards.

At the same instant the imp was upon him.

Where it had been, neither could say. It was just there in a jump. A black creature with yellow eyes and a long tail like a whip. The imp's teeth were small and triangular, sharp as a saw rip, and its claws like the talons of an eagle. It was upon Toby's back, legs round his neck squeezing, its teeth biting at the back of his head.

Toby danced about with the creature, round and round the room. It was hissing and spitting as it clawed and bit at him. He pulled at one arm, then another, then a leg. When he was free from one limb, another came back, and the tail too lashed about him. He moaned as it constricted his neck. He was choking, his tongue splayed out, his face reddening, eyes popping. About he went, spinning at dizzying speed, tugging, pulling. Blood was pumping furiously in his head.

He did not have long.

And he concentrated on the body of the beast, ripping it away in his strong grip. Tearing at the sprung limbs and tail. He was blood-streaked, breathless, but the creature was weakening and was hissing wildly. Around Toby went, straining every sinew.

And Orly saw what she must do. Rapidly, she opened the curtains. There was the window wide open. Toby slammed the creature's head on the sill. Its grip relaxed in limbs and tail. And Toby flung it out the window in a splay of legs. The creature bounced down the castle wall, and in another instant splashed into the moat.

Toby supported himself by the curtain; his legs were wobbly, blood coursing down his face and hands. His head ringing, he sank into a chair – and saw the Queen sitting up in bed shrieking.

'Murderers! Robbers! Tobards!'

She frantically yanked at the bell pull.

The door burst open – two guards rushed in. And Councillor Higgs.

'Seize him!' shrieked the Queen, her hands at her throat. 'Get me back my jewel!'

Toby had forgotten that he was still holding it. The yellow stone was blood-spattered in his hand. He had hung on to it during his battle with the imp, with no intention of giving it up while alive.

Two guards ran in at him and seized his arms.

Toby threw the jewel. The guards still held him by the elbows.

The Queen was shrieking, 'My jewel! My jewel!'

But Orly had caught it. And she had dashed with it to the desk. The guards were bewildered. Should they let go of Toby and go for the jewel? Surely a jewel can be picked up later? Get the attacker first.

'My jewel! Give me my jewel!' she screamed. She threw back the bedclothes. She would get it herself. She utterly must.

Orly slammed a boot on to it, Zeke's with its iron-clad toe. And again and again. The jewel cracked. And again. It split and shattered.

A terrible howl came from the Queen. She could move no further, stuck on the carpet, halfway between bed and desk, her hands clasping her face and neck. She was pain amidst panic, her eyes bulging, the sinews of her neck coming through the skin like rope strands. Her hair was greying as they watched, the colour washing away into whiteness, wispy and thin. Her face crawled with wrinkles as years etched her forehead, along the cheeks, deepening in the folds like the scoring of a prune. But then the underlay oozed away, her eye sockets hollowed and the skin on her face stretched like parchment. She was ageing rapidly before them, the skin tight as a drum over her face, her hands fleshless and bony. The decades were running through her in seconds, catching up with cheated time. And then the skin tore and curled like the hide on a spitted pig. It rolled up over itself, picking up the muscle. And the scream stopped but the mouth was wide as if hung in the scream.

She had become white bone, her skull hairless, no eyes in the deep sockets, no tongue, no lips, her skeletal hand pointing at her desk and the smashed jewel.

The bone began to crack and fracture like a dropped pot. Until it was a mass of pieces, somehow holding together in a glue. And the pieces fractured and split, smaller and smaller, the lines running through them, until they were like grains of sand – but held together as if by spit. The silent howl still upon her, the hand pointing.

And then she fell.

In a sudden heap, like dry sand poured from a bucket.

No one moved. The room was crowded, the door wide open. Many had come running at the screaming. A circle had formed round where the Queen had been. Perhaps a dozen soldiers now, Councillor Higgs, two soldiers wanly holding Toby's arms... All gazing at the pile of dust lying on the Queen's nightgown.

No one dared speak.

Everything was held in that moment. A terror gone in a terrible way. It could not be believed. That heap of powder had been their ruler.

And was no longer.

They were free. They were frightened. Who was now in control?

Orly walked into the circle and curtseyed before Toby. Visible once more, she bowed her head.

'I pledge my troth, King Toby.'

Toby placed a hand on her head, his face a mass of blood and scars. He was ripped and bleeding, but stood upright with Orly kneeling before him. The two soldiers stepped away; this was beyond them. Was there a new King here?

Those who knew looked to Councillor Higgs.

There was terror in the old man's eyes. He was bewildered, afraid.

Toby pointed his bleeding hand at him. 'I am your King.'

Higgs did not reply.

'Consider if I am not,' said Toby slowly. 'There will be war. And who will be your protector, Councillor Higgs? You, who did the Queen's bidding. Who will save you in the war?'

Higgs did not reply, cheeks palpitating, considering his choices. Which way should he go? Who was there to go with?

'Be with me,' continued Toby, 'and you stay Councillor. For one year. Then you may go back to your estates. No man shall harm you, for I shall be your protector.' Toby paused; he looked around the room, the blood like drips of paint on his face. 'But if you are against me, Councillor Higgs – no one will defend you.'

Everyone looked to the Councillor. He was the King-maker. For or against this bloody man?

And he sank to his knees.

'You are my liege,' he said, head bowed. 'God be with King Toby.'

And the room knelt to a new King.

Chapter 70

There was much to be done. The Kingdom must be told. And Toby had to take control quickly, before any forces of resistance could build up. And before any of that, he must wash, get out of his peasant garb and look like a king. Through dressing and washing, he gave orders all the while, keeping Councillor Higgs with him, for he did not yet trust the old man.

Though it was still the early hours of the morning, the whole castle was awake. Fires were being lit, early breakfast prepared. All the soldiery were ripped from their beds. Lords and ladies dared not sleep on with such momentous events on top of them. And their servants were sent rushing here and there, taking up the panic of their masters.

Far was brought up from the dungeon, and the few others awaiting death freed too. Far did what he could for Toby's wounds, using the scrapings from the healer's workshop. Difficult enough, considering the mess. And he apologised for not doing the best of jobs, but really a castle must have a proper healer. Toby agreed, and suggested that Far take it on. He said he would think about it. And Toby turned away, full of other matters. There were many dashing around him, finding clothes for him, sorting out the regalia. In an hour, he was due to address the court. He must think what to say. What had to be done.

These were important hours. His kingship was fragile.

Orly hugged Far but did not stay long with them. She had herself to get ready. After all, she must be a lady for the court. With her mother and father dead, she now had the title Countess Gomm. And had her estates to claim and her part to play in this new world. She must wash and find suitable clothes and powder and paint. Toby ordered the ladies-in-waiting to cater for her needs. And they took her away, already curtseying to this young woman in peasant garb who had the favour of the King.

In the court, Toby took the throne while those assembled sank to their knees. He was dressed in green leggings with a red and gold ribbed jacket. He wore the chain of state around his neck and his father's crown upon his head. Much more kingly than the bloody spectre who had first been addressed as King.

He called for Countess Gomm to come forward.

Orly made her way through the courtiers to a mumble of approval. The ladies-in-waiting had done well. She wore a full-length gown of blue and yellow with lace at the wrists and collar. To this was attached a red cloak, fully open at the front. She had amethyst earrings and a necklace of silver and diamonds. Her face was painted white in the manner of court, and her lips full red. On her head she wore a brocade of silk that covered the top of her forehead, half her face, and ran down to her collar at the back. It was held in place by a gold band at the hairline.

Orly knelt by the throne. And swore her allegiance to her King.

Toby said, so all could hear, 'Your family estates are returned to you, Countess Gomm.'

'Thank you, Your Majesty,' she said still on her knees.

To her alone, he said, 'Bring Far. I have a promise to fulfil.'

Orly nodded and backed away, between those filling the court. And went off to find Far.

The King proclaimed, 'All who lost their estates during the Queen's rule shall have them restored. I shall set up a Commission of restoration to right the wrongs of those evil days.'

The officers from the garrison were here. In groups of six, he had them swear allegiance. He must win over the soldiers. There were also a few lords present, those that happened to be around the castle or nearby. Each came forward individually and swore that he was their true King.

Bells could be heard through the windows, ringing here and there from the surrounding villages. Messengers were riding out, although it was still dark outside. A puzzled populace must now accept a Tobard as King. About and about face. The Queen was now the traitor; it was she who had murdered her husband. And the traitor was King.

Truths were lies. Lies were truths.

Toby knew he must take command. There was no obvious successor but him. The Queen had damned him, but then in her own murderous excesses she had damned herself. He must bring in all the Lords and get their allegiance. A real problem would be the marauding soldiers, who had become too used to murder and plunder.

But he was feeling like a king, and that, he knew, was well on the way to being one.

When the business of court was done, he went to the king's office with Councillor Higgs. Before he began any business he had the Queen's picture removed. It was full-length, with her in a green gown, in all her beauty that had so bewitched his father, and the yellow jewel at her neck.

'Burn it,' commanded Toby.

When it was taken away, he went through further business with Higgs. They began the list of Lords to be brought in for the coronation. He would declare an amnesty for the soldiers whom the Queen had encouraged to terrorise the countryside. Those who accepted his rule would join his army, and learn to behave in a more acceptable way. Those who did not would become outlaws and be hunted down.

Orly entered.

She said, 'Far has gone, Your Majesty.'

'Gone where?'

She shook her head. 'I don't know.' Her powder was streaked. She had been crying. 'I only know he left with a group of soldiers, Your Majesty.'

Toby sighed and shook his head. So much to do, so much that could go wrong.

'I would have made him Lord,' he said.

'He did not even say farewell.' There was sadness in her voice, but an edge of anger too.

Toby rose from his desk, already piled with papers.

'You may stay here at the castle, Orly,' he said. 'As long as you wish.'

She shook her head. 'No, Toby.'

Councillor Higgs gasped at the familiarity.

'I must go back,' she went on, 'and take over my estate. My family deserves that. Whoever has it now shall have it no longer.'

'I understand,' said Toby. 'I shall send fifty soldiers to escort you.'

'Thank you, Your Majesty.' She gave a curtsy, rose and went to the door. There she turned as she opened it, and said between pressed teeth, 'Be assured, Your Majesty, I shall have no more to do with peasant boys.'

Once in the corridor, she was weeping.

Toby was not able to resume work, though Higgs was standing by, eager with suggestions. He waved him away. And Toby thought of the three of them, going their different ways. He could, of course, make Orly and Far stay. He was the King after all. But that would be, he knew, at the loss of friendship. They would hate him. He must not play people like pawns, even if his heart told him to.

He wished to escape a tyranny, not create another.

Chapter 71

Far flicked the reins, and the two draught horses picked up their pace. He was driver on a food wagon with sacks of flour and pots and pans tumbling in the back. When they stopped, he must pack them better. But for now, he was glad to be travelling. And he breathed more easily. The castle was already out of sight, hidden in the trees. He had had fears that Toby would have sent men after him, to bring him back. This wagon was easy enough to catch on a fast horse. But no-one had come yet. And if they did he could explain himself. He had nothing to fear from Toby.

He feared worse from Orly.

The two large cart-horses ambled along, side by side, following the cart in front as they munched from their foodbags. The blanket over his knees had slipped, so he adjusted it and rolled down his sleeves. The reins were loose in his hands; the animals hardly needed him. The sun was just rising in a clear sky, it was chilly but would warm up in a few hours. He'd been hungry when he left, but within a few miles a soldier on horseback was going down the line with a sack of bread. The detachment was in a hurry, and must eat on the move. First halt at noon.

It was a sudden decision of his to leave. He had caught a glimpse of Orly being dressed by the ladies-in-waiting. She was already in her blue and yellow gown, wearing earrings, her hair being tied back. She was laughing and joking with them. And it hit him, like a kick; all their voices sounded the same. They were her sort, these high-born young women.

One of them shut the door on him. Telling him, without a word, he was in the wrong place.

He'd run out into the courtyard and found the detachment hurriedly setting up. Toby's orders were taking shape. They were going north to sort out some of the wilder bands of soldiers. Did they need a healer? 'Yes,' said the sergeant, slapping him on the back. 'Our last was beheaded. Can you drive a wagon?'

He did not wish to go all the way with them. And that might have been a difficulty, but the Captain had seen him with the King. And, after some discussion, there was mutual agreement.

In less than half an hour they were away. About fifty soldiers on horseback and three wagons; Far could not travel on his own. There might be a new king, but old soldiery stalked the highways. It would take some time to change their killing ways.

How quickly she had joined her class! He'd always joked with her that it would happen. But didn't really believe it. Or did he? Were his jokes a real fear?

In that gown, with her jewellery and the young women – she'd become Countess Gomm before his eyes. A countess with a large estate with a grand house, villages, forests, farms and hundreds of people whose lives she controlled. Orly had gone. The instant they were separated, he to the dungeon, while she made her escape – that was the last time they were on the same level.

He chewed the bread and eased it down with a swallow of water from the jug he kept by him on the board. Then wiped his mouth with his sleeve. Toby might make him a lord. Though he wouldn't put it past him to forget. And if he did, he would be a lord without estates. Penniless. What would be the good of that? It would be like a shepherd without a herd, a farmer thrown off his land. Worse. Could a landless lord be a healer? Earn any sort of living? Toby offered him the job as castle healer but it had to be that or a lord. Lords don't work. Others work for them. So the alternative was turn down the title and become castle healer. But he knew he'd hate it. All that bowing, kissing hands, all the gradations of rank, with him down at the bottom. He'd be a servant for the nobility. Ordered around and blamed for any remedy that was less than perfect.

Would Orly have him then? Of course not. Or as a landless lord? Would Countess Gomm give her estate in marriage to him? A jumped-up peasant. Words and promises on the High Ridge stayed on the High Ridge. Countess Gomm was Countess Gomm – and he knew she would not give it away. He'd seen the way she suddenly became a lady of court, as proud and as haughty as she ever was.

Her feelings might have been true on the mountain with Erdy and on the Ridge. But position was position in this ranked world. King Toby was not about to change that. Far had seen that in the throng of ladies; Orly in her court dress, the ladies-in-waiting about her with hand mirrors, laughing with her. That was the place of Countess Gomm.

No. He would not be the plaything of kings and countesses. He must make his way in the world. And he knew he could. The world would yet grant him respect for what he did himself. He would not wait around in the hope of marrying someone who would in the end reject him. He was going back to Erdy; he would study with him, work with him. There was a chance beyond chances and he must grab it. The Kingdom had almost been swept free of healers. The Queen's last legacy. But he knew too that he was only half a healer. There was so much he didn't know. Give him a few more years with Erdy... He had the aptitude, and knew he could be the best.

But not in a castle on his knees. If she had her pride, then so did he. He would not wait to receive the crumbs from the King's table. He would be respected for himself. They would all yet know him. That was his task; he had himself to make.

It did not stop him feeling low and lonely on this cold morning. But Orly had died when they came down from the High Ridge, and he would only mourn so long. And then get on with his life.

Chapter 72

The first years of King Toby's reign were difficult. The majority of the soldiers had seen the way the wind was blowing and had accepted Toby as King. Some though refused, and continued their banditry. There were places in the land virtually ruled by these robbers, who were as ruthless as they had been under the Queen. It took five years to run them all to ground.

Two Lords had rebelled in his first year, thinking Toby weak and believing that he had killed his own father. Or perhaps telling others that, to make their motives more appealing. They gathered up some of the renegade soldiers. Toby defeated the first, after a siege of the Lord's castle. Toby then gave him a choice: swear allegiance or be banished and lose his estates. Grateful for the mercy, he accepted the King. And the other Lord made his peace.

Since that time, the army has grown smaller and there has been peace.

Eight years ago, the King married Countess Gomm. She is now known as Queen Orly. They have two children. The eldest is a boy called Martin, after her beloved brother; the second a girl, named after Toby's mother, Eleanor. Orly often leaves the court with her children to go to her estate. There they walk and ride through woodland and meadow, always with an escort, as befits a Queen and her family. She ensures they learn country skills, not simply reading, writing, astronomy and geometry – but how to saddle a horse and plant a garden. And she gets her hands dirty with them. She says, and the King agrees, princes and princesses never know when they will need such things. Often they go boating on her lake. It is a large one with several islands where they picnic, the food being brought in other boats by servants. Orly will sometimes row. It is her estate, she says, and why should she not? But when the King joins them on the estate he never comes on their boating trips. He says he spent too much time rowing backwards and forwards across a wretched river, and never wants to see another rowing boat.

The King can be stern, and has a temper which he sometimes regrets losing. Orly is a pacifying force. He will listen to her. And sometimes take notice. On her estate she has set up a school for the peasant children. There they learn to read and write, and about the world they live in. She says it will make her farm richer if her people are knowledgeable. And peasants, she says, need not always stay peasants. The King is not convinced by such sentiments, especially as he grows older. It would be easier if peasants did stay peasants.

Far studied with Erdy for three years, at the same time practising his healing as they travelled together around the villages and towns. But Erdy always had to stay near his mountain retreat and Far would go sometimes on his own with the wagon. Until he became a travelling healer on his own. He was already well-known because of his part in the downfall of the former Queen. The story is told in song and played out at fairs on feast days – but Far says his role has been exaggerated.

Sometimes Far's travels take him to the castle. He will not go in, but stays in one of the castle villages – and there receives his patients, quite a few of whom come from the castle. Far treats the rich and the poor. The poor for little or nothing, as he does not forget he was born a peasant – and his family could afford little to pay a healer. The rich he charges in full, and will not be treated as a servant. If they do, he will not come back. Not many could get away with this. But he is Far, one of the legendary three. And now one of the best healers in the Kingdom, perhaps only second to Erdy, but even that is arguable.

Often he goes to Erdy's cavern in the mountains. They are equals these days, with much to speak of on the healing arts. Erdy loves to hear news of the King, the Queen, the family, and what is going on in the land. And Far always has news and often new remedies for them to try. Another stop on his travels used to be with Maeg. She too was a healer, and taught him magic. He would stay there quite a few days, and came to love the old lady.

Maeg died three years ago. She was very old. The King invited her to live in the castle in her last years, but she would not leave her forest. And so he detailed a local farmer to make sure she always had enough wood and food. The farmer would come to her cottage once a week with fire-wood, eggs, cheese, bacon, milk and anything else she might request. It was never much. Sometimes a few nails, or a piece of material. The farmer would never take payment. The King pays, he said. And Far too, in his irregular visits, would always bring supplies for the old woman.

The farmer came one day, the door wide open, and found her in her chair by the embers of the fire. A fox was sitting by her. The farmer chased it out, but the animal stayed around the cottage even as he left, the farmer said. She was buried in the forest near the cottage. Her funeral was a small affair befitting its site. The King and Queen attended, as did Far and even Erdy who hates to travel such distances. The farmer came and a few locals, and that was all, with the exception of the old fox who lay by the graveside.

Toby and Orly had not seen Far for seven years. The King and Queen, of course, knew of his growing reputation. Both felt slighted by him, the King for his refusal of a lord-ship, and Orly because of the way he had left her. At this small funeral they could not avoid each other. They all went back to Maeg's cottage for refreshments. And bridges were built. Far had his respect; he was someone in his own right.

And he was embraced by King and Queen. They have invited him to the castle, but he has never taken that up. He says castles are not for him, he does not like the ranks and ceremony. Orly gave him a cottage on her estate, which he has accepted. It is convenient for him on his journeys. At the cottage, he can rest himself and his horse, keep herbs and remedies, and so need to carry less on the wagon. He will not go to the big house, which is known as the Queen's residence. Orly has stopped inviting him, knowing his stubbornness. Instead, when he is around, she visits him at the cottage. She expects no bowing or ceremony from him, and they are friends again.

Far is thinking of getting married. He met a young woman, daughter of a healer, at a village fair. And now sees her whenever he comes to her village. He was worried his travelling ways would not suit her, but she insists it would. Orly thinks marriage would be good for him. Perhaps in the spring, he says.

He has also taken Maeg's cottage, which Erdy gave to him. Erdy says it is too far for him and his mother would be pleased it was used. Sly sometimes visits him there, but her visits have become less frequent. She is old. There is grey on her muzzle and her legs have become arthritic. She is more ancient than any fox in the land, and lives mostly with Erdy these days. Sometimes she goes out with him on his forays on the mountainside, more often when Far comes. But on colder days, she leaves them to it and sleeps by the fire in the cavern.

And lastly there is Martin, who played an important part in our story. Without him, there would be no King Toby and the dreadful Queen would still rule. He continues to row his boat across the dark river, as he has done for over ten years since taking over from Toby. He takes a penny from the dead, and in the middle of the river, drops it in the black water. He has almost forgotten why he is the ferryman, as he seldom speaks to any of the passengers, though he does remember it had something to do with his sister, Orly, whose life was saved by somebody whose name he has forgotten. His love for his sister is the only spark left in him. It will go, as all things go. And on he must row, back and forth across the dark river, as no one will take over the oars.

That is, until Toby comes. But for that – he must wait fifty years.

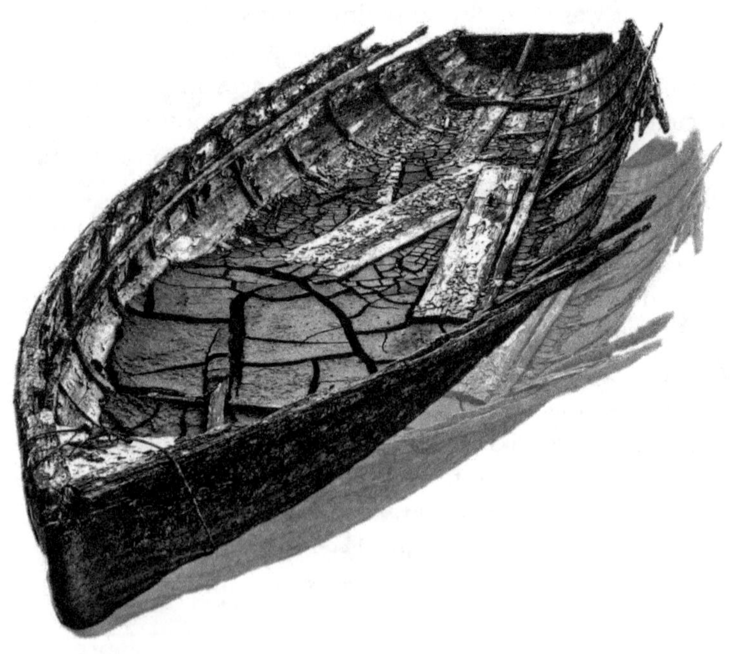

Thank you!

I am grateful to every reader who finishes one of my novels. I have taken you on a journey which I hope you have enjoyed. There are plenty of things you could have been doing, other than reading this book. So, thank you for your time.

If you liked *Hell's Chimney*, here's what you can do next:

I'd appreciate a review on Amazon. In that way, you can help me tell other readers about my books. Without reviews authors get few sales on Amazon. So I'd be grateful for your review to help this book be better known.

Books by DH Smith

Hell's Chimney is written under my name Derek Smith. Under that name I have also written children's books and a few for adults.

As DH Smith I am writing a crime series, whose main character is a builder sleuth, Jack Bell. The books are all standalone novels and can be read in any order. They are:

- Jack of All Trades
- Jack of Spades
- Jack o'Lantern
- Jack By The Hedge
- Jack In The Box
- Jack On The Tower
- Jack Recalled
- Jack At Death's Door
- Jack At The Gate

Some Amazon reviews

Well written from the first page to the last page.
I have definitely found a new author

The story grabs you, sucks you in, and leaves you guessing,
providing juicy dialogue and laugh-out-loud
moments along the way

A different type of mystery where the main personality
is not a professional crime solver, but a
builder/carpenter with his own personal issues

Books by Derek Smith

All my books, other than the *Jack of All Trades* series, are written under the name Derek Smith.

Mystery/Crime
Murder at Any Price

Fantasy
Hell's Chimney
The Prince's Shadow

Other
Strikers of Hanbury Street (short stories)
Catching Up (poetry)

Young Adult Novels
Hard Cash
Half a Bike
Fast Food
Frances Fairweather Demon Striker!

Children's Novels
The Good Wolf
Feather Brains
Baker's Boy

For Younger Children
The Magical World of Lucy-Anne
Lucy-Anne's Changing Ways
Jack's Bus

About the Author

I live in Forest Gate in the East End of London. In my working life, I have been a plastics chemist, a gardener and a stage manager before becoming a professional writer. I began with plays, working with several theatre companies, and had a few plays on radio and TV, as well as on the stage.

In the early 80s I became involved in running a co-operative bookshop and vegetarian café in Stratford, where I learned to cook, and had my first go at writing a novel. The first was a mess, and, after too many rewrites, binned. The transition from drama to novels took me a couple of years to get to grips with.

My first success was a young adult novel, *Hard Cash*, published by Faber. Buoyed up by this, I stuck with children's work, did school visits, and made a hand to mouth living as a full time author, topped up with some evening class work in creative writing at City University and the Mary Ward Centre in Holborn. A few adult fiction titles appeared from time to time, between the children's list, and I have since been working more in that direction with my *Jack of All Trades* series.

www.dereksmithwriter.com